Accelerated Reader

109334

Firestorm

David Klass
ATOS B.L: 3.4
ATOS Points: 11   MG

DATE DUE

APR 9 7			

DEMCO 128-5046

Also by DAVID KLASS

Dark Angel
Home of the Braves
You Don't Know Me
Screen Test
Danger Zone
California Blue

FIRESTORM

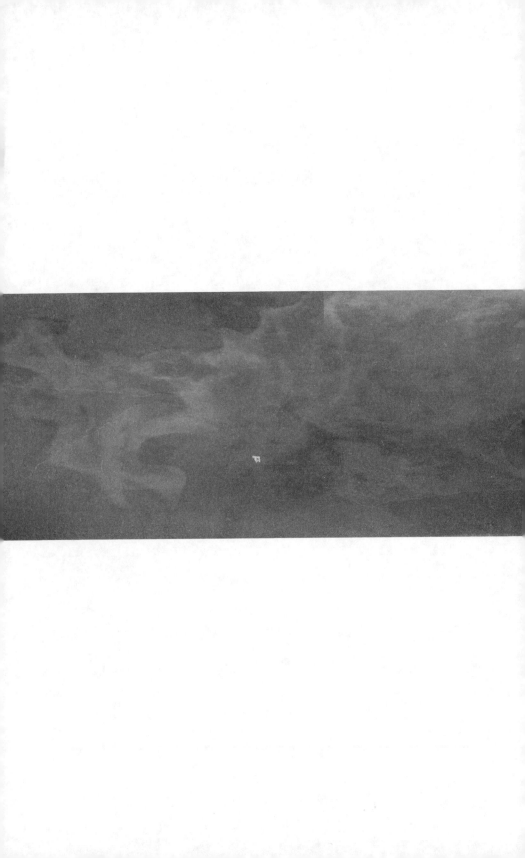

THE CARETAKER TRILOGY: BOOK 1

FIRESTORM

DAVID KLASS

FRANCES FOSTER BOOKS Farrar Straus Giroux New York

www.fsgkidsbooks.com

Library of Congress Cataloging-in-Publication Data
Klass, David.
    Firestorm / David Klass.— 1st ed.
        p.   cm.
    Summary: After learning that he has been sent from the future for a special
purpose, eighteen-year-old Jack receives help from an unusual dog and a shape-
shifting female fighter.
    ISBN-13: 978-0-374-32307-3
    ISBN-10: 0-374-32307-0
    [1. Space and time—Fiction.   2. Ecology—Fiction.   3. Dogs—Fiction.
4. Science fiction.]   I. Title.

PZ7.K67813 Fir 2006
[Fic]—dc22

                                                                    2005052112

For Gabriel

FIRESTORM

1

Halloween week in Hadley-by-Hudson. Senior year of high school. Nine in the evening. Had enough sentence fragments? My English teacher said they are a weakness of mine. But I still like them. They generate pace. You want pace? I'll give you pace. You want weird? Stick around, my friend.

The air pinching colder. Winter coming on fast, winding up to clobber us. A month from now it will be bitter, bitter, and you can feel the coming chill in the north wind. You can smell it in the rust and smoke of the colored leaves. Stock up on the Kleenex. Nostril-clogging chill. Wind the scarves tight. Get out last winter's mittens. Halloween decorations going up on doors and windows. Black cats crouching. Witches soaring on broomsticks. This is gonna get weird fast, but not the way you think.

Here's what I thought. I thought I was living in the most normal little town in America, having the most normal senior year a guy could have. First name? Jack. How's that for normal? Last name? Danielson. Pretty standard stuff, huh? Occupation? High school senior. Hobbies? Chicks, flicks, and fast cars, roughly in that order.

Oh, and I left out sports. Very important. When you're a guy in a town like Hadley with a tough public high school, it helps to be a jock. So I'm lucky that way. Six feet two. Muscles. Starting running back on the football team. Straw-colored hair, piercing blue eyes, and above-average brain power, except when I do something really stupid. Did I mention a winning smile?

Winning smile is often directed at one P. J. Peters. The "P" could have been for "pretty" as they come. Or "pert." Or "perspicacious." Look that one up in the dictionary, my friend. Sometimes "pretentious." Always "pleasing." The "J" could have been for "jousting," because we're always testing each other. Or "joker." No one could make me laugh like P.J. Or "jubilant" when she accomplished something really important.

So we're at the Hadley Diner on a night we've both accomplished something important. P.J. has won a local art contest for a pen-and-ink drawing of her great-grandmother, who is ninety-four. There were adult artists in the competition, so for a high schooler to win is pretty hot stuff.

I just rushed for three hundred and forty yards. New school record. New league record. Not a bad day's work. We defeated our archrival school. Guys are giving me high fives. Slapping me on the back. "Way to go, Jack. You the man. You the one."

Neon signs flashing out front. DINER. IF YOU'RE HUNGRY, WE'RE OPEN. Red leather seats. P.J. nestled close, reminding me not to get a swelled head. "You're still a bozo," she says.

"Mr. Bozo to you," I tell her back. "Let's have a little respect, Miss da Vinci."

A man walks by our table. Tall. Gangly. Adam's apple sticking out of throat like it wants to be plucked. He's just eaten. Heading for the door. Passes all the high school kids. Doesn't glance at us. That's curious 'cause we're making mucho noise. Maybe he doesn't like kids.

Then he turns his head and looks. Right at me. For a half second. Not at anyone else. *Just me.* Like he knows me. And I see his eyeballs roll around in his head. Now they look like normal eyes. Now the pupils disappear. Something flashes. Like a flashbulb. Or a computer scanner. A sudden burst of white light that turns silvery. Then the light is gone and I blink and he's gone, too.

"Did you see that?" I ask P.J.

"What?"

"That guy's eyes? They just flashed."

"What guy?"

"He was here a second ago. His eyes got weird."

"I think you'd better lay off mind-bending drugs."

Then we're out in my car, parked at the lookout. Hudson River flowing by. Big autumn moon hanging in the sky like a swollen sex gland. I'm thinking this is the night. But P.J. has other ideas. "Come on," I plead. "There'll never be a better time."

"No."

"Why not?"

"I'm not ready."

"P.J., you're ready. And you're killing me."

"You look pretty healthy."

"Yeah, I scored four touchdowns today."

"So?"

"It's fate. This is my day to score."

Wrong thing to say. Mood starting to fracture big-time. "So you're comparing my virginity to a football field?"

"No, P.J., I was just joking—"

"But you view our intimacy through a sports analogy? First base, second base, you want me to spread my legs like football goalposts? Is that it?"

"P.J., it's a beautiful night. We're seniors. I love you. The guys on the team give me all kinds of grief—"

"That we don't go all the way? You talk to them about us?"

Again, wrong thing to say. "No. Yes. Never. But—"

End of story. "Put it away. Back in your pants."

"But, P.J., there'll never be a better time."

"Put that sucker away and let's go home. There'll be lots of better times. I promise. Soon."

"Have you ever heard of blue balls? It's a medical condition. Can be terminal."

She gives me a sweet kiss on the side of the cheek. "You are such a pathetic dumb puppy."

"What is that supposed to mean?"

"There. I knew you could zip it up. Let's go."

"You'll never know what I suffer."

I take her home. We kiss. Gets intense. A curtain moves. P.J.'s dad peers out. I wave. P.J. waves to him and gets out of my car. I sit there and watch her walk to her house and disappear inside as the big front door shuts.

She's so beautiful. So smart. So much fun. She'll pick her moment. Girls know about these things. They operate on instinct. Just be patient, Jack.

I drive home with my blue balls.

Dad is waiting there. And Mom. He doesn't look happy. "So I heard about the game. Congratulations."

"Thanks, Dad. It was great."

"Maybe too great," he says.

"What's that supposed to mean?"

Dad paces. Mom stands still. Both look worried.

"What's that supposed to mean?" I try again. "Am I missing something here?"

"I've told you that it's not good to stand out too much," Dad says. "You show people up. Make enemies. People get jealous."

"Who's getting jealous?" I ask. "This was one of the best nights of my life. Everyone at the diner was slapping me on the back. Nobody was jealous. Everybody was happy for me. Except you." My voice getting louder. "What kind of fatherly advice are you handing out here? Fail intentionally? Don't try my best?"

Dad looks pained. Mom chimes in. "It's just better to fit in sometimes," she says. "Your father loves you, Jack. He wants what's best for you."

"And that's why he tells me not to do my best on math tests? Not to do my best on science projects? Not to set records in track? Not to score too many points in football games? It sounds like he wants what's mediocre for me."

"The thing is, it was on TV," Dad says.

"Yeah. I saw it at the diner. Local sports news. Why exactly is that a problem?"

"Exposure," Dad says. "Attracts bad elements. Did you see anything tonight?"

"What kind of anything are we talking about?"

"Anything strange," he says. "Nutty high school sports fans. Sex-crazed groupies. Whatever." He's trying to make a joke out of it. "Now that you're a big shot, you'd better keep an eye out."

"No, I didn't see anything strange," I tell him. Until I got home, that is. And my parents gave my big night the body slam. For no good reason. But I don't say this. I just think it. Then I remember. "Yeah, there was something weird."

They both look kind of interested. "I was at the diner with P.J., and this guy looked at me, and I swear for a second his eyes disappeared and something flashed. But nobody else saw it, so I must have been dreaming—"

Dad grips me by the shoulders. "Did he say anything?"

"Who?"

"The man?"

"No."

"But he looked right at you?"

"Yes? What's the big deal—"

"How tall was he?"

"Very tall. Maybe an inch taller than you."

"When you saw the flash, did it change color?"

"Kind of," I say. "White to silvery. Do you know this man? Dad, what's going on?" He's holding me tightly, freaking me out.

"We're gonna go for a drive," he tells my mom.

"Now?" I ask. "It's after eleven. Where are we going? The police? I don't get it."

"Go," Mom says. Which is weird, too. Then she hugs me. And my mom is not a touchy-feely kind of mom. "Goodbye,

Jack," she whispers. For a second I think there's a tear sliding down her cheek.

"Will somebody tell me what the hell's going on?" I request.

"In the car," Dad says. And he throws on a jacket and marches out into the cold darkness, so I follow him. After all, he is my dad.

2

Two-lane highway. Dark and empty. Curves and straightaways above the mile-wide band of black-rippling Hudson. Full moon flashing in the sky like a cautionary sign: DANGER AHEAD. OBEY SPEED LIMIT. SLOW DOWN! Dad going faster. Way over the legal fifty-five. Pedal to the metal. Sixty. Seventy. "I'm not your father," he says.

"What? Dad, slow down! You're going to kill us!"

"Listen to me, Jack. I'm not 'Dad.'" No, don't argue. Just listen. We don't have much time. Sorry, I do love you, but *I am not your father."*

Something in his face. In his tone. Maybe it's the speed of the car. I believe it even though I'm still fighting against it. "This is a joke, right? Some sort of test? Game?"

"No joke. No test. No game." He's driving like a pro. I've never seen him even push a speed limit in his life. Dad's a gentle guy. Meek. Law-abiding. Cautious. Where did he learn this?

"Dad, are you saying Mom was cheating . . . ?"

"I'm not 'Dad.' Mom is not your mother. Not me. Not her. None of it. *Damn it, hold on!"*

Tires screech. Car nearly flies into an oak tree. I prepare to die. Dad wins the battle with the road. Drives on.

My fingers are gripping the armrest. I can barely get the words out. "You're saying I'm adopted?"

"No," he said. "It's more complicated than that. No time to explain. That light you saw in the diner turned silvery?"

"Yes, but who cares—"

"You were marked. That's how they're finding us."

"Who?"

"I need to unmark you," Dad says. Driving with one hand now. At this speed it's suicide, but he's doing it. Rooting around in a black bag on the seat. Where did that bag come from? Pulls out a little metal cube. Camera? Never saw it before. High-pitched whine. Greenish flash. Strange sensation all over my body. As if an outer layer of skin is being removed, tugged off, the way you peel off sunburn. It's painful. Very. I yell.

"Sorry," he says. "It's your only chance."

"Chance to do what?"

"We are counting on you," he says. "Never forget that. You are our beacon of hope."

"Hope for what?"

"There they are!" he gasps. "They came so quickly."

I look around. Don't see anyone.

Dad jerks the wheel. Car skids wildly and jackknifes off the highway onto a narrow road. Scratch that, not a road. More like a path. Dark. Bumpy. Not well paved. Also not lighted. But apparently not dark enough for Dad's purposes because he switches off his lights. We career forward into Stygian blackness. Look that up, my friend, but not right now. No time for anything now. Except to hold on. My God, is it steep! Are we still on the path? How can this car not turn over?

"DAD, YOU'RE GOING TO KILL US. STOP!"

But he's looking back. Through the rear window. Half-turned.

So I look back, too. Lights behind us. Not cars. Motorcycles, I think. Less than a half mile away. "Can't outrun them," Dad says. "Got to stand and fight."

FULL BRAKE. Bone-jolting torque. Screeching grinding howl as if the car is a wounded beast and we're inside it. Stench of burning rubber. Car spinning wildly. Rolls over. Never been in a car that rolled over before. Not fun. Then everything stops.

Dad clambers out. Helps me. Something is burning. In the flame I see him clearly. Is this my gentle, caring dad? He's got a gun in one hand. Binoculars in the other. Scanning the road. "Go," he says to me. "Now. Go."

"Where?" I ask.

"The river," he says. "Jake's Marina. There's a boat at the end of pier three. Key under the cushion on the driver's chair. Go now."

"I'm not going anywhere," I say, scared out of my mind but very sure where I belong. "Whatever's happening, my place is here with you."

He puts his hand on my shoulder. Bends and kisses me on the forehead. For one second he's Dad again. How I will cherish that kiss. Then he looks at me. Eyes burning with purpose. "Listen, son. There's no time for me to explain this. Everything you believe is the opposite of what is true. I am not your father. Mom is not your mother. Your friends and schoolmates were for you to hide among. They go through life without purpose. You have a purpose. You are our beacon of hope. You must survive. And they are coming here now to kill you."

He fires the gun. Wide, sweeping tracer pattern. Not bullets. I don't think lasers. But something searing and hissing and deadly erupts out of the muzzle.

"Go find the boat," he says. "I'll hold them off. Get away. That's your destiny."

"I'm not going anywhere, and there's no way you can make me go. So just forget it."

He looks at me. "No time to argue." He lowers the gun. And shoots off his own foot! Intentionally! I see him gasp, and he buckles and almost goes down. His toes are gone. Half the foot is gone. Blood. Bone. He looks back at me and raises the gun to his head. "Next shot I blow out my brains. Do you want to see it, or will you go?"

I take a step away. Don't even know what I'm doing now. Mind roiled with fear and confusion.

"Go!" he says. "For years I've told you to hide your abilities. Now you must use them all. Fly, my boy, fly like the wind. And take this." He hands me a long knife.

Incoming fire rakes the ground in front of us. A rock is vaporized. Dad fires back.

I run. And that's one thing I have always been able to do. Fastest runner in my class. In my grade. In my school. In my town. In my county. I'm off downhill, arms pumping, legs churning, while behind me I hear more incoming fire and I think I hear a shrill scream of agony. Dad? Don't think it. Just run.

Through brambles.

Sliding down rocks.

Tumbling down sandy cliffs.

Even motorcycles can't make it down this.

To the shores of the Hudson.

Two hours ago I was making out with P.J. with this river providing the romantic setting. Now I'm running along the clay bank, feet sticking into two inches of muck.

Look back. Fire on the hillside.

Look forward. Jake's Marina. All dark and quiet. Scale the fence. Barbs at the top. Swing over and don't get stuck. Boats rocking on the night tide. Wavelets breaking on wharf logs. Minnows in moonlight.

Something coming over the fence behind me. A black shape. Then another one.

Run past pier one. Past pier two. To pier three. Fifty yards long. Half a football field. I dash down it. This is my day to score. I fly like the wind. No one can run this fast.

Black shape running faster. Gaining on me. Silver blade whizzes by my ear. Throwing knife? I see the black boat at the very end. Sleek craft. Built for speed. I leap to the deck. Run to the driver's chair. Rip off the cushion. There's the key. Stick it in. Switch it on. Deafening roar. This thing's got power! Boat starts to move. Then stops. Forgot to cast off mooring rope.

Dark form leaps from the pier at me. Black robe flaps in wind. I see it coming. Flying at me. Are those teeth or claws? No time to think. I dodge to one side and raise the knife Dad gave me. One strong thrust. Sickening thud. Man-bat-thing impaled. I lower my arm in horror and creature slides off knife, sinks into river, and Hudson swallows it.

That's the good news. Bad news is more black shapes coming fast. I cut mooring rope with knife. Jump to chair. Look back as I hit gas. Two black forms leap out at me. I stand and hurl knife at them. Roar. Boat explodes out into river. I glance back again. Two black ghouls hurtle over water and then lose momentum and altitude till they splash down. Into the drink. The rest of the shadowy figures collect on the end of the pier like a frustrated evil army.

I've made it. But why? For what? Where am I going? Everything I love has been left behind. I steer the boat out into the middle of the river and head south.

I put my head in my hands. And I weep for my father and my mother and P.J. and my teammates and for everything that was but now is not and never will be again.

3

Midnight. All alone. When I say all, I mean all. No one has ever been so alone. Just this boat. Just Jack. An hour ago I was worried about blue balls. Now I have nothing. I know nothing. "I'm not your father," Dad said. "Mom is not your mother. Your friends are not your friends. You're different from them." Sheer nonsense. Ravings. Madness. It had to be. Except.

Except that people came to kill you. On motorcycles. They fired guns. Dad blew his own foot off to get you to run away from them. And the fact that they came makes it all true. Doesn't it? Yes, it does.

But it can't be true. Eighteen years of normal life don't lie. But were they really normal? Always a little bigger than everyone else. Always a little faster. Always a lot stronger. Modesty aside, always just a bit smarter. Smarter even than P.J., the truth be told, and she is the top student at our school.

So if you were smarter than her, why weren't you top student, bozo?

Because Dad didn't want me to be. Don't get the perfect score, he said. Don't set the record in track. Don't get straight A's. You have nothing to prove. People won't like you. You'll stick out. Better to do well and fit in than to do brilliantly and show others up.

It never made sense to me. Never. But when you have a dad as good as mine, you keep your ears open and follow the program.

Now I know better. That wasn't really the point, Dad, was it? Let's be honest, now that the clock has struck twelve, so to speak. I can't be angry with you. I'm pretty sure you just gave your life

so that I could get away. But it wasn't about other people getting
jealous. That was a convenient explanation. It was about limiting
exposure. It was about not winning science contests or track
meets. Not getting too much acclaim. Not getting my picture in
the paper or a mention of me on radio or TV.

Because they were looking for me.

Who are they? I don't know.

Why do they want to kill me? Jack Danielson? All-around
nice guy? I don't know.

But they do. And here's the bad news. Not only are they out
there, but they've been out there for years. They were out there
way back in third grade when Dad said not to win the spelling
contest because the winner would go to the Nationals. "Who
cares about being a good speller?" Dad had laughed. "Let someone else get that honor, son."

You were protecting me, Dad. Even then. Because they were
out there.

Even then. Ten years ago.

So what's my next move? Call the police and tell them what's
happened? Logical and standard operating procedure for all
emergencies, but in this case maybe not a good idea. First: because Dad didn't go to the police. And he could have. Station in
town. Much closer and easier than the mad ride to the river. But
he chose not to go and he knew what was happening. So you'd
better follow his lead. Second reason: when you go to the police
your information goes out on all frequencies. Radio. Computer.
That's how they do their thing. They share information. And right
now people are searching for you to kill you. So if you go to the
police with this story you might as well paint a bull's-eye on a
mountaintop and stand in it waving a flag.

Okay, next option. Contact P.J. Or football teammates and
friends. And tell them what? A story that you would never in a
million years have believed yourself if it hadn't just happened to
you? And possibly bring danger down on their heads? Because

whoever is looking for you is ready, willing, and able to kill. So anyone you go to becomes a possible source of information about you.

Sorry, P.J. I do love you. You're right about most things, but you were wrong earlier tonight. There never will be a better time. We missed our chance.

The river dark and wide. Memories of P.J. First kiss. Junior year. Under the bleachers of the gym—of all places. We've gone there to talk. Just friends. Private place. Dark. Metal supports. We're sitting on the wood floor. Not clean, but who cares. Big and silent gym. Exchanging gossip. All of a sudden eyes catch eyes. Heads incline. Noses brush. Lips on lips. Faintly, firmly, locked. Then unlocked. Looking at each other. Then smiling tentatively. Then laughing, both laughing.

The joy of it. The sheer joy. Then a second kiss. Less tentative. Exploring newly discovered territory.

Lines from a poem. Tennyson, isn't it? I've always loved poetry. Remember oodles of it. Read a good line once, never forget it.

> *Break, break, break*
> *At the foot of thy crags, O Sea!*
> *But the tender grace of a day that is dead*
> *Will never come back to me.*

Standing at the prow feeling the deck rise and plunge.

Passing under a bridge. The sky glowing up ahead.

Is that Manhattan? It must be. Miles away, yet you can see it and feel it. A city that never sleeps.

Bird overhead. Gull? Albatross? Get away. Scat. I like my solitude. Leave me to my memories and my misery.

More lights on the banks. Suburbs of New York.

Dad and Mom rarely brought me here. Hadley is only fifty miles upriver, but a different world. Manhattan is too big, Dad used to say. Too many people living one on top of the other. Can't breathe. Too many cars. Too dangerous.

This from a man who, it turns out, could drive like a NASCAR champion and shoot like Jesse James. But at the time I believed it. And I've always been something of a country boy. Caught snakes and frogs when I was little. Climbed trees. Fished. Eagle Scout. Who needs Manhattan?

I catch my breath. There's the George Washington Bridge all lit up at midnight like a magical gateway. And beyond it are the lights and the skyscrapers and the millions upon millions of people who never sleep because they're too damn busy.

I don't know where I'm going, but this is one place I'm definitely planning to miss.

New Jersey Palisades on my right. Manhattan on my left. Unending stream of cars even at this hour on the West Side Highway. I can see the Empire State Building lit up orange and yellow. Halloween colors.

Sudden ungodly blast. I nearly jump off boat. Trumpet of doom. Big ship. Huge ship. Tanker. I can see its lights. Headed right for me. I steer for the Manhattan shore. Tanker floats past. Looks half a mile long.

I watch it slide by. I'm close to the Manhattan side now. See a marina. Didn't know they even had them in the city. Not that it matters. This is the one place I won't go. Don't know anyone. Never liked the city. Doesn't make sense. Better to head north or south. Up to Canada. Down to the Carolinas and Florida. Put some distance between me and whoever is chasing me.

But they know you're on the boat, bozo.

A little voice. In the back of my mind. I try not to listen to it. Go away.

They saw you roar off on the boat. They know you're headed downriver.

So what? Go away.

So plenty. They're probably coming after you now. Boats are easy to spot. And this one's kind of distinctive. The longer you stay on the boat, the more you're a target.

I don't want to listen. Because this boat was given to me by my dad. Our last connection. Go away.

Yes, focus on Dad, the voice insists. That's all you have to go on. He knew what was going on and he loved you and you don't have a clue, so follow his lead. His last few minutes. He tried to unmark you. So that you couldn't be tracked. Someone was chasing you and closing in on you, so he tried to muddy the trail. That's your next move. Muddy the trail. They're probably starting to comb this river even in darkness, looking for you. And when dawn comes, you're dead meat. What's the best way to muddy the trail? Where's the best place on earth to lose yourself?

I take a deep breath. Damn it. Can't beat the logic. I steer for the marina and the lights of Manhattan.

4

No sleep for the weary. I drop anchor near the marina. Big and small boats nearby. Yachts. A three-masted schooner. Houseboats. What looks like a junk. You name it. It's all here. Manhattan. Melting pot supreme. I sit on the deck and watch the lights of the buildings.

Thinking of Dad and Mom. Always there for me. Mom with her flower garden. Fresh vegetables and herbs. That's the way I see her now. Walking to the house from her garden with fresh-picked tomatoes and basil. Blue jeans. Old T-shirt. Work boots.

Passes me shooting hoops on the driveway. Lunch in twenty minutes, she announces. Wait till you taste these tomatoes. Let's see you make a shot.

I set up from twenty feet out. Blast off. At apex of jump, twenty-five inches off driveway, release jump shot that swishes net. Not bad, Mom says with a smile. Bet you can't do that again.

Her smile. Maybe not the warmest, maybe not the most touchy-feely mom, but she was always there.

But was she? Her smiles were missing warmth and her kisses were missing conviction because she wasn't your mom, bozo. She was filling in for somebody. And she never told you. Eighteen years of silence is akin to lying.

Maybe she had her reasons.

It's still a betrayal.

Dad. Throwing a football with his little boy in Hadley Park as the dusk settles and the lightning bugs start to flicker. White stripes on football spiraling through the gloom. Moon rising over river. Dad saying, Go out.

Come on, Dad, you can't reach me here.

Are you kidding? This old arm's a cannon. Go out. So I run. And the old arm lofts the ball. High arc. Too far. But I run under it. Ball falls into my hands. Way to go, son. Nice running. Now let's see you throw it back. Nice tight spiral. Right to me because I can't run the way I used to.

Thanks for the football coaching, Dad, but there were other important things you left out. Exactly how fast did you use to run? Or perhaps, more to the point, how far? What were we running away from? Who was chasing us? Did you do something wrong? Did Mom? Why didn't you ever tell me? *Because you didn't trust me?* Had to be that. Very unpleasant thought, but had to be. Should have trusted me, Dad. Maybe I could have helped. Now I think you're gone. They got you. I have a really strong sense that Mom is gone, too. She knew they were coming for her. That's what the goodbye hug was about, and the tear.

And here I am on this boat with nada. No knowledge. No money. Nothing to eat. Nowhere to go. No one to see.

I search the boat. Stem to stern, as they say. Find a few things. A flashlight. Helps with the search. A cabin downstairs. The bare necessities. Bed. Looks like it was never slept in. I lie down for a second. Don't even try to close my eyes. Sleep is a release and I'm trapped.

Get back up. Keep searching. Tool kit. Bottled water. Toothbrush in plastic case. Toilet paper still in wrapper. One small cabinet. Locked. No key to open it. I'm not in a patient mood. Pound on it with my fists. More solid than it looks. Get screwdriver from tool kit. Jimmy it open.

Not much inside. Manila envelope. Packet of papers. Hopefully, an explanation of who I am and what's going on. No dice. Legal documents. Title to the boat. Made out in my name. Hey, this boat is mine.

Something in the back of the cabinet. A small box. Inside is a watch. A bit old-fashioned looking. Big black numerals that stand out against a white background. Thick, stubby hour hand and much thinner minute hand, both sapphire blue. Heavy, dark metallic band that glitters as my flashlight's beam hits it. I slip the band around my left wrist. It fits snugly.

Back on deck.

The eastern sky growing lighter. Man in kayak paddles by. Fifty-something. Graying hair around edges of bald pate. Bristly gray eyebrows. "Morning," he says. "I thought I was the only one nutty enough to get up this early."

"Morning," I say back.

"Nice boat. Looks fast."

"Very. Thanks. Want to buy it?"

"You're joking?"

"No. I'll give you a great price."

Kayaks in circle around boat. "I already have a boat," he says.

"You can never have too many boats."

"Wrong," he says. "One boat is too many. All the care and the work and the expense. Pain in the ass. Two would be a heart attack. How much?"

"Make an offer."

"Two thousand bucks," he says.

"Four."

"Three," he counters. "That's not an offer yet. Just hypothetically."

"Hypothetically three thousand five hundred. Cash."

The grayish eyebrows knit together. "Did you steal it?" he asks.

"I own it. I have the papers. Three thousand five hundred in cash and it's legally yours. Go get a lawyer if you want."

He smiles. "I am a lawyer. Can I come check it out?"

Three hours later the banks open, and an hour after that I walk off down the dock with thirty-five hundred-dollar bills in my wallet. Goodbye, boat. Goodbye, last connection to Dad. You were my home for only one night, barely ten hours, but I liked you.

Now I'm homeless. Adrift in the whirlpool that is Manhattan. People riding by on bikes. Jogging by. Too many people. All strangers. Yes, but this is what you want and need to unmark yourself. Where do I go and what do I do?

Playground near marina. Kids laughing. I'm drawn to it. Something innocent about kids. And parents of kids seem more trustworthy than other total strangers. I sit on a bench facing the sandbox.

Time passes. Minutes. Hours. Replay events of last night in my mind. Over and over. Still can't believe it. I go get hot dog from vendor. Soda. When I open my wallet to pay him he sees wad of hundred-dollar bills. Quick eyes. Careful, Jack. This is the big city.

I come back to playground. Eat my hot dog. Midday sun beats down on me. No sleep the night before. Eyelids suddenly weigh a ton. Lean back. Nod off for a few minutes. Kid falls off swing and cries and I wake up fast.

Someone's watching me. Nearby bench. Girl. Cute. Very. She turns away fast when I look at her. Long blond hair. Open notebook. Pen. Some kind of school uniform. Skirt. Blouse. Knee socks. Gleam of bare thigh. Sexy.

I look away. After a few seconds I feel her looking at me again. Turn my head. Eyes meet. Both look away. Both look back. We both giggle, embarrassed.

"Hi," she says. Speaking first. New York girls. Not shy.

"Hey," I say back.

"You were really out. Snoring."

"Long night," I tell her.

"Party?"

"Worse."

"What does that mean?"

I answer question with question. "What's that uniform?"

"Oh, that's what they make us wear at Drearly. Hideous, isn't it?"

"Is that your school?"

She laughs. Lovely laugh. Nice teeth. Blond hair splashed by sunlight. "Where are you from?"

"What? Why?"

"Drearly's like one of the most famous schools in the city. I thought everyone's heard of it."

"I'm just a tourist."

She looks at me. Probing. Curious. A little fearful. A lot attracted. "Are you here with your parents? Or friends?"

"Just me."

"Cool," she says. Then, after just the slightest hesitation: "So, are you a serial killer?"

"What?"

"Just checking. A girl can't be too careful. Did you chop your parents up and burn down the house and run away?"

"No."

"But you did run away?"

"I don't like twenty questions."

"Neither do I," she says. "Can I come sit on your bench?"

I nod. She comes. Flounces down next to me. Nice smell. "I'm Reilly," she says. "My friends call me Rye."

"Like the bread?"

"Or the whiskey. Do you have a name?"

"Jack."

"Do you always hang out in playgrounds, Jack?"

"I don't know the city. I thought this would be a safe place 'cause of the kids."

Her face softens. "It is safer. But there are rats here. They come out after dark. The kids leave, the rats come."

"What are you doing here, Rye?"

"Homework." She nods at the notebook. "English assignment. Describe a scene in two hundred words or less. How do you describe chaos in two hundred words or less?"

Our eyes sweep the playground. Little boy crying because he's just tripped over little girl, who is also crying. Baby wailing as mom changes diaper. Two boys throwing sand in each other's faces in sandbox. Father by slide shouting into cell phone, completely oblivious as toddler prepares to ski-jump off slide and break neck.

"I see your point," I say. "Sounds like you have a pretty creative English class. All we do in mine is read *David Copperfield.*"

"I like Dickens."

"So do I, but one book all semester? I got hooked and finished it the first weekend."

"Wow," she says, "that must have been a slow weekend. Don't they have parties where you come from?"

"Once in a while."

"I like parties," Reilly confesses wickedly. "Just by coincidence a friend of mine is having one tonight. Would you like to come, Jack?"

Don't take this the wrong way, Reilly. There are things you don't know that I can't explain to you. First of all, I'm running for my life. Second, when I'm not in shock I'm in mourning. Lost parents. Lost childhood. Lost innocence. Lastly, there's P.J. "Thanks. That's really nice of you, but I can't. Maybe another time."

She pouts. Highly effective. "Why not?"

"I can't handle a chic Manhattan party right now."

"It won't be stuck-up. It'll be fun. Try it."

"I'm going through a hard time right now, Rye."

"I kind of figured that out, Jack. That's exactly why you need a party."

So I tell her. "Look, I didn't have a shower this morning. I don't have clean clothes. I'm kind of a mess."

"You can clean up at my apartment. We'll wash your clothes. Something tells me you clean up nice."

"What will your parents think if you bring a stray like me home?"

Reilly shrugs. Gives her a chance to flip her hair. Something going on with her parents that's not so great. "They're away in Paris," she says, as if everybody's parents disappear to Paris at regular intervals. "Business trip for my dad. Shopping opportunity for my mom. So it's just me in our big old apartment. And I'm lonely." She stands. "Do you want to come or not, Jack? I rarely ask twice and I never ask three times."

I stand up also. Sorry, P.J. But this is my only friend in New York. And I do need a hot shower.

✳

5

Central Park West. Exclusive-looking buildings with doormen out front. Joggers in hundred-dollar sneakers. Rollerbladers in designer sunglasses. Kids in double strollers being pushed by nannies. The park right outside, literally at your doorstep. Doesn't look cheap. But very safe and comfortable.

"This is my building," Reilly says. "Hi, Charles."

Doorman nods politely. "Good afternoon." His eyes frisk me and withdraw. He holds door open.

Dark lobby. Plush rug that seems to go on forever. Oil paintings on wall. Landscapes and seascapes. Is this an apartment building or a museum? We get on elevator. Fifteen floor buttons and a "P" at the top. Reilly hits "P." "I know that's not for parking," I say. "Unless it's for helicopters."

"Penthouse," Reilly informs me. "It's no big deal."

"So say you. But for a rube from the provinces . . ."

"You may be from the provinces, but you're no rube," she says. She reaches out and touches my cheek. Brushes hair from my forehead. "You have a nice face," she says. "I have good instincts about people. But you're not a serial killer, are you?"

"Not since the last time you asked."

" 'Cause if you are," she says, "be warned. I have a black belt in karate. A dog. And this is a high-security building."

"You don't have to worry about me," I tell her.

Elevator stops. One door on "P" landing. They have this whole floor to themselves!

We stand on Welcome mat as Reilly fumbles for key.

Something tells me the penthouse in this building doesn't come cheap. "What does your dad do?"

"Do you know what stock options are?"

"Not exactly."

"Neither do I," she admits. "But he does. Or at least his clients think he does." She grins. Secret out. Dad's loaded. She opens the door. Leads the way in.

Reilly, I'm sure you don't need my advice about being safe in Manhattan, but even if you have great instincts about people, not to mention a black belt in karate, you probably shouldn't invite strange men back here alone when your parents are gone.

"I trust you," she says, leading me down a long entry hall. "I don't know why, but I do."

Did you just read my mind, Reilly? "Did you just read my mind?" I ask.

She giggles. "Was that what you were thinking? Yeah, I know I might look foolish. But I grew up in this city and I'm pretty savvy about people. You inspire confidence, Jack. Boys who read *David Copperfield* in one weekend are usually safe. Voilà!"

Good God, Reilly. Whatever your dad is doing for his clients, it must be working. We leave the entry hall and emerge into the living room, which is the size of a basketball court and features floor-to-ceiling windows.

Manhattan flows into the room through those windows. Central Park with its emerald lawns and blue lakes. Uptown to Harlem. The Empire State Building points the way downtown. The buildings of the East Side rise up across the park, and the East River glistens beyond them.

"Wow," I say. "Talk about a million-dollar view."

"After a while," Rye replies, "you stop noticing it. That's Strawberry Fields right down there. Memorial to John Lennon. I love his music. He was shot right outside the Dakota over there. Check out the jogging track around the Reservoir. It's the prettiest place to run in the whole world at dusk when the lights of the city are just turning on. Do you want something to eat?"

A dog barks somewhere. Not a playful, happy yelp. More of a deep and angry growl. Let's hope Rover's chained up. I might be a country boy, but I never liked dogs. Never had one. Never wanted one. More trouble than they're worth. And the one growling in the recesses of Reilly's apartment sounds particularly unpleasant. "Maybe later. But a shower sounds good."

Minutes later I'm washing away dirt and stress. Hot needle spray. Expensive soaps and shampoos. Side view of the park through window. What am I doing here? Hiding? Nice place to bide time. But what's my next move? Am I endangering Reilly by hanging out with her? As I try to unmark myself, do I have the right to mark strangers with my presence?

Don't think too much. You've been through a lot. You can't control everything, but you seem to be doing pretty well at the moment.

Relax. Enjoy it, Jack. You've earned it.

Shower over. My clothes are in Reilly's washing machine. I get into the bathrobe she has provided. Blue silk. Body on full tingle after needle shower. Silk on tingling skin feels pretty damn good.

I wander through apartment. "Reilly? Where art thou?"

"I art in here. The bedroom."

The bedroom, huh?

Jazz playing. Reilly's room. View of park. Small private terrace. Teddy bears on big four-poster bed. "You do clean up nice," Reilly says. "You even smell better."

"Thanks, I guess. What kind of a party are we going to? I hope you'll say a dinner party."

She laughs. "Sorry, Meredith never has any food. But I'm sure I can dig up something for you here. Would you like a back rub, Jack?" She asks as if it's the most innocent thing in the world.

I remember P.J. "I don't really think . . ."

"I give good back rubs. I took a class at the Reebok Club. That's the gym my parents belong to. Come on, lie down."

A pretty girl offering a skilled back rub. One of those things in life that's hard to resist. I lie down. Reilly climbs onto bed. Kneels next to me. Small, warm hands on my back through the silk. Playful, surprisingly strong fingers. "Try to relax, Jack. Wow, do you have muscles. You must work out all the time."

"When I'm not reading Dickens."

"What sport do you play?"

"A little football now and then."

"I can't dig in because of your muscles. This robe is the problem. Let's lose it . . ."

I stop her hands. "I'm not wearing anything under it."

"Modest, aren't we? It's not like I've never seen a boy's back before. Let's get comfortable, Jack." She reaches back and pulls her own shirt off. Now she's just wearing a bra.

I catch my breath. Wow. This is happening too fast, but I can't find the brake pedal.

She divests me of my silk robe. Look that up, my friend, but not right now. Things are a little too steamy now for dictionary breaks. Reilly's hands slide up my back. She spreads oil on her palms. Circles it around my shoulder blades. She's kneeling over me now. Her blond tresses sweep up and down my spine. The jazz is throbbing. "Let it go," she says.

"What?"

"Your tension. Just try to relax. Listen to the music. Arms stretched out in front."

I stretch out my arms.

"Good. Now close your eyes and relax."

I shut my eyes. It's been a crazy, tragic, mind-blowing twelve hours. I needed human contact. Maybe not this close, but what the hell?

"Much better," Reilly says approvingly. "Eyes closed? Good boy. I'll tell you a secret. When you were sleeping in the playground I walked by and looked at you up close. You were so handsome. And you looked so innocent when you were sleeping. That's why I trusted you."

She's moving around on the bed.

Off the bed. Turning up jazz. My eyes are shut. I'm listening to the music. Trying not to think too much.

You deserve this, I'm telling myself.

"Stretch out your arms a little," Reilly says. "This is a special technique for getting your shoulders to relax." She's at the head of the bed, pulling my wrists. All of a sudden I feel metal. *Click.*

My eyes pop open. I try to yank hands away. She's handcuffed my wrists around a bedpost.

"Reilly, what are you doing?"

She makes a guttural sound in her throat. Not what you would expect from a refined Drearly girl on Central Park West. Growl of brutal triumph. Like a hunter after bagging a prime catch.

I twist head around to look at her.

Not Reilly anymore. Some kind of transformation taking place. Skin growing greenish. Eyes narrowing. Canines enlarging.

I hear myself pleading. "Who are you? I haven't done any harm to you. Please let me go."

She considers this as canines gleam. Tongue licks four inches out of mouth. Reilly-thing approaches. Voice a sharp hiss. "Just a worthless Gorm, they said. Go hunt alone. Now they'll see who's worthless. The Prince himself, and nobody helped her. Here he is. All trussed and blood-fat and ready for them."

She leans over bed. Bites my calf. Deep, slicing pain. I scream. Never been chewed before. Try very hard to yank hands out of cuffs. Some give, but not enough. Can't break bedpost. I'm strong but steel post is stronger.

She watches, amused. "You're not going anywhere. Just wanted my taste of royal blood. Sweet. Shall I give you a last chance? Tell me right now. Where is it?"

I look back at her. Force myself to focus. "Last chance" sounds ominous. I manage to ask, "What? Where is what?"

She reaches down. Nails curled like talons. Rake my back. I scream again. Jazz drowns it out. "You might as well tell me," she hisses. "Your life is over. The only question left is the amount of pain before darkness. I can turn you over to them and take my fee and go my way. But I want more, and what's good for me is good for you. So I'm asking you for the second time. Where is it?"

I look back into yellow eyes. Heartless. Soulless. Think, Jack. Time running out. "I want to cooperate. But I can't possibly tell you where it is if I don't know what it is. I swear to you I don't have a clue what's going on. So if you'll just explain to me . . ."

I stop talking. What I'm selling, Reilly isn't buying. I try the cuffs again. Can almost pull my hands free. Almost doesn't count.

Or does it? I just need lubrication. Only one possibility.

My blood. Lots of it on my back. On my calf. No help. I grind my watch's dark metal wristband into the skin of my right wrist. Rough edges of metal band cut smooth skin. It hurts. I can't let her see what I'm doing. "Go to hell," I say. "I'm not afraid of you."

"Hell is coming to you," she assures me. Leans close. Not the best breath I've ever smelled. "Do you know what they'll do to find out what they want? Neural flay. Even I wouldn't do it. But I've seen it. People scream like they're being eaten alive. Goes on for hours. You'll tell them everything. Tell me first. I'll kill you now. Tell them you died trying to escape. Save you hours and hours of torture. This is your one chance. Where is it? Where is Firestorm?"

Blood on my wrists. I slide my right hand slowly through cuff. Free. "Come closer and I'll tell you."

She comes closer. Eager hiss. "Tell me. I promise I'll kill you quickly."

"Thanks but no thanks," I say, and grab her. Sit up fast. Hit her with right hook that knocks her spinning back into wall. I

never hit a girl before. Then again, this isn't exactly Little Miss
Manners.

She bounces off wall. Doesn't go down. Bares canines. Spins
in with kick. Some kind of kung fu move. Catches me on chest.
Knocks me off bed.

No time to recuperate. She's on me. Fast slaps with clawed
hands. Lightning kicks to my stomach and groin. She's too quick
for me. Too skillful. Can't take much more.

Use your assets, Jack. Size. Strength. I grab her around waist
and power her back toward bed in football tackle mode. Pull
blanket over her head so that she can't see. She's flailing wildly. I
wrap her up in blankets and sheets. Tie it tight with bathrobe belt
and electrical cord.

Carry her in cocoon of sheet and blankets to walk-in closet.
Dump her in. Close door. Drag heavy bureau in front of it. Then
bed in front of bureau. Desk in front of bed. Five-hundred-pound
barricade. Even if she unwraps herself she'll never push her way
out.

I switch off jazz. Dab my left wrist with blood and slide cuffs
off so that they fall to floor. Stand there. Heart pumping. Chest
heaving. Looking at myself naked in bedroom mirror. I'm a
bloody mess.

First instinct is to get my clothes and run. Before Reilly finds a
way out of the closet. Or before her dad comes home. If she has a
dad. If she ever had a dad. If she is a she. I don't know what I'm
up against, but I know it defies easy categorization.

I wash my cuts and bandage them. Find my clothes. She did
not put them in washer. She dumped them on kitchen floor. No
need to clean them. She knew I wouldn't be needing them.

I put them back on. Feels nice to be dressed again. Should I
run? No. *Because she was of their world.* Whoever they are. So there
may be some clue here about what is really going on.

I won't linger too long. Every second in this penthouse is

probably dangerous. But I have to look. My need for information outweighs my urgent desire to get the hell out of here.

6

I search apartment, room to room. Draw blank. No personal stuff. Mostly fakes. Kind of like a movie set.

A trap. This was a trap set to lure you in. She was waiting near the river in case you happened along. A spider spinning a web for a very predictable fly. You blundered right into it. Oh, a pretty girl and she likes me, so I'll go home with her. So trusting and foolish. You won't survive very long if you don't get a lot smarter fast, Jack.

Here's the bad news. Whoever they are, whatever's going on, the people seeking you can predict your behavior. They have unlimited resources. They're creative. They know your world right down to stock options and Reebok Clubs, even though you don't know where the hell they're coming from.

They can play you, turn you inside out. She spun you completely around by asking if you were a serial killer. She pretended to be wary of you to keep you from being suspicious of her. Smart. You're outmatched, Jack.

But when she had you safely in her web, she presumably spoke the truth. And the truth sounded pretty weird.

What was all that stuff about you being a prince? Nobody ever called you royal, except for a second-grade teacher who once said you were a royal pain in the butt.

But you are the Prince! The beacon of hope!

Who said that? No one. Just a random weird thought
that popped into my head. Finish the search, Jack, and get out
fast.

Nothing in the whole apartment that provides the slightest
clue to who Reilly is. Master bedroom furnished, but no sheet under bedcover. No one ever slept here. Empty photo albums on
shelves. Bare refrigerator, except for four or five containers of
purple Jell-O. Apparently, when she's not sucking blood, Reilly
is diet-conscious. No clothes in dressers. All props and illusion.
A rigged trap. Intricately planned. Perfectly constructed. Wow.
Someone went to a lot of trouble to catch me.

I am ready to give up and flee. Pass a closed door. Growling
inside. Uh-oh, here's Rover. Time to get out.

No, fool. Let me go. We can flee together.

Who said that?

Me.

Who?

Me!

I look at the closed door.

Bingo.

Wait a minute. I didn't say anything. I didn't utter a single
word. I just looked at the door.

*Right. But you thought about looking. I don't have time to explain.
Open the door. The Gorm told them about you. They're coming. If they
find us here, it'll be a neural flay for both of us. And I don't know about
you, but I like my neurons unflayed.*

Good point, I think. Time to flee. But why do I need to take a
chance with you, whoever you are?

Because you have questions and I have answers, comes the response, loud and clear. *Now open the door and let me out. Every second
is precious.*

I hesitate for a second more and then unlock door and crack
it open very gently. Peer inside.

Small bedroom. Probably a maid's room. Now being used as

an animal prison. Birds chatter from coops. Rodents squeal from cages. Mice. Rats. Hamsters.

One big shape. When I say big, I mean big. Dog or bear? Dog. Chained to radiator.

Nearly three feet tall. Dark fur. Big jowls. Droopy ears. Sasquatch-size paws. Not a great Dane. Not a Newfoundland. I'm no expert on dog breeds, but I've never seen this one before.

I don't like dogs in general. I especially don't like large dogs. And I particularly don't like the look of this monstrous shaggy canine. I start to close door.

Wait. You can't leave me here.

Why not?

Because you're too incompetent to survive on your own. She caught you in a flash. They'll catch you again.

She caught you, too, fur ball, I think back to him. One of us is free right now and one of us is chained to a radiator, so watch who you call incompetent.

True. But I know things you don't. Important things. Useful things.

Like?

I can't tell you.

You'd better tell me, or it's the neural flay.

I can't. You won't leave me here. You have a good heart.

I close door. Start to walk away.

I know who your father is.

I know who he is, too. Or was. My father is dead. They killed him when they came for me. Goodbye, Rover.

No, your real father. I met him. Greatest honor of my life. I know why you're here. And why they're chasing you.

I stop walking. Turn around. Retrace steps quickly. Open door. Birds chatter. Rodents squeal. Only the dog is quiet. Big jowls. Enormous teeth. Glittering eyes. *Now get me out of here.*

How do I know you won't attack me?

Dogs are man's best friend.

That's a line.

No, it's true. We were the first domesticated animals. At least, that's how YOU would phrase the relationship. I'd of course put it in more equal terms. We started our partnership twenty thousand years ago. Dog and man. Man and dog. Best buddies. We're wasting time. This is our very last chance. Let me go. But if you don't have the nerve to do it, at least save yourself. Because they're coming. I can feel them getting closer. In fact, they're right outside the building. Save yourself. Go now.

That does it. The fact that he's telling me to go save myself makes me decide to stay and help. I approach the huge dog and look at the chain that connects his right hind leg to the radiator. Not handcuffs like the ones used on me. More like manacles. No keyhole visible, and for that matter I don't have a key. I could probably chisel it off him in about twenty years. But we don't have twenty years. Or even twenty minutes. Maybe not even one minute. I can hear someone ringing the doorbell.

Them. I don't know how I know it, but I do. My skin feels cold.

Go. Save yourself.

Not an option, rug back. Once I decide to help someone, I don't cut and run. How do I get these off you? She put them on. She must have had a way to get them off.

Only one way. Melt them off.

How?

Silfor.

What the hell's that?

Dissolvent. Eats through anything. You're right. She must have some around.

What does it look like? Where would it be?

Purple. Has to be stored cool. Forget it. You'll never find it. Save yourself. I beg you.

I run out to kitchen. Rip open fridge. Find purple Jell-O containers. Start to run back to maid's room. Then I freeze in mid-step. Because loud sounds are coming from direction of double-locked front door. They are either knocking it down or taking it off its hinges. And they're not fooling around.

I dash back into maid's room. Here it is. What do I do?

Pour it on the chains and step aside.

I rip open container. Tilt it onto chains. Purple liquid oozes out. Coats chains. Instant chemical reaction. Sizzle sounds. Chains turn black. Metal becomes soot-like powder. Big dog free.

Okay, Rover, what now? You're the one with the answers.

Name's not Rover. Also not fur ball or rug back.

Do I care? This doesn't seem the time for formal introductions. The neural flay guys are breaking down the front door.

There's always time for politeness. Gentility is a universal sign of cultural sophistication.

Okay, I'm Jack Danielson.

Gisco.

Gisco? That's a name for a dog?

Jack's a name for a prince?

KA-BOOM. Loud ripping-tearing sound that I think is front door falling in or being ripped in half. Footsteps thudding into hall. More than one man. Big, powerful, and purposeful.

Jack, I strongly suggest we get out now.

You don't have to convince me. But how? They're already inside. No way to get past them to front door.

We're in the maid's room. Near the service entrance.

Good point, snout face.

Gisco. Some respect, please. This way.

I follow dog to rear of apartment. Closed door. I turn knob. Locked. Try to unlock latch. Jammed.

Footsteps approach. My skin tingles with cold dread.

Get it open.

I'm trying.

Try harder.

You try.

No fingers.

They're two rooms away and getting closer. I hammer on latch with my fist. Give one last yank with all my strength. Latch releases. I rip open door. Bolt out into back stairwell. Start down.

No, fool. They're waiting for you down there.

Then where?

Up.

Gisco is galloping upstairs. I know "gallop" is most often used to describe horses running, but that's the way this big shaggy dog moves as it bounds up the steep flight of stairs. I follow at maximum speed.

We reach the top. Closed trapdoor.

Voices from below. They've found service door.

I hit trapdoor with heel of my fist. And again. Pop it open. Climb out onto roof of building.

Help me up. Dogs can't climb.

How?

Lower your shirt. I hope it's relatively clean.

I rip off my shirt. Lower it. Gisco sinks his teeth into the fabric.

I brace myself and haul him up. He weighs a ton.

You haven't been missing many lunches, muzzle mouth.

He reaches roof and spits out my shirt. *One more offensive nickname and I will gnaw off your gonads.*

I lock and bolt trapdoor from top. Good news is they can't follow us up this way. Bad news is we are trapped. I turn slow circle. No way off roof.

Okay, Gisco. Point taken. If you're going to hang out with humans, you might want to try to develop a sense of humor pronto. Now, how do we get off this roof?

Only one way.

Which is?

This way.

Gisco runs across roof at full sprint. Halfway between racehorse and locomotive. He reaches the edge of the roof. Launches himself through the air. Canine missile. Snout leading the way. Legs folded to belly. Oddly aerodynamic. Heading for roof of another building more than twenty feet away.

No way he'll make it. Dogs are not known for staying airborne. In a few seconds he'll be Central Park West roadkill. Goodbye, Gisco.

But he somehow just makes it to lip of far rooftop. Skids along till he stops himself. Looks back. *Your turn.*

You've got to be kidding me.

Only way out. No time to hesitate. You're a human, not a chicken.

You can insult me all you want. I can't do it.

No choice. They're coming up the stairs.

He's right. Cold tingling. I can feel their proximity.

I think of my dad's last words to me. "For years I've told you to hide your abilities. Now you must use them all. Fly, my boy, fly like the wind."

I start to run across roof. Building speed. Arms pumping. The New York breeze hitting me from the side. Twenty yards to the lip. Ten.

I've done some long jumping in my time. The whole key is planting the takeoff foot. No margin of error. I reach the edge. Right foot comes down so that toe is at edge of abyss. Plant and lift. Height is crucial. Arms straight out in front of chest. Legs stretching. Reaching for the far roof.

I'm flying between two Manhattan buildings. The city all around me. Clouds above. Sidewalk below. I don't make it. No boy could. I plummet.

Sixteen stories. See the windows flashing all the way down. The same face watching me from every window. A face I've never seen before, yet it seems familiar and terrifying. Is this the face of death itself? Thick shock of white hair, like an old lion's mane. Handsome, aristocratic features with a cruel edge. Strong jaw. Aquiline nose. Red lips slightly open to reveal gleaming, sharp teeth. The piercing eyes of a raptor, watching dispassionately as I meet my doom. Watching me all the way down. Death scream torn from my throat like a long scarlet rope. Pavement rising up to slap me into eternal darkness.

Thump.

My feet hit ledge of far building. I do make it. Go sprawling and sliding onto gravel and tar paper of roof. Never so happy to be scraped up.

Good jump. Sloppy landing.

Let's get out of here.

We find stairway down. Sixteen long flights to lobby. One more to basement. Find a side exit. Both of us winded. But no time to rest. We push out onto leafy side street.

And we run. Boy and dog. Side by side. Block after block at full sprint. Fleeing together. Drawing strange looks from New Yorkers who are used to almost anything. Till we can run no longer.

On a corner far from Reilly's building we sink down to the sidewalk. Dog is panting. I'm gasping. We made it, Gisco.

No, we haven't made it. This is just the start. From here on, it's going to get a lot worse.

✳

7

Tell me what's going on. Right now. Talk. Or think. Or whatever it is that you do.

Can't. We've got to get away.

We are away. We long-jumped our way to freedom, remember? Now we're walking down Broadway, adrift in a city of eight million people, not to mention lots of mangy dogs. They'll never find us here, whoever they are. So relax and tell me what's going on. Begin with who's chasing me. Fill in some of the blanks about where you all come from. And I'd appreciate it if you'd throw in a little personal info like who I really am and why so many people want to kill me.

No time. Your curiosity is understandable, but you're wrong. It's not safe. They're scouring the city for us and we're highly distinctive. They'll find us. Only one option. We've got to get out of town.

Hold on. There's nothing highly distinctive about me. Normal American boy. You're the one who's distinctive because of your size, not to mention girth.

Are you implying that I have a weight problem?

No offense, but you're not exactly a cute little doggy. If you had a horn you could pass for a rhino. Also, not to make you self-conscious, but you don't act like a dog.

What do you suggest I do?

Piss on a fire hydrant once in a while.

What a revolting suggestion.

How about interacting normally with other dogs? Don't be so aloof. You call attention to yourself.

They sniff my rear end. Surely you don't expect me to reciprocate?

That's how dogs get to know each other.

I prefer small talk and soft jazz.

Do you really think they're looking for us?

Absolutely. And they'll find us in a matter of hours.

There's a lady looking at us right now.

I see her.

Staring.

Yes.

Should we run?

No. She's coming toward us. If she were one of them, she'd never expose herself like this.

She's a big woman, with big hair, several big shopping bags, and a very big mouth that opens into a gooey smile. "Excuse me, but where did you get that magnificent dog?"

A highly intelligent woman. Treat her with respect.

Shut up and stop feeding me thoughts. The last thing we need now is an interrogation by a dog-loving boob. "At the pound."

"No! I can't believe it. My husband's sister is a dog trainer and I've been to the shows with her. I thought I knew all the breeds. But I've never seen anything like this. What exactly is he?"

"Just a big mutt," I tell her. "A garbage can of dog genes."

How dare you insult my ancestry.

"Are you sure? There's something so pure about him."

"Pure mongrel," I tell her. "Part great Dane, part Newfoundland, part rhino. And he sheds like an alpaca."

She laughs. "He needs a good bath, too."

You're right. She's an idiot. Get rid of her.

"He always smells like this. This is a good day."

"You need a collar and a leash or you're going to get a ticket. They're cracking down. Can I pet him?"

Don't even think about letting her touch me.

"Go ahead. He likes it when you scratch behind his ears. Dig in your nails."

I'll bite her arm off at the elbow.

I can hear her nails dig in as she rakes him behind his ears. "Oh, what a cute doggy-woggy."

Get her away from me before I rip out her jugular.

All of a sudden, I feel a cold prickle on the back of my neck. Black van. Driving by on the other side of Broadway. Tinted windows. Can't see inside. But I can feel that they're looking for me. I step behind the lady and try to use her to shield me from view. Gisco, that van!

I know. Gisco is now nuzzling up to her. Practically licking her knees. Her shopping bags screen him.

A strange thing happens. In my mind's eye, I get a flash picture of the street. People walking in slow motion. Cars driving by. The dark van. Ribbons of light shoot away from the van and touch every pedestrian. Like an X-ray.

Two ribbons of light head for Gisco and me. Can't dodge them. We'll be found out. No way to hide from this.

My left wrist suddenly tingles and then gets hot. I glance down. A bluish glow emanates from my watch. The two tentacles of light reach us and are deflected by the bluish glow. The van drives off down Broadway.

I'm not sure exactly what's happened, but I sense that this watch from my father just saved us.

Meanwhile, the lady with the big hair is thrilled that Gisco has cuddled up to her. Doesn't know he's hiding. Thinks she's found a true-blue four-legged pal.

"Oh, what a friendly doggy-woggy. Let me give your ears one more good scratch." Her nails sink in an inch deep.

The neural flay couldn't be much worse than this.

The van's gone. Do you think they'll come back the other way?

Every second we hang around is dangerous.

You convinced me. Let's get out of Dodge. "Excuse me, ma'am, but I've got to take him to the vet to be dewormed."

She pulls her hand back fast. "Nice talking to you. Bye."

And good riddance.

We turn off Broadway onto leafy side street. Okay, how do we get out of New York and where do we go?

You're asking me? You want me to be the brains of the operation after all your insults?

So far they've been able to anticipate my every move, so I'm open to suggestions.

They're masters of cause and effect. So let's reverse causality with the old chicken-and-egg game.

How does that work?

Observe something. Choose quickly.

I draw a blank. Look to the skies for help. See an airplane. Airplane.

Good. That's the chicken. Now, where's the egg?

I don't follow you.

Where were airplanes hatched?

They're not hatched. They're built. In factories.

Where did they first get off the ground?

The Wright Brothers. Kitty Hawk.

Good. That's where we're going.

Okay. But first let's duck into this pet store.

Absolutely not. Horrible place. Like a slave ship. My brothers and sisters, rise up. You have nothing to lose but your chains.

Dogs and cats in small, dirty cages start barking and meowing.

Bored salesclerk looks around uneasily. "Boy, they all woke up at the same time. Can I help you?"

"I need a leash and a big collar."

"In his size, I just have two. One with spikes and one with rhinestones."

Spikes.

"We'll take the rhinestones."

Why?

You're not a spikes kind of guy, okay?

Not okay. What do you know? You see how he treats me, my dear brothers and sisters. This wretched race of fools! Vent your full rage upon them!

Dogs and cats going nuts. Canaries chattering. Parrots hurling profanities at me in English and Spanish. Even the tropical fish swimming angry zigzag patterns.

Salesgirl wigging out. "What the hell's going on?"

"I don't know," I tell her, paying. I fasten rhinestone collar around Gisco's huge neck and snap on chain leash. "Maybe they need to be fed or something. Bye."

I yank dog out of store. Enough rabble-rousing.

That place was a disgrace.

So what? Is it any of our business? Stop calling attention to yourself.

He sniffs. *And to think the word "humane" is akin to "human."*

✴

8

Penn Station at rush hour. Gazillions of stressed-out people. Commuters. Travelers. Hard to spot or remember anyone in this chaos. Even a blind teenage boy wearing a baseball cap and dark glasses, tapping with his cane as his large Seeing Eye dog leads the way. Dog bounds forward and boy nearly falls down a flight of stone steps.

Sorry about that.

Slow down. You nearly killed me. I'm supposed to be blind and you're supposed to be a trained dog, remember?

First of all, you're not really blind, so why don't you watch where the hell you're going. Second, I'm a little nervous, okay? They're probably here looking for us. I'll relax on the train.

What do you mean they're here looking for us? I thought we outfoxed them by reversing causality. The old chicken-and-egg game. Remember?

They don't know where we're going. But they may anticipate that we're going to flee by train.

Great. So what do we do?

Proceed with caution. Here's the ticket line. By the way, I only travel first class.

Maybe they have a kennel car.

Old-man ticket seller. "Whaddaya want?"

"I'd like to reserve a first-class private sleeper on the five-sixteen to Raleigh."

Now you're talking. Ask if they have room service.

"No uncaged pets allowed."

"I'm blind. This dog is my eyes."

"Come on, kid. Don't try that."

"Don't try what?"

"I've been doing this thirty-two years. You think you're the first wisenheimer who wanted to take his dog on the train and bought a pair of dark glasses? I watched you walk up. And I know a trained Seeing Eye dog when I see one. They're super-smart. Not like this hairy putz."

What did he call me?

"For your information, mister, I'm not totally blind, but I am legally blind. And this is a super-intelligent and highly trained Seeing Eye dog."

"Yeah, right," the man says, looking Gisco over.

"I'll prove it. Give him a command. Anything."

"Sit," the man says.

Gisco looks back at him. Contemptuous dog stare. Haughty. Condescending. *That's the best you can do?*

The huge dog daintily parks his rump on the ground in a thoughtful and decidedly un-doglike pose. His belly sags down on his folded hind legs and he raises one eye and surveys the ticket seller with the equanimity of the Buddha.

The old ticket seller gapes. "I'll be damned. Never saw a dog sit like that before." He types on his computer and studies the screen. "I've got a sleeper, but there are two beds."

"Fine. I'll take both of them."

The man cracks up. "Your dog sleeps in a bed?"

Your mother eats with silverware?

"We're in a rush. How much is it?" I peel hundreds off my roll. At the sight of the large bills he stops laughing and making wisecracks and gives us our tickets.

"You'd better hurry. Train leaves in ten minutes."

We head for the stairs to the platform. Uh-oh. Stop short at the same second. I instantly spot him. Getting better at this. Dressed as a security guard. Standing on steps. Scanning crowd. Don't think he saw us.

I don't think so either. But we'd better get on another train.

What are you talking about?

Seeing Eye dog yanks blind boy down wrong stairs.

This is a train to Montreal. Leaves in two minutes.

I know.

I don't want to go to Montreal.

Neither do I. Too cold.

Our train leaves in seven minutes.

Six. That's it over there.

Cold prickle. Gisco. He saw us. He's coming.

Just keep running. Don't look back.

I look back. Glimpse security guard climbing onto train and chasing us. He's fast.

"ALL ABOARD."

When I say "now," jump out the door.

I look back again. He's gaining on us. Raising some kind of gun. In full sprint. Awkward aim. He fires.

FZZZT. Empty blue seat near us melts like wax candle.

Now.

Gisco jumps out just as train's doors start to close. I dive out after him. Doors clip my right ankle, but I make it. Sprawl onto platform.

Security guard is trapped in mid-car. By the time he makes it to the closed door, the train is rolling.

Tall man. Nasty face. Tries to pry doors apart. No luck. Train gathers speed. Ferocious scowl at us. Can't blame him. He's off to Montreal.

We sprint back up stairs. Down the next stairwell. Hear "Last call, five-sixteen to Philadelphia, Washington, D.C., Raleigh, and all stations to Miami."

Friends and family of departing travelers are walking up the stairs. We dodge them, fighting our way down. Gisco loses footing and tumbles like snowball on mountainside. People get out of his way. Canine avalanche.

I follow and jump down last twenty steps. We tear across platform and dive onto our train just as the doors shut.

Made it. Whew. Then we see black shoes. And uniform.

Female conductor right there, looking down at us. Cute. Slightly chubby. Red hair. Glasses. "Sorry. No uncaged pets allowed."

"I'm blind and this is my Seeing Eye dog."

"I just saw you running along the platform."

"Yeah, but I'm legally blind. My dog is trained to catch trains. We just made it."

She considers. "Where's your luggage?"

"Somebody stole it out of our taxi. To hell with New York. We're going back home to where folks are friendly."

She shrugs. "There are bad people everywhere. Let me see your tickets."

I produce them. "This way," she says.

We walk through train. Reach our private little sleeper compartment. Small but comfy. I pretend I can't see. Let Gisco lead me in. Feel for chair. Sit down carefully. "Thanks," I say. Open wallet and give her a tip.

"Thank you," she says. "I'll come by later and show you how the beds fold out."

"Don't bother," I tell her.

"It's no bother," she says. "Enjoy the ride, Mr. . . . ?"

I hesitate. "Smith," I tell her.

Great imagination you have.

"I'm Jinny. See you later, Mr. Smith. See you later, Mr. Smith's dog." She smiles.

Either you tipped her too much or she likes you.

Jinny closes door.

Train speeds through long tunnel.

It pops out into daylight. New Jersey. Swampland. The sky-scrapers of New York recede into the late afternoon shadows.

We're finally alone. And safe.

Now I need some answers.

9

Locked sleeper compartment. Man and dog rolling through wastelands of New Jersey. Chemical plants. Oil and gas refineries. Befouled meadows and polluted swamps.

Dog staring fixedly out window, as if pondering deep puzzle. Boy looking impatiently at dog. Talk to me.

How can they stand to live around such a smell? Yet they don't clean it up. They keep going and going . . .

I yank curtain closed. Goodbye, view. The sightseeing portion of this journey will commence after the conversation. Now, let's have some answers.

Big mutt shifts uneasily. *What do you want to know?*

Start with the basics. Who am I? Why are people trying to kill me? Who are they and, for that matter, who are you? Are you from the Twilight Zone or some top-secret government experiment? What the heck is Firestorm?

Sorry. Can't tell you any of that.

Don't screw around with me, dog.

I'm not, human. I feel for you.

But you don't know the answers to my questions?

I know the answers. I just can't give them to you.

I lose it. Jump forward. Try to grab dog around neck.

Gisco growls. Shakes me off.

I grab fore and hind leg and try to flip him over.

He bares teeth. Warning snarl. *Let go now.*

Talk! I try to flip him over.

Teeth close around my right arm. Not biting me yet. Not breaking the skin. But I can feel jaw muscles tighten. Feels like steel vise. *Last chance. Let go.*

I pummel Gisco with left fist. To hell with you. Who am I? I have a right to know.

Dog surges forward. Unexpected thrust. Must be the sled-dog part of his ancestry. I am jerked forward and bang my head against metal wall so hard that I nearly black out.

You okay?

No.

Sorry I had to do that. Never grab a dog around the neck. Very old impulse to protect jugular vein. Also, don't grab a dog's legs. Equally old impulse to remain upright.

You seem to be my friend. My only friend right now. Why won't you tell me what I need to know?

I shouldn't even tell you that. But I pity you.

Okay. Why?

Because the human brain is a powerful but notoriously delicate and unstable mechanism.

Meaning?

You couldn't handle the truth.

Try me.

Can't risk it.

What's the worst that could happen?

Jarring dislocation from your own past. Identity loss. Deep betrayal. You might melt down.

I may be a human but I don't melt down easily.

Read Oedipus.

You're gonna tell me I'm destined to kill my father and marry my mother?

Sad dog eyes looking at me. *Much worse than that. Sorry, kid. Don't you think I'd tell you if I could?*

The awful thing is that I do. I sink down to dirty blue rug of sleeper compartment. Curl up into fetal ball. Break into tears. This breakdown has been a long time coming.

Now the grief hits like a thunderstorm. Horrific images. Dad shooting off his foot. His face twisted in agony. Raising the gun to his head. Do I have to blow my brains out to get you to go? Reilly-thing with my blood on her lips. Long jumping between buildings. The face of death watching me. Constantly being chased and tracked, by a nameless, faceless army. Can't trust anyone except big fur ball of a dog who won't answer any questions because he says if I learned the truth about my fate it would be worse than what drove Oedipus to strike out his eyes.

Tap, tap.

Go away. Leave me alone. Don't know how long I've been lying on the floor, crying and shaking.

Gisco is next to me. Snuggled against me. *There, there, kid. I feel for you. So lost. So isolated. I really get it. We're all in much the same predicament . . .*

"We" who?

Forget it. Slip of the tongue.

No it wasn't. "We" who? Come on!

Me. The people chasing you. The people helping you. The Gorm. The couple who raised you.

I know you can't answer all of my questions, but just answer one. Where are you all from? I beg you to tell me.

The big dog hesitates. *Not from the Twilight Zone. And not from a government experiment, either.*

Tap, tap, tap.

Then where?

Here. And not here.

So far you haven't answered anything.

Long wet dog tongue licks my cheek. Perhaps meant to be consoling. *It would blow your mind. And there's no time now. Someone's at our door. You are the beacon of hope. Pull yourself together. A lot of people are counting on you.*

Yeah? Well, tell them to go jump in a lake. I want my parents back. I want my life back. I want to go to sleep in my room with the sports posters taped to the wall and my stereo on the table near the desk with the picture of a smiling P.J. and the view out the window of Mom's garden.

Tap, tap, tap, tap. "You okay in there? Open up."

Look, kid, you can cry yourself a river, but you can't have those things back. They're gone for good. We've got problems in the here and now. Someone's trying to get in.

Growl at them. They'll get the message.

No, you've got to open the door and convince them that we're okay. The salient point I'm trying to get across is that this is not such a great time to be having a breakdown. We can't risk calling attention to ourselves.

The word "salient" does it. Dog using fancy SAT word. Like a puff of breeze that blows away the fog. He's right.

Key turning in our door. Jinny standing there in her conductor's outfit. "Are you okay?"

Brave grin. "Sure."

"What are you doing on the floor?"

"Napping."

She steps inside. Concern in her voice. "What's wrong?"

"Nothing." I look up at her. "I always nap on the floor."

"You've got tears on your cheeks. Your eyes are red."

I fumble for my sunglasses and put them on. Look back at her through dark lenses. "Now they're not red anymore. We paid for a private compartment because we didn't want to be disturbed. If you don't mind."

"We? That would be you and your dog?"

"I think I answered enough of your questions, Jinny."

"Okay," she says, and her eyes harden. "Okay, Mr. Smith. It's just that I had some information for you."

What information? Sounds ominous.

She steps out and starts to close door.

"Stop, Jinny. What information?"

"Forget it. I'll give you your privacy."

She closes door.

I get up to chase her.

Where do you think you're going?

To find out what she knows.

If you go alone she'll see that you're not blind.

The human brain may be delicate and unstable, but apparently it can register nuances of meaning that the dog brain can't distinguish.

Meaning?

She already knows that I'm not blind, Purina face. The question is what else she knows.

10

Dispense with sham of cane and dark glasses. Hurry through train. Searching car to car. Jinny, where are you? What did you come to tell me? Reach the cafe car. People eating sandwiches.

Reading newspapers. Stench of stale bread and beer. Not the most appetizing odor in the world, but my stomach responds.

Rumble rumble. Last meal was hot dog in Riverside Park. A stale sandwich would sure hit the spot.

Spot a conductor. Old. Stooped. Tired and bored. Waxy complexion. Punching tickets. "Excuse me, sir. I'm looking for Jinny? She works on the train and I've—"

"Rawlings," he drawls out of the side of his mouth, as if he answers a thousand stupid questions a day and can't be bothered to open his lips more than partway.

"I beg your pardon?"

"Virginia Rawlings. Next car, last door on the left."

Hurry to next car. Find last door. Knock. No answer.

Open door a crack. "Jinny?"

Voice from semidarkness. "Go away."

"It's me. Mr. Smith."

"I know who you are. Go to hell, asshole."

Peek inside. Storage space. Blankets. Bedding.

Jinny leaning against a stack of pillows near the one small window. Crying her big brown eyes out.

Enter storage room. Close door behind me. "Actually, my name isn't Mr. Smith. And I'm not blind."

"Could I possibly care less?"

Refreshing sarcasm. I step toward her. "I know this sounds hokey, but I can't stand to see a woman cry."

"Then why don't you leave."

"Tell me what's wrong?"

"No," she says.

"I'm sorry I was rude before. Can I sit next to you?"

"No."

"Are you one of those girls who say no when they mean yes?"

She glances at me. "No. I mean yes, I'm not. *Don't confuse me.* I'm miserable enough."

"That makes two of us," I say, and I sit down next to her.

Shoulders touching. Jinny stops crying. We look out the one small window at the landscape that flashes past.

Polluted swamps have given way to woods and farmland. I remind myself this is called the Garden State. Pretty October sunset overhead. Furrows of purple cloud stretch to the horizon, as if the sky has been plowed over.

" 'Barred clouds bloom the soft-dying day,' " I whisper.

"What?"

"Nothing."

"It sounded like poetry."

"Yeah." I hesitate. " 'Ode to Autumn.' John Keats."

"I've heard of him," Jinny says. I can't tell whether she's still being sarcastic. Don't think so.

"He's one of my favorites," I tell her. "I think he had the most musical turn of phrase of any English poet ever. He wrote a poem addressed to Autumn, as if he's talking to the season. It has a line about 'barred clouds.' This view reminded me of it. Sorry. I wasn't showing off."

Jinny relaxes slightly. Her shoulder is now pressed against mine. I can feel her warmth through her conductor's uniform. "Keep going," she says. "Keep talking."

I'm getting something from her. Don't know what it is. Sadness? Anger? Regret? Can't quite make it out.

So I keep babbling away about the poem. "Keats tells Autumn it doesn't have to be jealous of Spring, because Autumn has its own special music. Small gnats mourning. Hedge-crickets singing. Grown lambs bleating on the hillside." I hear myself rambling on and shrug. "It sounds a lot better when Keats describes it."

"It sounds okay when you describe it," Jinny says softly. "Keep talking. Please."

"That's about it," I tell her. "Keats only wrote a few odes. Dashed them off in one burst of genius, in his early twenties. Then he got sick. Traveled to Italy to try to recover his health.

Died in Rome at twenty-five. I used to think that was so young. Imagine dying at twenty-five? Never having gotten married. Never having kids. Now it seems so old. I'll consider myself lucky to make nineteen." My voice cracks. I shut up. Saying too much.

Silence in the car. Jinny's breathing. Train sounds. Outside the window barred clouds bloom the soft-dying day over a New Jersey pine forest. "I knew you were in trouble the first time I saw you," Jinny whispers.

"How did you know it?"

"I've been chased myself," she admits. Honest girl. This isn't easy for her. But she wants to talk.

"By the police?"

"No. By a guy."

"He was in love with you?" I probe gently.

She moves her head, somewhere between a nod and a shake. "He wanted to marry me. Then he wanted to kill me. He almost did both. So when I saw you I knew."

I'm getting something very strong and personal from her that I can't figure out. Some sort of connection. Sympathy? Deeper than that. Empathy? Darker than that. Fear?

"Is that why you took this job on the train?" I ask. "To get away from him?"

She turns to look at me. Wet brown eyes, big as saucers. Russet hair shimmering like a bleeding vein of gold in dusk light. "Hold me," she whispers.

I start to hold her, then pull back. "You're not a Gorm?"

She looks angry and baffled. "Is that like a ho?"

No one could be such a good actor. I chuckle and hug her gently. "Not at all," I tell her.

Feels good to have my arms around Jinny. She's a big girl. There's a lot to hug, and she hugs back. Her hair brushes my neck. We've both been crying recently, so our cheeks feel cool and a little wet as they brush together.

Not quite sexual attraction. Not quite friendly companionship. Some interesting place in between.

"Who's after you?" she whispers.

"You'd never believe me."

"Bet I would."

"I was living a normal life in this little town."

"Uh-huh," she says.

"Then people came to kill my father."

She sucks in a breath. "Oh my God."

"He told me to flee. Ever since then strange life-forms have been chasing me. Some of them look like giant bats. Then there was this girl who brought me home, but it turned out she was a Gorm. That dog and I escaped from her apartment, but he's not a normal dog. We communicate by telepathy. And the weirdest thing is I don't know why he's helping me and I don't know why they're chasing me, but it seems like I'm the critical player in some kind of gigantic, secret war."

Jinny trembles. I hug her harder. Is she afraid? Freaked out by what I've told her? No, she's giggling. Trying to hold it in, but her body is shaking with mirth. "Okay, wise guy," she finally gasps. "You don't have to tell me who's chasing you. It's none of my business."

Can't blame her for not believing me. But I decide to take advantage of this change in mood. "Jinny, what did you come to my compartment to tell me?"

She stops laughing. "Doesn't matter. It's okay. I took care of it."

"Please. I need to know."

She hesitates. "Someone's asking questions about you."

"What do you mean?" I ask quickly. Jinny feels me tense up. "Who?" I demand.

She pulls away. Studies my face. Sees that I won't let this go. "Someone from New York security called. Talked to our head conductor. Wanted to know if there was a blind man on the train. And a Seeing Eye dog. The head conductor asked each of us about the passengers in our cars. I covered for you."

"Why?"

She nods. "Like I told you, I've been chased. I knew you weren't really blind, so I was telling the truth. I bet they called all the trains that left Penn Station around that time. I heard the conductor tell them he had checked and there was no blind man on our train. Which is true, right?"

"Right. Thanks, Jinny. I owe you big-time."

She stands up. Turns away from me. Makes a sound in her throat. Whatever it is, it's really troubling her. "You don't owe me anything," she says softly.

"But I do. You may have saved my life. And you did it without knowing me. Just because you're a good person."

She turns toward the window and pretends to fix her uniform in the reflection. "Yes, well, now I have to get back to work."

Strange, I thought she liked me. She saved me. Now she doesn't even want to look at me.

Then I understand. No, stupid, she *can't* look at you. It's not anger. Not empathy. It's guilt! She *is* a good person, and she feels terrible because she's betrayed you.

Jinny reaches for door. "I gotta get back to my job."

I grab her. Pull her back into storage compartment.

She tries to scream.

I clamp my hand over her mouth. "You told them I'm on the train. And then you felt bad about selling me out. So you came by to try to find out what kind of trouble I'm in."

I remove hand. She lies quickly, desperately. "No. I would never—"

"Or maybe it wasn't that. Maybe you came by to keep an eye on me. Was that part of the deal? Keep tabs on your catch? Tell me the truth. How much did they offer you?"

"They didn't . . . I didn't . . . We never . . ." Jinny tries several denials and they get jumbled together. Then she tries stamping on my instep, but I'm too fast. She starts an impressive scream, but I cut off her air supply.

I'm looking into her eyes. She's scared. Thinks I'll strangle her. I won't, but it doesn't hurt for her to think it.

"How much? Last chance."

She gasps. "Three thousand dollars. More than I make in a month. I figured you probably did something really bad. I'm sorry. I like you. I just needed the money . . ."

"Where are they going to board the train and get us?"

"Philly."

"How long till we get there?"

"Less than thirty minutes."

"How do I get off before then?"

"You can't."

"There must be some way."

I'm looking into Jinny's scared brown eyes. "No. It's a straight shot to Philly," she says. "We're going sixty miles an hour. There's no way off this speeding train."

I let her go. Control my anger. "I'll find one," I promise. "And when I go, there goes your reward. Guess you'll have to find another way to make some extra money. Oh, one other thing, Jinny. If I were you I'd run for it as soon as this train reaches Philly. The people chasing me aren't very forgiving. When they figure out I'm gone, they'll come looking for you to find out who tipped me off. They have a technique called the neural flay that's supposed to be particularly unpleasant. Good luck being on the run again."

She's looking at me. Eyes desperate. "Wait. Let me come with you. I can help. Don't leave me alone."

"Like to talk more," I tell her. "Have to run."

11

Dining hour on train. Cafe car full. Newspaper readers opening brown bags and unwrapping sandwiches as they scan sports sections. Mothers handing bottles to babies.

Gisco and I trying to figure a way off this express to hell. Not much time. Philadelphia swimming toward us through the evening gloom. Announcement over the loudspeaker. 30th Street Station in twenty minutes. I have a pretty strong hunch a world of pain is waiting for us in the City of Brotherly Love if we don't find some way off soon.

Twenty minutes and ticking. Nineteen now.

You don't have to remind me. Dogs may not wear watches, but we're very sensitive to our own impending doom. There it is!

We stand in tiny space between last two cars. I shine flashlight. Black iron ladder leads to roof.

Why are you hesitating?

Because I don't like climbing ladders at night into windstorms to reach the roofs of speeding trains.

No choice, old bean.

Don't call me that.

Eighteen minutes, old bean. Better go for it.

So I grasp iron ladder. Start to pull myself up.

Climb rung by rung. Cold autumn wind whips me. Forty lashes. Swat. Swat. My face, my clothes, tearing at my fingers that hold the ladder. I hang on for dear life.

Don't stop.

Easy for you to say. How come I'm the one that has to do all the hard work? If dogs are really so great, you'd think we'd find ourselves in a situation where you could—

Keep climbing. Seventeen minutes.

I keep climbing. Reach roof and somehow pull myself up. Never been on top of a train before. Kind of neat. You can feel it speeding along beneath you. Like galloping atop a gigantic super-fast horse. Dark countryside flying past. We must be in outlying suburbs. Two-story houses, spaced apart. Lights on. Kids doing homework. Here and there spooky lakes of blackness. Fields? Parks? Clusters of tall trees stand together by the tracks, as if engaged in private conversations. Their branches blot out the moon.

Hurry up.

I take off my belt. Lower it to Gisco. Let's go, jabber jaws.

He clamps his teeth around knot. I try to haul him up. Like pulling a two-hundred-pound potato sack up the side of a cliff.

Paws are pathetic. Why can't dogs learn to climb?

Dogs have many abilities that humans don't have. Do I ask you why you can't smell worth a damn? Do I ask you—

Okay, okay, I get the message. But all the same it wouldn't hurt you to miss a few meals . . .

I just missed lunch and dinner. If I miss one more meal I might take a chomp out of your drumstick of a leg.

I haul dog up and onto roof. Good news is we are now standing atop train, side by side. Bad news is there is no easy way off. No convenient hay bales by side of tracks to cushion our fall. Nor does the train slow down around curves to permit easy egress. Look that up, my friend, but not now. Now we have to get off this speeding caboose.

In the distance, the clouds are unnaturally bright. Is that Philadelphia?

Unfortunately, I think you're finally right about something. Fourteen minutes. It's now or never.

Never. We'll die if we jump from here at this speed.

They'll kill us if we don't.

We can make a break for it at the station.

You don't know who you're up against.

That's because you won't tell me.

Kid, I'll tell you one thing.

Go on.

Tunnel.

What? Where?

Dog flattens himself out on haunches. *THERE!*

I dive onto stomach just as we disappear into maw of dark tunnel. Not much clearance. Feels like tunnel is giving me a crew cut. I'm hugging grimy roof of train for dear life. Pressing nose into the cold steel. Rumble of train is magnified by narrow enclosure. Feels like I'm being eaten and digested by dark and angry stomach.

I'm not exactly enjoying this.

Me neither. Dogs are highly sensitive to noise.

Then we are through and out the other side, and back in the open space and relative quiet of the moonlit evening.

Wow, was that awful.

Out of the frying pan into the fire, as you humans say.

Meaning?

There's Philadelphia.

We can see it in the distance. City skyline in moonlight. Tall buildings marching closer.

I see a wedding band of gold curving through the blackness. Moonlight on water. A river. Right in our path. Only chance.

Dogs can swim, right?

Understatement. One of nature's great swimmers. Not known for our diving. Do you think the water will be cold?

That, fuzz face, is the least of our worries.

Train reaches old trestle bridge, which is not as solid as it looks. Standing on train's roof, we can feel bridge shake rhythmically. Dark glint of river probably only thirty feet below, but from here it looks like an abyss. Now we're starting across bridge. Now we're in the middle.

I take three steps and leap off. Momentum of train slings me far out. YAAAAAAAAAA! Flapping my arms. Trying to fly. Failing miserably. Falling into blackness.

Gisco right with me. Not enjoying this either. Yelpings of canine fear. YA-BA-WAAH, YA-BA-WAAH! Not a pretty sound.

Fur ball, if we don't make it, you've been the best thing about the past two days, which isn't saying much . . .

Thanks, old bean. Feeling's mutual.

Then we splash down. Not the cleanest river in the world. But could be the coldest. Initial impact socks me like a punch to the jaw. Nearly knocks me senseless. Before I know it, I'm sinking far beneath the stars that fade to distant spearpoints. Make that ice-pick points. Frigid temperature jabs me back to full consciousness. It's only late October. Why does this feel like polar sea?

I kick for surface. Come up sputtering.

So you made it. Thought I might have to dive down and find you on the sludgy bottom.

Thanks for the kind thought, but I didn't notice you swimming around in circles looking for me. Where are you, by the way?

Up here on the bank. That river's a little cold.

Hurried strokes till my feet touch. Crawl out onto mud and pebbles. Retch and choke and cough. Suck in a cold few breaths. Check myself. Arms and legs functional. All teeth appear to be adhering to gums. I made it!

I stand. Shiver. We're going to have to find some food and shelter soon without calling attention to ourselves.

I agree. Good news. Lights up ahead. Voices. Some kind of outdoor get-together. Maybe it's a cookout.

Great.

Bad news. I think someone's pointing a gun at us.

12

Think big. A stomach the size of a refrigerator. A great shaggy head with an untrimmed beard. Holding a shotgun, light as a toothpick. Foghorn voice commanding, "Freeze."

Which is indeed what we're doing. I try to stand still but shake in my wet clothes in the numbing wind.

Shotgun aimed at my nose. "Just where do you think you're sneaking around to? I oughta blow your brains out."

Good news, Gisco. I don't think he's one of them.

Right, but he's still holding a gun on us.

On me, actually. What do you suggest?

Calm him down. The capacity of unstable humans for unprovoked violence is well documented.

"Hey, there," I say in my friendliest voice. "We weren't sneaking around."

"Then how the hell'd you get here?"

"By accident. We jumped off a train into that river."

Big man scowls. "Don't lie to me, boy."

"The train tracks cross that bridge. Feel my clothes. They're wet from the river. I just swam out."

Stubby fingers grab my shirt. Suspicious eyes cross the trestle bridge and then dive down to the inky river. Then back to me. "Why'd you jump?"

"We decided we didn't want to go to Philadelphia," I tell him and shiver. "By the way, I'm freezing."

"Not my problem," he says with impressive lack of sympathy. "Walk up the bank. And don't try anything, or I'll blow your fool head off. Same goes for your butt-ugly dog."

We climb the bank toward the lights.

I don't want to seem standoffish, old bean, but I think I would prefer not to meet this gentleman's companions.

No choice. If we run, he'll shoot us in the back.

We stumble through overgrown swampy field. Cattails. Hiphigh grass. Brambles. Here and there a stunted tree.

Men's voices up ahead. Engaged in something serious. It involves money. We've blundered across a business deal. The giant was a lookout. He yells, "Yo, Hayes."

"Wait till we're done," comes flying back at us.

Money changes hands. Contraband tucked away. Guns? Drugs? I don't try to see. Three motorcycles roar off.

"Okay," the one called Hayes shouts.

Shotgun prods my spine. "Move it."

We hike up to clearing. A dozen motorcycles circled like a Stonehenge of Harley-Davidsons. Chrome in moonlight. Beefy men looking me over. Leather and long hair and tattoos. Motorcycle gang. They don't look particularly fond of shivering teenagers and know-it-all shaggy dogs.

"Who the hell are you?" a voice of authority demands.

I spin around. Hayes. Top Handlebar or whatever you call the leader of a motorcycle gang. Hawklike features. Brown skin. Chiseled muscles. Nasty smart. You can tell by looking into his flint-hard eyes. Which is what I'm doing as I stand there shivering. "Where'd you find Dorothy and Toto?" he asks.

"Down by the river," the big man supplies. "Say they were headed to Philly and jumped off a train. I didn't see 'em jump, though. They could've been snooping around."

"They don't look like cops," Hayes points out. "Punk ass should be home doing his homework, and no police dog is that fat." Some of his buddies laugh.

You're no day at the beach either, pigeon face.

Hayes stares down at Gisco. "I don't like the way he's looking at me."

"He's just hungry," I say quickly. "Missed dinner."

"Yeah, well, I ain't dog food, so tell him to look someplace else before I skin him for a rug."

"Down, boy," I say. Unless you want to end up a motorcycle blanket, chill out.

Gisco has his back arched, attack mode. He slowly lets it relax, and looks down, as if to count blades of grass.

"We don't want any trouble—" I start to explain.

An impatient voice from the fringe of the circle cuts me off. "We can't take chances. Let's get rid of them."

"Getting rid of them is taking a chance, too, Cassidy," Hayes points out.

Cassidy steps forward. Shaved head. Flat cauliflower of a nose. Whoever broke it did a thorough job. Flick. A knife pops open in his right hand. "Nobody jumps off a train in the middle of the night. Who knows what they heard or saw. They came out of the river. Let's put 'em back in."

Hayes listens to this advice and watches for my reaction. Will I beg or try to run away?

I can tell that these gang members admire strength and detest weakness. Also sense that while they're suspicious of me they're not particularly fond of Cassidy. The only way out of this is to take him on and make it personal. Not us against them. Him against me. Mano a mano.

"If you're gonna call me a liar," I say to Cassidy, "why don't you back it up like a man?"

Whistles around the circle. "He's calling you out!"

"You heard him, Cassidy," Hayes says. "Lose the blade or give him one."

Cassidy wasn't expecting this. He looks me over. Reluctantly hands his knife to a friend. "This is gonna be fun," he grunts, and shuffles toward me.

13

*D*o *you know what you're doing, old bean?*

Don't try to help me. They'll shoot you.

Careful. Here he comes!

Cassidy feints with his right, and when I duck he kicks me in the balls. Not exactly Marquis of Queensberry rules.

The bad news is I wasn't expecting his kick and it connects in the family jewels. I groan and sink to my knees. He follows with an even harder kick, aimed at my temple.

This would finish me, but the good news—if you can call it that—is that you can get kicked in the balls and fight through the pain if you've been there before. Unfortunately, I have. Defensive linemen trying to bring me down on football fields. Stray elbows on wrestling mats.

The flash of pain is intense but starts to subside almost instantly. I pull back and avoid the kick to the head.

Baldy wasn't expecting to miss. Throws him off balance. I grab his ankle and twist and he crashes down into the mud.

Then we're grappling, rolling around and around in the clearing. Suits me just fine. I've got two varsity letters in wrestling. Could have been county champ if my dad hadn't suggested I let the other guy win. I get in a control position and pin Cassidy on his back.

He rears up and bites off a piece of my ear. Mike Tyson move.

They don't do that on high school wrestling mats. I hear him growl and then feel his teeth slicing into my right earlobe. He spits something out and there's a piece of what used to be me on the ground.

"Hurts" doesn't do it justice. "Burning agony" is closer. I go kinda nuts. Surge of strength. From my knees I lift Cassidy off the ground and slam him back down into a tree stump. Impact knocks the air from his body, but he keeps punching at me. So I pick him up again. Second body slam breaks a couple of his ribs. He tries to gouge out my eyes, but I bury my face in his chest as I pick him up again. Third slam makes his body relax and his eyes glassy.

He's not dead, maybe not even unconscious, but he won't be talking about throwing someone in the river for a while.

I get back to my feet. Heart thumping. Blood flowing down the right side of my face.

You okay?

Don't I look it?

You look like you just slid through a garbage disposal.

A couple of the gang members carry Cassidy away. Hayes doesn't even give him a look. He's focused on me. "Not bad, punk ass. What's your name?"

"Jack."

"Eighteen?"

"In a few months."

"Big for your age. Tough, too. How come you're not home with your mommy and daddy?"

"I don't have a home." I also don't have a mommy and daddy anymore, but I keep this to myself.

My answer touches something in Hayes. Momentary connection. Something tells me he didn't exactly have a stable home himself when he was eighteen.

"You coulda got killed jumping off a train. Why'd you do a damn-fool thing like that?"

" 'Cause we coulda got killed staying on it, too."

"Somebody's after you?"

My voice shakes as I say, "I gotta stop this bleeding."

"Answer my question."

"Somebody's after me. I need dry clothes."

"I'm not running a charity."

"I'll pay."

His eyes gleam. "You got money?"

Watch it, old bean.

"Enough to buy clothes," I tell him. "And also a motorcycle."

Hayes looks amused. "Say what?"

"Nothing fancy," I continue. "A used bike with a couple of dings would be just fine. Long as it runs."

Aren't you forgetting that dogs can't ride motorcycles? Our paws are not suited for grasping handlebars. I suggest you purchase another type of vehicle. A luxury sedan would be my first choice, but I'm willing to consider an SUV . . .

The beefy men in leather are looking at me like I'm crazy. "A straight cash deal," I tell Hayes. "No bills of sale or DMV documents or any of that. Name your price."

Hayes considers for a second. "What's to stop me from just taking your money?"

Blood running down my cheek like war paint. My arms out from my sides, fingers clenched into fists. Looking back into those flinty eyes. "What's to stop you?" I ask him back.

I get the feeling Hayes doesn't smile very often, but he does now. "Punk ass reminds me of me," he tells his buddies. "Get him some dry clothes before his big balls freeze. Screech, you had a bike you were looking to move?"

"Yeah," a guy agrees in a high-pitched voice, "but hell, that old thing—"

"Will do fine," Hayes finishes. "What about the mutt?"

How considerate of you to remember me. Mutt, by the way, is not an appellation I answer to. Mr. Mutt, perhaps. Let me again bring up the luxury sedan option . . .

"I got an idea," says a fellow who seems to prefer denim to leather. Looks more like a farm boy than a motorcycle gang member. "I saw something in my Auntie Rachel's barn that would work. One of them old sidecars from like a hundred years ago."

Hayes thinks it over for a second and then offers me his deal. "Four hundred bucks to Screech for the bike. A hundred to Auntie Rachel for the sidecar. Another C-note to me for dry clothes and the pleasure of our company. You got six hundred dollars, punk ass?"

Six hundred? That's highway robbery. Counter low. May I suggest that in negotiating, it's always best to give the impression that you are willing to walk away—

"Deal," I say, and offer my hand. It flaps out there in the cold wind like a lonely flag.

Hayes ignores it. "Show me the cash," he says.

14

It works just great most of the time," Screech assures me. "If it starts to stall, kick it here." He demonstrates. The engine sputters and catches.

Great bike. You really know how to pick 'em.

Don't give me any lip. You look preposterous.

That's putting it lightly. After an hour of searching in Auntie Rachel's barn, the gang members found an old sidecar. Looks like it belongs in a Laurel and Hardy movie, a prop from a century-old stunt. Next they improvised a way to fasten it to Screech's

Harley, which is rusted and has more dings and dents than a carp has scales.

After putting a crude bandage on my ear, they dressed me up in patchy denim and scruffy leather. Jeans two sizes too big. I double-cuffed the pants legs, but the waist and seat balloon out. Leather jacket with one long sleeve and the other ripped off at the shoulder. And one last mocking touch—some joker tied a red bandanna on Gisco's head.

So here we are, saying our goodbyes to the motorcycle gang, who have come to see us as comic relief. "Smooth sailing, punk ass." "Don't let those pants blow off." "Next we got to get that dog some tattoos." "Check it out—Dorothy in leather and Toto in a do-rag!"

I smile and wave and am about to hit the gas and get us the hell out of there when Hayes saunters over. Uh-oh. What does he want? "You look like a fool," he says.

"Thanks to you and your buddies," I reply.

"You complaining?" Now he's holding my handlebars.

"No. I'm dry and this bike runs," I tell him with a shrug. "That's all I need. Thanks. See ya."

He doesn't let go. Awkward moment. Tough guy wants to say something, but he's not good at expressing himself. I hold out my hand for a shake to get him to release my bike.

This time he takes my hand. Grip like an angry anaconda's. I can't disengage.

He leans forward. "It's not my style to hand out advice, but whatever's chasing you, it's better to face it than to run. Go home."

I look back at him. "You ran."

Impassive features. Tough guy. So why does he suddenly seem sad and vulnerable? "Look where it got me," and he spits on the ground as if dismissing his whole life with one gob of saliva. "Keep running and pretty soon you're not gonna be able to go back. So do what I didn't. Go back home to what you know and to those who love you."

"Not an option." I would say more, but I'm remembering what I knew and those who loved me. My throat constricts.

He watches me and he gets it. We do have something in common after all. "Okay, then. Happy trails."

ZAA-ZAA-ZOOM! Sounds like cannon fusillade. Old motorcycle roars forward and nearly jumps off embankment. Sidecar hangs over edge of cliff.

Gang members shout advice. "Pull her back." "Don't forget to steer." "You're gonna lose the dog!"

Gisco agrees. *I thought you said you knew how to ride this thing! I don't mean to be a backseat driver, but THERE IS NO ROAD BENEATH ME! DO SOMETHING NOW! JACK!!!*

Wrestling match with old motorcycle. Like busting a rusty bronco. Right on edge of cliff. Wheels spitting sand. Fifty-foot plummet to rocks. Weight of sidecar dragging us over. Gisco covering his eyes with his paws.

Give handlebars one last yank. Wheels pop out of sand. Back onto tarmac. ZAA-ZAA-ZOOOOM!

Heading south on two-lane highway. Cold wind slapping me, but old leather jacket is like suit of armor. Throaty roar of motorcycle. Vibrations shaking my bones.

Not bad. Fun, actually. I accelerate.

Still feeling adrenaline rush from leap off train. Not to mention brawl with Cassidy. Violent night. As I speed into utter blackness, I wonder who will be gunning for me next. Bring them on!

Snippet of poetry flashes to mind. Tennyson's "Charge of the Light Brigade." Second stanza:

> *"Forward, the Light Brigade!"*
> *Was there a man dismay'd?*
> *Not tho' the soldier knew*

Some one had blunder'd:
Theirs not to make reply,
Theirs not to reason why,
Theirs but to do and die:
Into the valley of Death
Rode the six hundred.

Yes, that's the proper way to face it. Like Lord Cardigan leading the British cavalry into certain death at Balaclava. Stiff upper lip! Just keep galloping forward! Danger on all sides of me since Dad told me to get in the car in Hadley-by-Hudson. Barely more than twenty-four hours ago. It seems a lifetime.

On, gloriously, forward! If death awaits, then give a good account! This whole thing is too murky to reason out. Mine not to reason why! Mine but to do and die!

Are you okay?

Never better, flea face. Starting to enjoy this.

I mean, are you sure a punch to the noggin during that fight didn't scramble your brains?

My brains are sunny-side up and functioning perfectly, thank you very much. Why do you ask?

'Cause I'm picking up this weird vibe. Seems like an old British war movie or something. You sure you're okay?

Absolutely. Just sit back and enjoy the ride. Wait a minute. You were reading my mind? My inner thoughts?

No, just a mood I was picking up on. Forget it.

No, don't forget it. It's a hell of a lot more than just sensing my mood. You even nailed the British part. I wasn't trying to communicate with you. You weren't any part of it. But you knew exactly what I was thinking.

Jack, let it go.

So you can peer into my head? Just the way I read Jinny's mind, and found out that she was betraying us?

You did a great job there.

Don't change the subject. And I read the minds of the motor-cycle gang members. I knew they didn't like that guy Cassidy, and I should take him on one-on-one.

Which you did. Bravo! Now, why don't we—

So you can read me just like I read them? Better, actually. You can even read specific details—

I'm a great believer in personal privacy. But the simple fact, dear boy, is that you don't shield your thoughts. You hang them out like underwear on a clothesline.

How can I shield them?

Instead of directing them outward or floating them like boats, turn them inward. You learned to send them easily enough. You should be able to shield them.

I search for shield mechanism. Now that I'm looking, I sort of know what Gisco means. And where to find it.

There. That's it.

Why didn't anyone tell me before?

Well, no one's been reading your mind before. You were reared in a blissfully nontelepathic generation. Your boyhood compatriots were not tuning in to your wavelength.

But my parents could do it. Right? They were like you, so they knew how to do it, just as well as you do. Correct?

'Fraid so, old sport. But they loved you and wanted what was best for you. I suppose knowing what you were thinking was a good way of protecting you.

So that's how they did it. Always wondered. The few times I tried to break their rules.

Once I hid two marijuana joints in an old boot in the back of my closet. Mom just happened to find them. "Jack, you've disappointed us." Grounded for a month.

Another time, bunch of guys from the football team were going out for a midnight joyride. I snuck downstairs to join them at the agreed-on meeting place.

Dad just happened to be awake, getting a glass of milk. "Where are you going at this hour, son?"

"Oh, just . . . getting a drink of milk, like you, Dad. Humid night, huh? Made me thirsty."

"You said it. Let me pour you a glass. Have a seat on the couch. Let's see what's on *The Late Late Show*."

"How do you always catch me?" I once asked Mom.

"You have a transparent face," she said with a laugh. "Comes with being such a sweet boy. Part of the territory."

Transparent face, my ass, Mom. You were reading my thoughts. Kind of invasive, huh? Like reading my mail.

Oh my God, all my fantasies about P.J. on those hot summer nights.

And other fantasies, about the cheerleading team. The kinds of silly, outrageous things that creep into guys' heads every so often. Mom and Dad read all of that.

I pull over near a crossroads. Lord Cardigan never had to deal with anything like this. Suddenly I don't feel so good. Not sick. Just betrayed. Sad. Angry. Violated. Powerless. Completely powerless and manipulated.

You okay?

Read my mind and you tell me.

Don't be that way.

Screw you. I glance up at sign. Turn off highway onto larger highway. Heading for Washington, D.C.

What are you doing? We were on the right road.

This one heads south, too.

But it's not as direct. We're losing time.

So what? It's not like anybody's expecting us at Kitty Hawk. I've never seen Washington, D.C., and I feel like checking it out. Want to see the White House. And the Capitol. You got a problem with that?

I forbid it. This is a mistake.

Maybe, but it's my mistake. Mine. Me. Remember me? Jack Danielson. I'm tired of following other people's rules and doing what other people say I should do and letting them take advantage of me and manipulate me. I'm taking control here. If you want to come along for the ride, shut up about "forbidding it" and try to enjoy being a tourist.

Otherwise, you're welcome to get out right here.

15

Washington, D.C., at three in the morning. Sleeping city. Empty city. And pitifully clueless city. Supposed to be supremely aware, completely plugged in, hyperinformation hub. FBI. CIA. Pentagon. Buzzing with state-of-the-art intelligence. Bastion of security. Protect citizens against all threats, foreign and domestic.

Truth is no one here has a clue. I'm parked on Pennsylvania Avenue. Looking at the White House. Pretty in the moonlight. Lincoln, Teddy Roosevelt, F.D.R., J.F.K.—all slept here.

Current President snoring away inside. What's he dreaming about, I wonder? The next gala dinner for the Prime Minister of Hoozie Whatsie? Or the coming midterm elections, and will he have to make another stump speech in Dubuque?

I feel a powerful urge to rap on the door and wake him up. Hey, Mr. President. It's me, Jack Danielson, from Hadley-by-Hudson. Open your eyes, sir. Get your butt vertical. They're here. All around us. Gorms. Bat creatures. Guards in Penn Station with laser guns. They're battling each other all over your fifty states! Do something!

What should you do, sir? Heck, I don't know. You're the President. I'm just doing my duty as an American citizen. Bringing you key info. Now do your job and protect me. Because the police in Hadley didn't protect me and the New York cops couldn't do it either, but you're the President, and if anyone can do it, sir, you can.

But of course I don't go rap on the door. Because I know that he can't help me. He doesn't have a clue. That's why he's snoozing. Yes, there's a battle going on within his borders, but it's a shadow battle, fought by people and creatures far more advanced than he is. One sign of their superiority is that they know about his world but he doesn't have the slightest inkling that they even exist.

So I stand there, barely able to resist the temptation to run forward and give the door a swift kick. Wake up, Mr. President. HEEELLLPPP MEEEE!

No point in even trying. It would be futile. I'd be dismissed as a kook. Sure, Gorms and bat creatures. The Secret Service would like to take you to a nice, clean cell, Mr. Danielson. Come along. Spiffy leather jacket, by the way, but what happened to your right sleeve?

The night breeze blows. I stand there next to the motorcycle. Gisco sits in his sidecar, also looking at 1600 Pennsylvania Avenue. As I watch, he shakes his head.

You okay, kid?

You're the one who looks sad.

Who's reading whose mind now? Just thinking about missed opportunities, old bean.

Who missed what opportunities?

Forget it. Can we go now?

We drive off down the avenue. Dark and mostly empty streets. Swing around to the parks that hold our cherished national icons. The reflecting pool shimmers with a million stars. Pass the different memorials. Lincoln looking sad but wise. The Washington Monument poking up in a none-too-subtle display of national potency. We ride uphill along the east side of the Mall till the great dome of the Capitol Building fills the night sky.

Park on a corner of the south terrace. Behind me, the Capitol stands in columned splendor. I get off motorcycle and walk. Gisco trots along next to me.

Stop at edge of terrace. A zillion marble steps lead steeply down to the Mall far below. I stand there, looking at the sleeping city. Two thousand years ago they said all roads led to Rome. Now all roads lead here.

This is the Rome of my world, the nexus of power, our national and global security blanket. Whatever goes wrong, this is where they can fix it. Whoever attacks, this is where they can repel them.

In the distance are a spattering of lights from homes, office buildings, and government facilities. In some strange way I feel connected to everyone and everything out there, to the White House I just visited, and to the Capitol Building right behind me, to the Pentagon and the FBI headquarters, and to the thousands of people who help run the vast machine of this nation, who are now slumbering away in Georgetown and Arlington and Bethesda.

I am part of them. I was brought up to believe in them. Yet they can't help me. Somehow I'm stuck in this mess all by my lonesome.

Gisco is also looking down and shaking his head. I ask him: What are you so upset about?

Sleeping. The fools! They could have fixed it. They had the opportunity and the power. Instead they did nothing. Shortsighted idiots!

What are you talking about? Who could have fixed what?

Gisco doesn't answer. Sad dog face. Still wearing the red bandanna. Something about what he just said, and his use of the past tense. I almost figure it out—

And then I hear a little snap, crackle, pop, and what looks like a string of red firecrackers goes off with cherry flashes.

Jack! Watch out. Paralysis darts!

16

Too late. Shooting pain in right hip. Then numbness.

Go, dog. Save yourself. I can't run.

Climb on my back.

What good is that going to do? Take your chance and flee. It's me they want.

Get on and shut up!

Shadows running at us. Hurling something. Blue spiderwebs flash.

Plasma nets. If they hit us, we're sunk. Get on now!

I get on. Cling to his furry back.

Big dog bounds through the darkness. Surprising agility. Red paralysis darts and blue plasma nets flash around us like fireworks on the Fourth of July.

Dog makes it to motorcycle. *Can you drive?*

I swing awkwardly off his back onto Harley. Gisco leaps into sidecar.

VRROOOOM. For once the old motorcycle starts right up.

I try to roar off terrace in easterly direction, but it's not going to work. More shadows coming from that direction! From the west, too! Taking fire from three sides. Like the Brits at Balaclava!

I drive in wild circle on marble terrace, searching for way out. Semicircle of shadows closing in fast.

They could definitely shoot me down but they don't, so I guess they want to take me alive. Find out what I know. The old neural flay. And I have no way to escape.

Except one.

I accelerate and head south, toward the Capitol steps.

What are you doing, Jack?

Taking the only way out.

You'll kill us.

Ours not to reason why. Ours but to do and die.

Have you gone mad?

Stiff upper lip, juicy jowls.

We plunge over the edge of the terrace. Motorcycle and side car career down endless steps. Bumpita-thumpita-bumpita. Bones shaking. Teeth rattling.

Old motorcycle somehow stays upright. Sidecar stays attached. Gisco lying flat, covering eyes with paws. *O GREAT DOG GOD, SAVE YOUR HUMBLE SERVANT.*

I murmur similarly desperate prayer, although not directed at Great Dog God.

We accelerate. No more thumping and bumping. Now it's a concussive BAM, BAM, BAM. We are slamming our way down Capitol steps at more than fifty miles an hour. Old motorcycle can't possible hang together. Antique sidecar can't possibly endure this punishment. But they do, and we make it down, and then suddenly we're on the National Mall, speeding away across the grass.

Gisco uncovers eyes. Peers between paws over edge of sidecar. *We made it! We're alive! I knew you could do it!*

You weren't exactly full of encouragement. But I guess it's hard to be plucky when you're cowering in fear.

For your information, I was just lying flat to cut down on wind resistance.

Ah. I see.

But since we're away free and clear, let's put some distance between them and us.

Not a bad idea.

We zigzag our way out of D.C. at high speed.

17

Outskirts of city. I lie down on grass. Gisco inspects my hip. Probes gently with paw. Not a bad bedside manner for a dog. *It's not too serious.*

It's completely numb. I can't move my leg.

Temporary synaptic paralysis. You'll be fine.

I sit up on grass. Great. But there's something I don't get. How could they possibly have found us and set up an ambush? They couldn't have known where we jumped off the train. They couldn't have figured out we bought a motorcycle from that gang, or spotted us on local roads. So how could they have guessed we'd come here?

Psychological profiling. Do you know why you wanted to come to Washington, D.C.?

Curiosity. I'd never seen it.

That's not the reason. Not the underlying reason. You've been trained to act that way.

What way? What are you talking about?

It's epoch-appropriate behavior. Children of your generation were taught in school to trust authority. If something bad happens, tell your parents. Tell your teacher. Tell the police. Right?

Yes, that's what they teach us.

So, given everything that's happened to you, it's natural that you felt the need to alert a higher authority. They thought you might try to reach out to your congressman or senator or even the President. So they were waiting for us. But we won't make that mistake again, right?

Right, I agree. Something about Gisco's response is troubling me. More than troubling me. It's giving me an answer to something that's been nagging at me for a long time. Right, I repeat, we won't make that mistake again because you're going to tell me what's going on.

Where?

Here. Now. It's time for the truth. Where do the guys who just ambushed us come from? Which is also, I suspect, where you come from.

I can't answer that question. You can't handle it.

I'm not looking for an answer. Just for confirmation. I've figured it out.

Dog eyes studying me. *I truly doubt that.*

You say you're from here yet not from here. You speak of my generation not being telepathic. The technologies that you use—laser guns, paralysis darts, and plasma nets—are beyond anything I think the government is working on, even in secret programs. And you use the past tense when describing the present.

Grammar was never my strong point.

Sometimes I catch you looking at this world wistfully, the way I think I'd look at the Garden of Eden if I could go back there. I don't think you're from the Twilight Zone. You're clearly not of this world. Yet at the same time, you seem to fit here very naturally. So . . . I know where you must be from.

Dog eyes watching me. Waiting. I look back into them and finish the thought. The future. This planet's future. My future. That's why you fit and yet you don't fit. You belong and yet you don't belong. And all those people who are trying to kill me are also from the future.

Gisco doesn't deny it.

You've all come back in time, I would guess hundreds if not thousands of years, and now you're fighting it out in my world. You want to do one thing. They want the opposite. I'm in the middle of it, even though I don't know what you're fighting over. But my guess is that something must be awfully screwed up in your future world for you to have come back here. Is that right? Tell me!

Gisco hesitates. Droopy ears quiver beneath red bandanna. Finally he nods. *Yes, Jack, you figured it out*, he admits. *You're right, but you're also wrong.*

About what? Don't talk in riddles.

It's not just that I'm from the future. It's that we're *from the future. You and me both, kid. Stop accusing me of coming back to your world. This ain't your world any more than it is mine. We were both born almost a thousand years from now.*

I feel dizzy, but he goes on.

As for the future being screwed up, you're also wrong about that. It is but it's not. Or at least it doesn't have to be. That's sort of where you come in. You have to find Firestorm. You are the beacon of hope. I really can't tell you more till we get to Kitty Hawk and have time to noodle this around and figure our next step. Jack? You okay?

But I'm not okay. Fainting. Or at least swooning. My tie to consciousness dwindles to a silver thread. I'm lost in my own mind. Because I know that what Gisco just said must be true. I've had a hunch ever since the Gorm called me the Prince. I just never admitted it to myself before.

Didn't want to. Couldn't face it.

It's not that they're interlopers while I belong here. That was a feeble attempt on my part to cling to some semblance of the familiar. The truth is I am not of this place and time either. I AM OF THEIR PLACE AND TIME! I am of them. Yet at the same time I know nothing of it or of them.

My ignorance of self crashes over me like a wave and I feel myself drowning. I come from a future that is blank to me, yet the only thing I know is a present that I am not truly a part of. I was put here for a purpose I do not know, and am being chased by enemies who want to kill me for reasons no one will explain.

The only thing I know for sure as I lie on the grass is that a big dog is licking my face to keep me conscious, and sending me not very comforting telepathic messages: *There, there. It will probably all come out right in the end. After all, we've avoided the neural flay so far.*

How will it come out right? My parents are dead. And they weren't really my parents. All my friends are gone. I have nothing tying me to anything.

At least you're still alive. There's an old dog saying: Better a dog without a leash than a leash without a dog.

Is that supposed to be comforting?

You're doing great, Jack. I didn't think you could handle the truth, but you're tougher than you look, dear boy. We'd better get going now. Because the more you find out about yourself, the more you're going to realize how important it is for them not just to catch you or torture you but to obliterate you from the face of the earth.

18

Happy Halloween. The spooky predawn hours. Moon a goblin's yellow jaw, chewing through mist. Rural Virginia, dark and quiet. Trick-or-treaters still asleep. I don't need a mask this year. Got something better. Boo. I'm from the future. Boo, bat creatures. Boo, telepathic dogs. Want a real scare? Boo, Gorms and neural flay.

Wide-open blacktop, heading south. Old Harley rocketing forward, making occasional hacking and retching sounds. Way over speed limit but who cares? Wind trying its best to uproot my straw-colored hair from scalp. Dust turning blue eyes into tear geysers. Leaning forward. Gripping handlebars. Let's go faster. VROOOM.

Here's the weird part: telepathic dog riding next to me is from the future. My future. Except that apparently I'm from that future, too. In fact, I was born into it. So in a way he's really from my past. Boo. Happy Halloween. I'm as Gormy as a Gorm. As batty as a bat creature.

You okay, kid?

Uh-oh. You're not reading anything, are you? I had my screens up.

Just a tickle. Knew you were thinking about me. Couldn't tell what. You're getting much better at this.

Kind of a necessity, actually. Cranial privacy is underrated. Wonder if everyone in the future world is telepathic. Must make for a pretty messed-up situation.

Odd thing is I can't seem to stop thinking about that future world. Not at first, mind you. First hundred miles out of D.C. I was too numb to think of anything except the white line on the highway. Now it's broken. Now it's solid.

Maybe it was the synaptic paralysis dart. Or my meltdown discombobulation on learning the truth.

But paralysis is wearing off. Discombobulation lessening. I find myself pondering that future world. Mind you, I'm still horrified by the idea that it's my true world. Still don't feel like one of them. Yet how could a fellow not be a bit curious?

What is it like, that far future time I was sent here from? Are my birth parents there now? If I ever meet them, they better have a pretty damn compelling reason for sending me away, and getting me into this mess.

I try not to stew on it. What's to be gained? But my questions will not go away. As Dorothy said, there's no place like home. So if you don't know your home, it's probably normal to speculate about it. Do they have schools? Varsity sports? Hard to believe guys are still running around football fields ten centuries hence.

If not, what have they replaced them with? What do they care about? Do they still believe in love? Family?

If I'm some kind of Prince, that must make my parents royalty. King and Queen? Of what? Do they live in a palace? If I ever make it back, will strangers bow and curtsy to me? Or will they just try to kill me, as they all seem so intent on doing now?

A thousand years! The scale of it! They are to me and this world what I am to Charlemagne and the Crusades!

Yet they have come back here and are battling over something in this world. How they must look down on it, and all the ignorant, backward people who populate it!

Stoplight towns and one-horse burgs flash past as we roll through southern Virginia and into North Carolina. Great names for small places. Littleton. Boykins. Scotland Neck. Hobgood.

Restaurants and chain stores I've never seen before. Stuckey's. Hardee's. Signs advertising real southern pit barbecue. Two-story plastic statue of a hog.

Never been in the South before. Always been intrigued by it. Love the accent. Especially when ringing off the lips of a southern belle. Love the writers. Faulkner. Flannery O'Connor. Tennessee Williams. Find the history fascinating. Larger-than-life figures. John C. Calhoun. Frederick Douglass. Robert E. Lee. Martin Luther King.

Yet all of it is steeped in blood and ghosts. Flannery O'Connor's good men who are hard to find because they always turn out to be psychotic. Blanche DuBois with her Tarantula Arms and Laura Wingfield with the glass menagerie. Lee at Gettysburg, sending his men charging into rifle fire. There go the flower of the South, borne off in a tide of bullets. King lying in blood on the balcony of a motel in Memphis.

Be careful, Jack. Nice people here, but there's also lots of hidden pain.

Rain starts to fall. Hard to drive a motorcycle at night in the rain. Hey, cymbal ears. Maybe we should find shelter and wait for it to stop.

No. We're almost there. And it's not going to stop.

What are you, a weatherman?

Weather dog. Trust me. Dogs know about these things.

Fine. I don't mind getting sopping wet. You've been pretty quiet the last few hours.

Just remembering all we've been through together. That Gorm in New York would have sold me for a neural flay if you hadn't come along. I'll never forget that you got me out.

You repaid the favor. Saved me in D.C. We're even.

Fair enough. But if anything should ever happen between us, I want you to know . . . Dog literally can't finish the thought. Choking up telepathically.

You don't have to say it. Or think it. I know you'll always be there for me, Gisco. You're my only friend.

A rainy dawn breaks as we cross Roanoke Sound to the barrier islands of the Outer Banks. Pass through Kill Devil Hills. Wonder what devil was killed there. Right nearby is Kitty Hawk. Signs for the Wright Brothers Museum. Other signs pointing to great dunes.

Drumroll of thunder. Sky opening up. We should pull into a motel. We have the cash.

No. We'd have to check in. Show I.D. The whole point of coming here was to lie low.

True, but lying low won't help us if we drown.

There!

Where?

An old barn. Exactly what we need!

I still don't see it.

You missed the turnoff. It looked perfect.

Careful U-turn on wet highway. Back the way we came. Driveway leading between sandy dunes and stubbly pines to shadowy structure. Jagged flash of lightning. There it is, sure enough, an old barn.

No lights on. No signs of life. Impressive that Gisco could have spotted it in this downpour as we sped past. Good eyes, snaggle tail. Must be those herding genes.

My ancestors didn't herd. It was beneath them.

Fine. Whatever. Let's go get warm. Think we can break in? Hope the horses inside don't mind company.

Don't smell horses. Barn must be vacant.

Vacant but secure. No way in. Maybe I can climb through the second story . . .

Wait. Here's a door.

Thank God. This is like the biblical flood. Uh-oh, locked.

Let's give it a good push.

Dog charges forward. Hits it low. At the same second, I give it a stiff shoulder high. Old wooden door doesn't stand a chance. Bursts inward.

Ta da! We're in.

Nice and dry. Warm, too. Here's a light switch. What do you know, it works! Clean for a barn, huh? Just a bit odd that this perfect barn should have been sitting here among the dunes, waiting for us to stumble on it. But we've had enough bad luck. Time something good happened. You were right about horses not being here. Doesn't look like this place has been used for animals in years.

Want some free advice, old bean?

If you're handing it out.

You're too trusting. It may be the death of you.

What?

Au revoir. Or should I say adieu. Big dog turns and gallops back out of door, which swings shut behind him.

I don't know what's happening but I don't like it.

What are you doing, carrion breath? Is this some kind of dog practical joke? Get back here. Where are you going?

Suddenly I'm spooked. I run after Gisco. Wooden door is flimsy. No problem breaking it in, no problem busting it out. I lower shoulder. WHAM! It's like running into a brick wall. Something has reinforced it from the outside.

I fly back through barn and end up on my rear end. Get shakily to my feet. Look the place over in a new way.

BECAUSE I WAS BROUGHT HERE. No other windows or doors visible. Just one light, a bare bulb hanging by a wire from the high ceiling. Swinging slightly, back and forth.

As I watch it swing, the light goes out.

Pitch darkness.

I stand there and shiver, even though the barn is warm.

Happy Halloween.

Trick or treat.

Jack, you were just tricked by man's best friend.

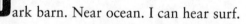

19

Dark barn. Near ocean. I can hear surf.

Never felt this betrayed. Different from feeling alone. Felt alone when I sailed down the Hudson, away from Hadley and P.J. and my parents. Terrible empty feeling.

Now I pace from one side of barn to the other. Damn dog. Saved him from Gorm. Joked around with him. Thought he was my only friend. Opened my heart to him and showed him my deepest fears. All the time he was playing me. Using me. Entrapping me.

The old chicken-and-egg game my ass. Looking back on it now, I see that I was literally taken for a ride. Gisco must have seen the plane flying overhead. Given me some kind of telepathic prompt or hypnotic suggestion to look up at it. And then that nonsense about reversing causality.

He chose Kitty Hawk.

Brought me here.

To this empty barn.

Why? I don't know. But it couldn't have been for an honorable reason or he wouldn't have run away.

Man's best friend. Hah! Twenty thousand years of partnership! Hah! Just let me at that flabby fur ball again for five minutes. That's all I ask.

Calm down, Jack. Try to focus. Dangerous situation. Safe to assume you're in the hands of your enemies. They're going to show up any second. Try to find out what you know. By causing you pain. Also, very possibly try to kill you. So let go of your anger and figure out your next move.

I stop pacing. Start circling. Feel walls of barn inch by inch. No cracks, no windows, no ledges.

Just a secure box with me in the center of it.

Flecks of light in roof, three stories up. Sun rising outside.

Me starting to crack inside. Minutes passing. Hours dragging by. Waiting for interrogator. Or executioner. Nothing to do and nowhere to go but just stay put. Which is excruciating. Stress rises. Fear begins to take over.

Maybe this is a form of psychological warfare. They're softening me up. When they're ready to hurt me, they'll come in and bang me around.

Either that or they're watching me. Studying my reactions like a boy studying a spider caught in a jar.

It won't work. I won't give them the pleasure.

I sit down on floor. Hurl telepathic defiance at the four walls. I'm not afraid of you! I won't put on a show for you! If you want a piece of me, come and get me, craven cowards that you are! You'll regret it if you try!

Almost immediately I hear a sound. Uh-oh. Hope I didn't piss anyone off. Look up. Fifteen feet above the floor, a door opens. Or maybe it's a window. Can't tell. Dawn light spills down.

A big black bird flies in and glides to the floor.

No, not a bird. A person.

Check that. Not a person. A masked and robed figure, dressed all in black.

Demon? Ninja?

He lands with barely a sound and stands there, bare feet spread to the width of his shoulders. Black mask with eye slits. Dark eyes watching me.

Trick or treat. Something tells me this is not going to be a treat. Not much warmth in that death mask or in those spooky eyes.

"Who are you?" I ask. My voice quivers.

Silence.

"Are you human? Do you understand me? I'm warning you. I'm in a bad mood. Don't appreciate being locked up. You're smaller than I am. The last guy who messed with me was carried away with a bunch of broken ribs. So get this through your creepy mask. Do. Not. Screw. Around. With. Me."

Ninja does not respond verbally or telepathically, but dark eyes glitter menacingly.

Then arms spread to full wingspan. Odd way of moving. Not fast, or at least not rushed, but marvelously graceful. A half step forward, then quickly to the side. Reminds me of a boxer's shuffle. Never off balance. No open targets.

I feel a burst of fear. Go weak in my knees. Which is strange. I've been in lots of fights and I've never felt this scared before. "Don't come any closer."

Warning ignored. Forward and to the side. Like a dance, circling nearer to me.

My fear level amping up. Panic. Debilitating. Is he doing this to me, or am I doing it to myself? My fists clench. "I'm warning you. *I'll kill you—*"

Threat broken off as black shape leaps effortlessly toward me off right leg. I am expecting this attack, but I am still much too slow to block the punch.

Because it's not a punch. It's a flying kick. Executed from apex of jump, so that the angle of strike is perfectly horizontal.

Jump was from the right foot, so kick is with the left to confound me. Black outfit swirls behind him like cloud of smoke as he soars through the air. Knee snaps straight out with a whipping sound. FSSHHHT. Maybe it's the fabric of the ninja suit. Maybe the kick is so fast it literally whips the air. Hard to tell.

No time to think. His left foot explodes into center of my chest. POW! Like a cannonball.

I've been kicked before in my life. And punched. Once even hit with a chair in a gym brawl. I have great balance. Low center of gravity. Don't usually get driven backwards. Almost never go down.

This kick knocks me clear across the room. I tumble end over end. Remember how it felt to be in the car when my dad rolled it.

Spinning.

Total lack of control.

Slam hard into far wall of barn. Stunned. Almost black out.

Ninja doesn't follow up attack. He lets me lie there and recover. Cheeky bastard. Telling me he doesn't need to press his advantage.

He can finish me whenever he chooses. He's enjoying my pain, so he wants to prolong this.

Big mistake, buddy.

climb groggily to my feet.

Okay, crow face. I've seen the kick. Not bad. Now enough defense. Let's try some old-fashioned offense.

I move toward him, arms up. When I get within range I feint with my right and swing with my left. Good punch. Don't telegraph it. All the power of my body behind it. Aimed right for the jaw of that ninja mask.

BOOM. Punch connects. Flush on jaw. Ninja crumples as if made from origami paper.

That's what I expect. But that's not what happens.

He ducks. Graceful bending and rolling motion. His chin floats away from my punch. I end up off balance and overextended. He steps in quickly and grabs my wrist. Pulls and shifts his center of gravity and suddenly I am flying through air again, this time upside down.

The kick was a karate strike, but this is a judo throw. Full fighting repertoire. Very impressive. I think this as I fly upside down, arms and legs flailing.

Crash hard into wall. Slide down. Lie there in a heap. He lets me recover. I get slowly back to my feet.

Here he comes again. The dance. Forward and to the side.

Think, Jack. If you let him kick you again, it's over. Your punch didn't work either. Your advantages here are size and strength. Small space, like a boxing ring. No place for him to run. So tie him up and pin him against a wall.

And don't wait, or he'll strike first. Do it now.

I go in for wrestling takedown. Shoot for one leg. All I need to pry him over onto his back. I've done it a hundred times on wrestling mats. No real defense.

Ninja sees me coming and runs away, toward nearest wall. I chase. You can run but you can't hide.

He jumps at wall and does somersaulting backflip. Before I can pivot he's landed behind me, his arms moving around my waist in a control position.

He expertly trips me up. I've wrestled state champs who don't move this well. He rides me into the ground. I try to buck him off. Like trying to shake off my own skin. His right hand slides up from its grip to a spot behind my neck. This weakens his hold on me for just a second.

I figure now I'll get him off for sure.

ZAAAAAAPPPP! Electrocution.

That's what it feels like. A hundred thousand volts of pain flowing into me through a live wire. Not a wire, it's his thumb pressing into some kind of nerve spot on my upper spine. My body jerks spastically.

He releases me and when I slump down he catches me, kneels behind me, and shifts his grip to my throat.

Choke hold. Heel of his right hand cutting off my windpipe while he holds me securely with his left.

This is a finisher. This one will kill me.

Absolutely nothing I can do. The urge to live makes me thrash wildly. Endows me with near-superhuman strength. I actually lift him off the ground from behind, like a water buffalo with a lion on his back. Smash him against a wall. For a second his grip loosens.

But then the lion digs in his claws. His hand tightens mercilessly. I sink down to my knees. Then fall onto my stomach.

Being choked to death is no fun. You fight for that last breath. Then you feel the lights switching off. A little voice from deep in the control room of the soul: Jack, you're dying, dying, dying forever.

But there's nothing I can do about it. Helplessness. Regret. Farewell.

Dad.

Mom.

P.J.

Darkness.

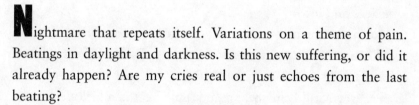

21

Nightmare that repeats itself. Variations on a theme of pain. Beatings in daylight and darkness. Is this new suffering, or did it already happen? Are my cries real or just echoes from the last beating?

One constant. My adversary. Different robes. Multiple masks. But the same little guy. Built like a fire hydrant, with the grace of a gazelle. He of the sideways shuffle. Of the spinning karate kicks. Of the excruciating jujitsu holds.

I fight back using every method I can think of. Punches. Kicks. Football tackles. I even try to bite him.

Take off my leather jacket and sweep it like a net to trip him up.

Throw my shoes at him.

Nothing works. He's too good.

Each beating leaves me dazed or out cold. Little guy has a dozen chances to kill me. But he doesn't. He just disappears, and comes back later to dish out more punishment.

It's not that I give up. I simply run out of ways to fight back. He has an answer for every technique I know.

So I finally take the one option left.

I start to imitate him. Try to learn from him.

Always been a fast learner. See something demonstrated once, never forget it. A long parade of amazed coaches. "Hell, Danielson, I just taught you that crossover dribble and now you're doing it better than me." "Damn, Danielson, you went with that pitch just the way I showed you yesterday!"

So I watch the ninja.

Stand with my feet to the width of my shoulders. That sliding shuffle step. Never off balance. Not presenting a target. Makes it hard to predict which way I'm going.

Oh, so that's how you snap out that kick? The knee comes up first and then the foot shoots out straight.

Ah, I see, so when you punch, your power is generated in your legs and hips.

So there's the pressure point you used to immobilize me. I can reach around and find it on my own spine. Damn, it hurts. And if it hurts me it's gonna hurt you, pal.

Progress. Still being beaten, but now I get in a kick here and a punch there. Beatings becoming more like sparring sessions. Longer. More drawn out. Competitive.

I've noticed something odd. This sadistic guy who's beating me up isn't doing any permanent damage. He doesn't hesitate to choke me out or knock me unconscious, but he's never broken a bone or even knocked out a tooth.

Must be intentional.

Maybe something I can use.

I take my lumps, and eat and drink the tiny amounts of food and water that appear while I'm unconscious, and I study him. Suffering but learning. I'm getting better. One day soon the student will kill the teacher. I hate him. I owe him a world of pain.

I can now shut out the fear that this guy broadcasts telepathically. I've found the screen that blocks it.

One last awful beating. I get in some good shots and he seems to resent it. When he gets me down, he kicks me black-and-blue.

Slaps on a choke hold. Before I black out I get in a solid elbow to the ninja mask. I swear I hear a groan of pain. Take that, you bastard.

Wake up in morning light. I was out for a while. I know his pattern now. He'll wait for me to get up. As soon as I start to recover he'll return.

So I don't get up right away. I lie there, silent and motionless for a while, planning.

Because I'm ready for him. D-day has dawned.

There's one moment when he's predictable. When he makes his initial jump. He may be dressed like a bird, but he can't fly. So from when he vaults through the window to when he lands there's a brief opportunity.

I wait till I'm good and ready, then get to my feet. Act groggy, but my mind's clear and cold as a mountain stream. I weave back and forth. Setting a trap for him. Send out a telepathic summons of pure rage, as if I'm not thinking straight. Come on, you bastard. I'll rip you apart.

But I'm calm on the inside. Calculating.

The window opens. He glides down, a gray-brown vulture.

I run directly beneath him.

He can't kick me. Because if he does, it'll have to be a face shot, and with the weight of his jump behind it he'd risk killing me. The one thing he won't do.

So he falls right onto me and tries to twist away.

I grab him. Recognize this grip? You're the one who taught it to me, you bastard.

Like holding an electric eel. He's going for pressure points and twisting and flailing, but I've got him wrapped up. Can't hold him this way for long. Don't need to.

Two steps toward wall. Another lesson he's taught me. Use the surface of the wall. Harder than any fist.

I let my center of gravity drop suddenly. He wasn't expecting that. I drag him down with me as I fall over backward. Then kick him out and over me with both my legs, flipping him toward the wall.

Want to fly, ninja? Be my guest.

BAM! Ninja hits wall of barn like a vulture flying into a skyscraper. He slides to floor, stunned. Then he's trying to get up. Impressive recovery time.

But not impressive enough. I jump off left foot and fly through the air. Nail ninja with right-footed kick to chin area of mask. POW!

He goes over on his back. Stirs but can't shake that one off in time to even try to get up before—

I'm on him. Both my knees crashing down on his sternum. Another thing he's taught me. Use gravity. OOOSHHHH. The air driven from his lungs.

Now I'm ready to finish him off. I've never been mad enough to kill before. Now I am. You want pain? I'll give you pain. Jack is a nice guy, but you asked for it.

Blood rage roaring in my ears. He tries to kick me off. I slam his head back to the floor. How many times has he knocked me out? Now he's the one seeing stars.

I decide to pry off that mask. I want to see the fear in his face before I finish him off.

My right fist clenches to deliver death blow. I pry off mask with left hand. It doesn't come off easily, but I wrench it and leather straps give way. I yank it free and start to deliver a brutal final strike with my right hand.

And then I stop.

Because his eyes are open. Looking up at me. Gray eyes. Cognizant eyes. Human eyes. He knows what's coming. And trick or treat—he's got one final trick.

He is a *she*!

Female features. Even, in their way, attractive. If you happen to like sadistic women built like mailboxes.

I'm almost mad enough to bust in that face with a vicious punch. Almost. My fist opens. Can't do it.

My fingers clamp across her throat. You can kill a person this way in half a second. Rip out her windpipe.

"Who are you?" I hear myself asking. "Talk or die."

Her lips part. Soft voice. "I am called Eko."

"Why have you been hurting me?" I demand.

"This is what I was sent to do," she gasps. "Time is short. It was the only way."

"To do what?" I ease up. Let her suck in a breath.

"To make sure you could defend yourself," she explains in a whisper. "Before teaching you the other things you need to learn. Now you are ready."

"Oh, so you're really on my side? I don't think so."

Those gray eyes look up at me. No fear. "If you want to kill me, go ahead. You have the right. You can do anything. You are our beacon of hope. If not, come. We have much work to do, and time is short."

Oh, do I want to kill her. Or at least hurt her. But, looking into those gray eyes, I find to my horror that I'm actually starting to believe her.

That's crazy. After what she's done to me, how can I possibly trust her?

Then I see the decorative image on the jeweled pendant around her neck. A beautiful woman with long, flowing hair.

I've seen this woman's face before. My parents had an antique brooch. In their bedroom, back in Hadley-by-Hudson. Same flowing hair. Same distinctive, beautiful face. They said it was just an antique they picked up at an old bric-a-brac shop.

"Who is she?" I ask Eko.

The gray eyes hesitate for a second. "Your mother," she whispers. "Your real mother."

I get up and back off, my head spinning far worse than when

I was being kicked or punched. "Is she alive?" I gasp. "What's her name? Where is she? How do you know her?"

Eko takes a few seconds to recover from the beating and then slowly stands. "Later," she whispers. "Now we must go. It's dangerous here. Will you come?"

We look at each other, silently and awkwardly.

I nod. "I'll come. But next time you want to teach me something, Eko, see if you can find an easier way."

✴

22

Four-wheel-drive vehicle. Powerful as a tank. My body black-and-blue from recent beatings. With each bump in road, stabbing pains. Ouch, my legs. Ouch, my ribs. Ouch, ouch, my neck.

Makes little sense that I'm allowing myself to be chauffeured to an unknown destination by the young lady who spent the past few days beating the stuffing out of me. But nothing has made much sense in my life since a tall stranger's eyes flashed at me in the Hadley Diner.

Follow your instincts, Jack. If you can't trust someone who calls you their beacon of hope, who can you trust? And that pendant with my mother's image! That sealed the deal.

Eko takes it off her neck and lets me hold it. I fire a dozen questions at her. She dodges them. "Not now. We're in danger. People are chasing us. I need to concentrate on getting us safely away."

"Who's chasing us? Why? Just tell me my mother's name!"

"Mira," she whispers. "It's the name of a famous star that

varies in brightness. Sometimes it shines brilliantly. Other times it's barely there at all."

I sit staring at the lovely face on the pendant and contemplate the mysterious new name in my life. Mira.

Eko's traded in her colorful ninja robes for simple white shorts and a turquoise top. Give her a camera, she'd look like a tourist.

She drives the way she fights. Hands graceful and sure on the wheel. Same hands she punched and choked me with. Gray eyes rarely straying from road. Not Asian eyes, not Caucasian. Some exotic blend. Almond skin.

Two-lane highway smack down middle of barrier island. Sometimes I can see ocean on our east and glass-smooth sound to the west. Then island widens again.

I pass her back the pendant. "How can anyone be chasing us, Eko? No one knows I'm here, so how can we be in danger?"

"Because we are." Woman of few words. Reminds me of Gisco at his most sphinx-like. Finding practical reasons not to answer my questions. Then again, when you're riding in a Jeep with a girl who's been beating the hell out of you for days, maybe it's not such a bad idea to take things slowly.

We pass through Duck and Corolla. Expensive beach houses in gated communities. Satellite antennas perched like giant spiders on rooftops. Swimming pools glinting. Jacuzzis swirling. Bikers in Spandex. In high season, I bet this place is packed with rich sun worshippers.

North of the shops of Corolla the houses thin out. Scenery becomes more rugged. A lighthouse towers over the dunes.

"Why do they need a lighthouse?" I ask Eko to break a long silence. Perhaps she'll be more willing to talk about things that are not grand futuristic secrets.

"Wrecks," she responds.

"What kind of wrecks?"

"Shipwrecks." Then, because she can see I'm not satisfied, she adds, "The Outer Banks used to be called the Graveyard of the Atlantic. Especially where we're going."

Fitting, in a way, given all the people trying to kill me. Jack Danielson, on his way to the Graveyard of the Atlantic for a beach vacation with conversationally challenged Ninja Girl.

What did I do to deserve this?

Eko back to silent mode. She's got this Zen thing going on. Self-contained. Inward. As if I'm not even in the car. As if we could drive for five hundred miles and her eyes would never stray from the road, and that would be fine.

Isn't she curious about me? Doesn't she feel a need to explain her recent strange behavior?

The highway ends. Road jigs to the right and stops near a wooden fence. I assume we're going to stop, too.

Wrong, Jack. White four-by-four drives right out onto sand. And continues northward, as if it's the most natural thing in the world to drive along a beach.

Other vehicles have been this way before. We follow their tracks. Pass Jeeps and trucks parked on the dunes. People swimming. Surf-casting. Kids gathering shells. But we don't stop. That would be too normal. We keep going.

Dusk falls. We've been driving on the dunes for hours. No more swimmers or fishermen. Just sand and surf and us.

Sun sinking. Wind rising. Waves like rows of gnashing teeth. Getting creepy fast. Where are we headed? I don't know. Why? I don't have a clue.

At least I'm out of that barn. The scenery is more interesting here. Not to mention the wildlife. Bird circling overhead. Huge wingspan. Eagle? Albatross? I'm no ornithologist, but it sure is majestic.

"Blue heron," Eko supplies. First thing she's said that wasn't in answer to a direct question.

Or was it? Uh-oh.

She never took her eyes off the sand. So how did she know I

was watching the bird? My screens were up, but you can't be too careful. "Did you just read my mind?"

"No," she says. "You mask your thoughts."

This must be true. If she could read my mind, she would have known my fighting plans in the barn. I could never have surprised her. "Then how did you know I was watching the bird? You weren't looking at me."

"The bird saw you looking up at him," she says.

"So you read the bird's mind? It's hard for me to believe you could read the mind of a blue albatross circling five hundred yards above us."

"Blue heron," she corrects me. "The giant of the marsh." The most Eko has said in hours. Maybe she feels like talking all of a sudden. Or maybe she's a bird lover.

"What marsh?" I ask. "This is a beach."

Eko nods toward the dunes. "Over there. You'll see. The important thing now is to get where we're going."

"And where is that?"

"Someplace safe."

"The barn wasn't safe?"

She shrugs. Goodbye. I'm hanging up.

Her eyes flick to the blue heron and soar with it through purple clouds that swim to sunset. I watch her carefully. She has a good poker face, but I detect strong emotions stirring as she watches the heron glide.

Awe. Yearning. A deep, simmering anger.

Enough waiting. She's been giving me the silent treatment for hours. Time to seize the initiative.

I grab the steering wheel and yank it toward the water.

"What are you doing?" Eko wrestles me for the wheel. We zigzag over dunes. "We'll get stuck," she warns.

"Then stop and talk to me. NOW!"

She stomps on brake. We jerk to a stop five feet from glistening tidal pool.

Nice to have her following my directions for a change.

"You owe me, Eko. I trusted you by coming, and now I need a few answers. That barn was safe and isolated enough to keep me locked up in while you beat the crap out of me. Why did we have to go on a beach safari all of a sudden?"

She answers reluctantly. "For your protection."

"No one knows I'm here," I point out. "Except for you and that flea-bitten mutt, who I assume took your money to betray me. So why did we have to leave a safe spot? Where are we going now? There aren't any houses here. It's getting dark. And, by the way, who are you when you're not assaulting strangers in barns? Or is that your day job?"

Eko's lips start to move. I get the weird feeling she is going to smile at my pithy wit. And I get the even weirder feeling that it might be a nice smile.

Nope. Frown. No warmth in it. "People will keep coming after you," she says. "They will chase you down till you die." If she's trying to comfort me, she's not doing a very good job. "You must know that by now, or you're a total fool. I'm taking you to a safe place, or at least a safer place. But while we're traveling we're vulnerable."

"But why are they after me?" I ask. No, I plead. Like I'm begging her for this one answer. "Why do they want to kill me? Why do you want to help me?"

Her gray eyes lock on mine. Neither friendly nor unfriendly. Her voice a whisper. "Because you hold the key."

I open my hand. Empty. "I don't hold any key." In the fading light, the lines of my palm glint like diverging paths. Which is the lifeline? Probably not one of the long ones.

"You are the key," she whispers again, very seriously.

I search her face. Not much there to help me. "Come on. Finish. The key to what?"

Her voice even more solemn. "Finding Firestorm. And saving

the world. Only you can do it. So everything depends on you. The fate of the whole future."

What? How? Why? Me? "How can that be?" I gasp, astonished and confused by her tone and the magnitude of her words. "I can't even vote. Or buy alcohol." Or get laid, I almost add, but I stop myself. I have my pride.

"Nevertheless," she says. "Now, please, we need to go." Her fingers brush mine on the steering wheel. Her touch is unexpectedly warm. She starts to pry my hands off. "You are our beacon of hope, but you talk too much."

I release the wheel, she hits the gas, and we drive on in silence.

✳

23

Beach house on fringe of marsh, perched precariously on stilts like an old wading bird. Inconspicuous and remote. Not visible from the beach. No other houses around, and no people either. No roads. No marinas. Nada.

Not exactly furnished with all the comforts and amenities. No jacuzzi. No satellite TV. No TV sets at all, in fact. No radios. No CD system to pump a little beach music when the sun is out.

Guess I should be grateful for lightbulbs and hot water.

One high-tech exception. In living room. Blue cube. Eko hurries to it when we arrive. Strokes it once and then puts her hands around it. It begins to glow. More than a light. An aura. She stands there for several minutes, bathed in blue glow. Concentrating. As if reading something with her whole body.

"What the hell is that?" I ask when she's done. "A tanning lamp for people who want to be bluer?"

This doesn't strike her as funny. "You don't have the scientific background. Wouldn't understand."

"Try me."

She sighs. "Ecosystem monitor and security radar."

I ponder for a second. "It gives you weather reports and warns you if people are trying to find us here?"

"No need for that," she says. "They are trying, and they will find us soon."

Nothing like an optimistic attitude, Eko.

I pepper her with questions about who I am, who my parents are, and what my role is in saving the future. She will not answer. Promises we will get to that when the time is right.

"Just tell me if my mother is alive?" I insist.

She studies my face, takes pity on me, and finally answers in a soft whisper. "I believe so. She was the last time I saw her, three months ago and a thousand years from now."

So she's alive! Mira, who fades and grows brighter. That's some unexpected good news from Ninja Girl. Maybe I'll meet her one day, and we can do a little catching up. Hi, Mom, it's the son you took out of the cradle and dropped into the time machine. Since then I've been lied to, chased, betrayed, and nearly killed a dozen times. Thanks. And how are you doing, Ma?

I explore beach house. Three stories connected by steep stairs. Jack's room on second floor. Bed. Writing desk. Dresser with clean clothes. Not fancy, but style is not a high priority right now. When you've been on the run, don't underestimate the value of clean underwear.

Who bought all this stuff? Who owns this house?

I ask Eko, but she dodges questions the way rain flicks off a duck's back, into the marsh.

Yes, there is a marsh. As I lie in bed, I hear birds and gazillions of insects. No way I can sleep. What am I doing here?

There's not one person I trust, not one thing I know is true. Except that some kind of net is closing around me. Even in this isolation. Pursuit drawing ever closer.

I finally sink into a bad dream. See the evil face I first glimpsed when I jumped between Manhattan buildings. Leonine mane of white hair. Gleaming teeth. The raptor-like eyes are now blood red. And a voice like a hungry lion's low roar. Echoing through my nightmare. "Jack, Jack."

I'm home, in Hadley, on our back porch. Reading *David Copperfield*. The red eyes loom suddenly over the bushes. Voice calling from the shadows: "Jack. It's time. I've come for you. You can't hide from me. Give up, Jack . . ."

"Jack?" Bang, bang. "Jack? Wake up."

I open my eyes. Eko's voice. Must be some mistake. Still pitch-dark out. Check watch. Four-thirty. "It's the middle of the night."

"Get dressed. Breakfast is ready."

✳

24

Basic training. Only way to describe it. Who drafted me? Into what army? For what reason? Don't ask. Just follow orders.

—*0430 hours*. Reveille is Eko pounding on my door. "Wake up, Jack." I haul myself out of bed, imagining big breakfast. Eggs, bacon, and hash browns. Dream on, Jack.

—*0500 hours*. Breakfast is apple juice and granola.

"Where are we going so early?" I ask as I sip my juice.

"Running," she replies. Great conversationalist.

"In darkness, in a marsh? What about alligators?"

She's not amused. "Finish and let's go."

I finish last spoonful of granola. Stomach still empty.

—*0550 hours*. Running. In the gauzy darkness of early morning, with the stars still in the sky. We don't just run. We sprint through knee-deep marsh water.

Can't see where I'm going. Step on rocks that cut my feet. Bushes prick me. Spiderwebs glom onto my face.

Remember, I'm fast. And tough. Once gained three hundred and forty yards in a football game.

But Eko's faster. How can a short girl generate such speed? Perfect form. Pumping arms drive piston-like knees. Never hits an obstacle. Does she have night vision?

By the time we splash through final murky channel and reach the spot where marsh becomes bay, all I want to do is sink down onto sand and puke up my granola.

Two orange kayaks waiting for us. Eko tugs one toward the water. She sees me on my knees. "What are you doing?"

"It's called resting."

"That's your kayak."

"Chill. Just give me two minutes."

Sergeant Ninja Girl doesn't chill. "Now," she says.

—*0700 hours*. Kayak challenge.

Eko's kayak shoots through the water, powered by controlled, splashless strokes. Pocahontas from the future.

I try to keep up. Exhausted from the run. Knees on fire. Spine rebelling. My paddle splashes in every direction.

She stops suddenly and points to a white bird overhead. "Cattle egret. They feed on the bugs that swarm around wild horses." She beaches her kayak. Creeps up the steep bank.

I follow. So what is the big deal about cattle egrets?

Crest bank. Grassy field. Horses grazing. Never saw a wild horse before. Pretty special. Colors and movement. Muscular legs and tossing manes. Grays and blacks and browns. "One big family?" I ask.

"Harem. That's the stallion." She nods to one that is a little bigger than the rest. "Don't get any closer."

He's looking our way. Caught our scent already. Eyes narrowing. A thousand pounds of hooves and testosterone.

I stop walking. Chill, harem master. I'm no threat.

Eko and I watch till the horses start to canter off. She follows them with her eyes. I sense the strong feelings from her, again. Awe. Yearning. Simmering anger.

The wild horses break into a gallop and thunder away through high grass in morning breeze. "Beautiful," I say.

"Yes," her voice a sigh. Then, embarrassed to have been caught showing emotion, she gruffly barks, "Let's go."

"What are we going to do next?" I ask.

"Fight," she says.

—*0900 hours.* Combat drill.

Eko shows me a series of moves in slow motion. Sweeping kicks. Diving rolls. Spinning jumps. Snapping strikes. One flows into the next. She slows them all way down for me.

I try my best, but she's never satisfied. "You're just flapping your arms and your legs. Just using your body."

"What else am I supposed to use?"

Eko launches herself off the ground, using a dive roll for propulsion. Lands in tree branch. Looks down at me.

I try same stunt. Abort takeoff. Crash-land in sand.

"You are our beacon of hope," Eko informs me, shaking her head, "but you're as graceful as a one-winged turkey."

—*1100 hours.* Lunch. Pretty, secluded beach. I'm ravenous. Eko produces a little bag. One brick of Cheddar cheese for each of us. Green apple. Rice balls.

As we gulp down the rabbit food, I try to take advantage of our break in the day to get more answers. "You told me my mom's name, and that she's alive. What about my dad? Is he still alive? What does he do?"

Eko finishes her last rice ball. Stands. "We can't talk about that now."

"Why not?"

"Because it's time for you to clear your mind of all questions and worries."

"Then there won't be anything left," I joke.

"Exactly," she agrees. "That's the goal."

—*1300 hours.* Upside-down Zen.

"First, sit like this," Eko says. She folds her legs into a position that would make a contortionist pop aspirins. Then she tilts her body and stands on her head.

"You're kidding, right? I can't do that."

"Try," she says.

I nearly dislocate every bone beneath my hips.

"Okay, just sit still and empty your mind."

So I sit there, still and silent.

Emptying your mind turns out to be a very hard thing to do. Like willing yourself to fall asleep. The conscious act of trying to do it makes it nearly impossible.

Don't think about food. But a nice rib steak and a baked potato sure would hit the spot.

Don't think about sex. Wonder if P.J.'s with some other guy yet? She looked so hot at the Hadley pool last summer.

Surreptitious glance at Eko. She's wearing a two-piece. Her eyes are half-shut. Her mind no doubt completely empty. She's got the sensuality of a washing machine.

Uh-oh. Her eyes pop open. Hope she didn't hear that.

"You have to try," she says. "Sit up straight. Palms up, the backs of your hands on your knees. Breathe shallowly. Focus all of your concentration on a very simple task."

"Like what?"

She draws a line in the sand. "Bend that line, grain of sand by grain."

"You're kidding, right? No one can do that."

"I can," she says.

"I'm not like you. I can't do the things you can do."

Out of the blue, Eko smiles. For the first time. After all my wisecracks and sarcasm failed, for some reason this gets her. "You are so much more than I am," she says.

An unexpectedly nice smile. But it doesn't last long.

—*1700 hours*. Flying practice.

Crevice between the dunes. The afternoon breeze has picked up. Eko has me run, with my arms held out to full wingspan. Wind blasts sand in my face.

She sits on a rock and watches. "Feel the breeze. Let it take you. Steer with your whole body. Your legs, your trunk."

I try for a few minutes. Feel ridiculous. "Enough, Eko. I'm not a bird, so don't make fun of me."

She comes down from the crevice. "I'm teaching you the most beautiful thing you'll ever learn. Here, do it with me." She extends her arms. Runs through the natural wind tunnel. Looks uncannily like a bird. Reminds me of when I first saw her, gliding down in black ninja robe. "Come, Jack," she says, "fly with me."

No girl has ever said that one to me before. So I try to fly with her.

—*2000 hours*. Dinner.

Stewed eggplant. Bowl of rice. Berries.

—*2100 hours*. Lights out.

Before I get into bed, I remember my nightmare and peer out the window. No death's face lurking in shadows.

But wait! There's a monster perched on the roof!

No, not a gargoyle. It's Eko. Watching the starlight over the marsh. She looks terribly sad.

I resist an urge to call out to her. To join her. She's not your friend, Jack. She lives deep inside herself. She beat you in the barn without mercy. She's drilling you now without sympathy. She just doesn't seem to care. Maybe she can't care. Maybe she hasn't got that bone in her body.

Follow her orders. Learn from her. But whatever you do, don't get too close.

I fall into bed. Hungry. Tired. Aching. Not sure how many more of these days I can take. And what's the point?

I'll never learn to run in darkness.

I'll never bend sand.

I'll damn sure never fly.

25

Why don't you take off your clothes?" Eko asks.

We're standing on a beach at seven in the morning. I'm covered with sweat and my chest is heaving. She looks fresh as a daisy. We just ran five miles through deep sand.

I've only been in basic training for a few days, but I can feel how much stronger I am. Toned. Cut. Recovery time way down. I may now be sweating and gasping a bit, but I pushed Eko on the last mile. We raced in, neck and neck.

Made it. Whew. Rest time.

But of course Eko wants to keep going. Announces that the next task will be a long-distance swim.

Fine. Bring it on.

In the nude.

"No offense, Eko. I don't go around skinny-dipping with people I barely know."

"You're ashamed of your body?"

"Not at all. It's not about me."

"I've seen lots of naked men before," she says matter-of-factly. "It's no big deal."

"Then why bring it up?" I ask. "Why do you want me to shed my shorts?"

"Because I need to teach you how to swim."

"I already know how," I tell her. Pretty well, I almost add. Two gold medals at our town pool's summer Olympics. Could have won more, but Dad was watching. "Why don't you let Tom Jennings win the backstroke? Make his dad proud."

But I don't brag about my swimming to Eko. I've seen her run and I've seen her fight, and something tells me she's also good in the water. "I'll be fine in shorts."

"Your choice," Eko says. "But it's easier when nothing is getting waterlogged. Especially where we're going."

She raises her T-shirt over her head. Unclasps her sports bra. Slides her shorts off. Then her underwear. Stands there naked, except for red bead necklace with jewel pendant hanging between her breasts.

I look away. Slowly look back. Can't stop my gaze from flicking down her body. Never saw a naked member of the female gender before. During our petting sessions, P.J. was always rather modest. Kept some articles of clothing on, as if she needed a bra and panties for security and protection.

Not Eko. Secure in her own skin. Short, muscular body. Athletic arms and shoulders. Small but firm breasts. Wide hips. Triangle of dark hair between powerful thighs.

I catch my breath. Look back up and our eyes meet. Son of a bitch, Eko's smiling.

Second smile ever from her. "Let's go swimming," she says. "You look like you need to dive into cold water."

She runs into surf and dives into wave. I follow. Water unexpectedly cool.

Soon we are half a mile out. She turns and sets course parallel to shore. Swims the way she runs. Graceful. Rhythmic. All parts working in concert.

I can barely keep up with her.

She stops. "Ready to go down? It's about a hundred feet deep here."

"Eko, I always wanted to learn scuba, but they didn't have lessons in my town. And aren't you forgetting breathing masks and oxygen tanks?"

She takes off necklace. Carefully unthreads two red beads. Swallows one. Passes me the other.

I roll it around in my hand. "What's this? A vitamin?"

"Two hours of oxygen," she says.

"Oxygen is a gas. Doesn't come in pills."

"Stay close and try not to get into too much trouble," she advises. She does a little pitch forward, and dives straight down like a mermaid returning to her secret world.

I swallow red bead. Feel it breaking apart inside me. Like antacid tablet. Can this work? I'm not a fish. No gills. I can't go down a hundred feet without an oxygen tank.

Come on, Eko summons me telepathically.

I can't do this. It's crazy. You're nuts. I'll drown.

I never thought you were a coward.

No girl has ever called me that before. It stings. Meanwhile, the red bead is doing hopscotches in my stomach. Not just in my stomach. My throat. My lungs.

I lower my head beneath the surface. Keep my mouth closed. Wait for that warning light to start flashing. OXYGEN DEPLETION. And the siren: HEAD FOR THE SURFACE NOW.

No warning light. No siren. I'm fine.

Come on.

Eko swimming circles beneath me. I join her. Pressure builds in my ears. It gets dark fast. Water temperature must be sixty degrees at surface. Drops ten degrees real quick.

I stop descending. It's getting inky and I feel drunk. Eko, it's too dark. Too cold. I can't handle the pressure.

She swims back up to me. I see that her jeweled pendant is

glowing. The glow lights the way in front of her and also flickers over her whole body, so that she seems encased in a moving jacket of warm light.

Use your watch, Jack.

How?

Find the way.

I look at the watch on my left wrist. Dad's gift. Old-fashioned watch face on a dark metal band. Didn't know she'd even noticed it. Hope it's waterproof. I remember the way it saved Gisco and me in Manhattan by deflecting two search beams from a Dark Army van. Okay, turn on. Switch on. Abracadabra. Hocus pocus. Eko, I don't know how to do this.

Stop thinking of it as separate from yourself. Control it as part of yourself.

Okay, let's see. Feel my arm. Upward to my wrist. Around my wrist, the dark metal band. Feel the extra weight of the watch. The constriction of the band. The band that's now starting to grow warmer. As the watch starts to glow . . .

A million points of light suddenly surround me. Dance around me. Embrace me. Warming me. Cold vanishes. Pressure goes kaput. I can see clear as day.

Down and down we go. Entering magical realm. I've never done anything like this before. Why does it feel so normal, so much like coming home?

Because it was home. We all come from the ocean, Jack.

Yeah, but a real long time ago. How deep are we?

Fifty feet. You couldn't see here without the watch.

Suddenly I am caught up in a pinwheel of color and movement. Three, four, five hundred of them. They've got a single yellow stripe across their faces. Each of them must weigh fifty pounds. A vast school of them, and they've decided I'm the field trip. They're swimming circles around me. Eko? What are they?

Large amberjacks.

They don't eat humans?

No. They're just curious.

As quickly as they came, they dart away. Large, saucer shape getting closer. Almost five feet long. Reddish-brown-colored shell. Paddle-shaped limbs with two claws. Looks like it would be ungainly on land. Graceful in the water.

Loggerhead turtle, Eko informs me. She swims to it, and it nuzzles her with its massive block-like head. She puts her hands on its shell and hitches a downward sloping ride.

Threatened species. Their nesting sites are vanishing. This one's more than two hundred years old. It's circled the world a dozen times. Say hello.

I try. No dice. Dr. Dolittle I'm not. Sorry, Eko, I don't speak turtle. Can't communicate with wild creatures. Don't seem to have that connection.

It's the purest connection there is.

My dial doesn't have that frequency. What's your turtle pal saying?

He's not saying anything. He's just being a sea turtle.

Then I guess I'm not missing much.

You've got to get over your sense of superiority. Humans are really in many ways an appalling race. We were given great power, and we did the stupidest thing imaginable with it.

What was that?

Seventy feet under the Atlantic, I can feel the sadness and anger as Eko hesitates and then answers. *Ruined everything. Sea turtles would have done better.*

Ruined everything how? What did we do, and who was responsible?

But she's not answering. Just as she hasn't answered so many of my questions about myself and my parents during the past few days of basic training.

She dives deeper. Loggerhead turtle swims away, long tail trailing behind.

Sorry to see it go. Something comforting about such a gentle giant.

Speaking of giants. Enormous shadow poking up at us from the black depths! Looks like a submerged redwood. Doesn't fit into this soft underwater playground. Too straight. Too hard. Made of dark iron. What is it, Eko?

Anti-aircraft gun. Welcome to the Graveyard of the Atlantic.

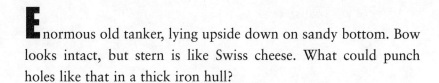

26

Enormous old tanker, lying upside down on sandy bottom. Bow looks intact, but stern is like Swiss cheese. What could punch holes like that in a thick iron hull?

Torpedoes. German U-boats hunted in these waters.

We swim closer. Fascinating mix of death and rebirth. The ocean has repopulated this ghost ship. Cold skeleton of iron wreck flames with white, orange, and purple-tipped anemones. Fish teem around it, swimming through gaps in the hull that serve as entrances to vast, hidden chambers.

Wreck of tanker feels oddly spiritual. Who knows the pain and final struggles of the men who sank with it? Now all resting in peace. Silence of a hundred-foot-deep mass grave. Rusted tanks are now high-ceilinged cathedrals for congregations of dark-robed mollusks. Gutted machine rooms the shadowy hermitages of crustaceans in seclusion. As we swim past, an enormous Maine lobster bows its antennaed head, as if in obeisance.

Look that one up, my friend, but not right now. Now I've glimpsed something. In a dark hole. Silver flashing brightly. A lost fortune! A sunken bit of treasure! I begin to stick my arm far down to retrieve it.

Don't do that, Eko warns. *You'll lose fingers.*

I rip arm away. Just in time. Large water snake emerges from hole. Not pleased at being disturbed. Four-foot monster. Not scaly. Charcoal skin. Upper jaw protruding over lower. Opens its mouth and shows me razor-sharp teeth.

Conger eel, Eko tells me. *Bottom feeder.*

Looks like it would have enjoyed snacking on my arm. How did you know it was there?

How did you not know?

We swim together in silence. Explore wreck. Eyeball an octopus. I lose track of time. Never been so fascinated.

We have to go soon. Do you like it down here?

One of the best things I've ever done in my life.

Me too.

Something about her answer. Do you do this a lot where you come from, Eko?

No opportunity.

Why not?

We ruined it.

How?

Nothing left like this. The beauty. The diversity. All gone. Nothing wild. Nothing free. Everything farmed.

I'm not talking about on land. I'm talking about deep beneath the oceans.

So am I. Most of them empty. Toxic. Sea lice and jellyfish. The rest farmed and guarded.

Even the deepest oceans?

Eko's looking around at the panorama of ocean life on display. Sadness on her face for just a minute. More than sadness. Resignation? Even a kind of guilt?

We better go back up, Jack. We'll run out of oxygen soon. Go slow.

We start up. Whoa, what's that? I feel a sinister vibe. Like an electric current. Pure hate in thought form. Then I see it. Seven-foot-long shadow. Circling. Eko!

Sand tiger shark. Don't worry.

Don't worry about a shark?

They don't usually eat humans.

"Usually" is not the most comforting word you could have used. How rarely are we talking about?

That's a small one. You're almost as big as he is. See, he's decided to look for something smaller to eat.

Sure enough, sand tiger shark swims away.

I wasn't really scared, Eko. Just being cautious—

Stop.

Stop what?

Stop everything. Stop swimming. Stop moving.

27

The evil vibe again. More directed. Far more intense.

I glimpse another shadow. Not seven feet long. Twice that! Stout body. Big front dorsal fin. Another smaller one near tail. Tiny eyes. Short snout.

Bull shark.

Are they dangerous?

Most dangerous sharks in the world.

Any more bad news?

It's hungry.

Can we fight it?

It's hard to fight a shark underwater.

I'll take your word for it. Should we flee?

Worst thing we could do.

What does that leave?

Summon help.

Good idea. You got any friends around? How about Aquaman? I'm getting the hell out of here—

Don't move! They're coming.

Who's coming? Watch out! It's circling closer.

Eko swims between me and shark.

What the hell are you doing?

Protecting you.

I swim next to her. We're scarier together.

No, stay behind me.

Not a chance.

You are our beacon of hope.

I just hope we're not lunch.

Bull shark shows us its teeth. I don't want to look. I do anyway. Wish I hadn't.

Teeth are triangular and serrated, like pyramids of saw blades.

Stay behind me. It's going to attack!

How do you know?

Bull shark darts in and Eko swims to meet it. Jeweled pendant on Eko's necklace flashes. Disco ball. Blindingly bright.

Shark blinded for half second by explosion of colors. Ever see a shark confused? This one stops coming forward and shakes its ugly head, as if trying to clear cobwebs.

Eko attacks! Tries to gouge out bull shark's tiny right eye with three-finger claw strike. She doesn't get eye, but shark backs off. Swims away thirty feet to regroup.

I rejoin Eko. I think you really pissed it off.

That won't work again. Next time it'll get one of us.

What should we do?

While it's eating me, swim away as fast as you can.

You're kidding, right?

Eko looks at me. *Goodbye. Never forget that you have the weight of a world on your shoulders. When your moment comes, remember me and be brave!*

Enough with the heroic speeches, Eko. Let's get the hell out of here.

Too late. Shark swims right at us.

Eko swims to meet it. Offering herself as the main dish. Should I try to help her? Should I flee? I flash to my dad, ordering me to run away, shooting his own foot off to convince me to go. He sacrificed his life to save me. To keep me alive. For some higher purpose. If I die here, I negate it all.

So I head toward surface. Then I stop.

Can't leave her like this. I swim back.

Shark strikes and Eko barely dodges it. She's fast.

Shark is faster. She's evaded it once, but it's gotten behind her.

Great ugly mouth opens wide. Ready for lunch.

I grab rear dorsal fin. Feels like bony sandpaper. Put shark in a cross-face wrestling hold. Increase pressure and try to rip the fin off its back.

Shark forgets about Eko. Tries to fold itself in half and bite me. Can't bite its own back. Decides to shake me off. Launches into dizzying twirl at rapid speed.

I rip loose and somersault away, head over heels. Stunned. Recover. Turn.

Shark giving me a look: I am an eating machine at the top of the food chain, and you have really pissed me off.

Eko swims up to join me. *Now you can't get away. It wants you. We have to stand and fight.*

I thought we couldn't fight a shark underwater.

We can't.

Not much choice. Here comes Jaws.

Twenty feet away. Fifteen. Great jaws open. Ten feet away. I see my fate in those rows of saw blades. Mouth a prayer. Let it end quickly. Five feet away . . .

POW. Underwater impact. Shark knocked to one side. Before it can recover, POW. A dolphin! A gang of them. A pack! Swimming at shark and ramming its underbelly with their beaks. Shark is more than a match for any one of them. But every time it wheels to face one, another dolphin rams it from underneath. POW. POW. POW!

Bull shark has had enough. Swims off angrily.

Eko, it's gone! We did it!

It'll be back. Sharks never give up a fight. We've got to take the express train out of here.

What are you talking about?

Grab on.

Dolphin swims up to her. Another stops in front of me. Lovely animal. Sleek yet robust body. Gray with light spots. Friendly face with white lips. I watch Eko find a secure hold on her dolphin's back. I latch hold of my own. A lot more comfortable than wrestling a shark. Skin is smooth. Like plush Italian leather. Okay, Flipper, let's roll.

Dolphin doesn't move. I don't speak turtle. Apparently I also don't speak dolphin.

Ready? Eko asks me. She informs dolphins. And we're off.

Smooth ride, powerful engine. Twenty, thirty, forty miles per hour. Other dolphins race around us. Feels like I'm swimming with them. Cavorting.

Water getting warmer. Sunlight. Orb of orange visible through blue-green curtain. We break surface.

Skim along on living Jet Skis. Indescribable joy. To be alive! To be in sunlight! On the back of a friendly dolphin. Who jumps five feet in the air and playfully executes one-and-a-half turn before perfect reentry.

Hey, Flipper, what the hell was that?

But I'm loving it and they're loving it, too, and we skim and jump and dive all the way to shore. They bring us in to shallows. Frolic around us as we walk through breakers. Rub up against our knees. Swim between our legs.

"Thank them for me, Eko. They saved our lives."

"Thank them yourself."

"I can't."

"If you try, you can talk to them. They're as smart as you are, just different. Try."

"I'm trying. I can't." Wish I could.

Then we're onshore, watching their gray dorsal fins as they put on a farewell show for us, leaping and darting. And then they're gone.

Eko gets dressed. I watch the waves.

"Thanks," I say to her when she's got her clothes on. "I'll never forget that. It was all new to me. And magnificent."

She nods. Walks up next to me. Also watching the waves.

Strange bond between us. Part shared adventure. Part common sensibility. Any way you slice it, Ninja Girl and I are having a moment.

She almost never calls me by my name, but now she surprises me by whispering, "Jack."

"Yes?"

Not looking at me. She's looking out at the Atlantic. A highly unusual emotion in her voice. Vulnerability. "When the shark attacked me, why did you come back?"

"It didn't feel right to just leave you there."

"I see. Because we're not friends, are we?"

"Not really," I admit.

"You can tell the truth. You don't even like me. Why should you? From the day I attacked you in the barn, all I've done is order you around and cause you pain. So why did you come back and risk your life for me?"

She turns to face me. The Atlantic is still in her gray eyes. The depth. The loneliness. For a dizzy moment I'm tempted to say something warm. Endearing. To kiss her.

"I would have done it for anyone," I tell her. "I just wasn't brought up to let people risk their lives for me while I turn and run."

Eko nods. "Right. That's what I thought." Moment broken. Then, "Let's sprint home. In knee-deep water. It's harder that way."

"But it must be five miles."

"If you can't run, crawl," she scolds. And off she goes.

I follow. Back to business.

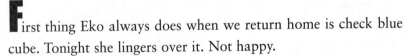

28

First thing Eko always does when we return home is check blue cube. Tonight she lingers over it. Not happy.

"What is it?" I demand.

"Nothing. Go to bed."

"We're in danger?"

"Just some bad weather coming. Good night."

I lie in bed. Positive a little inclement weather was not the threat that worried Eko. She would probably enjoy a typhoon. So at home with nature. Even the vicious parts, like eels and sharks. I relive our diving adventure. Never knew the ocean was so beautiful. Far prettier than land. Deeper and more layered.

Wonder what Eko meant when she said that humans, as a species, were appalling. That we ruined everything. How did we ruin it? Where do I fit in? She was willing to sacrifice her life for me. As my father did. Why? What's broken that they expect me to fix? How can I possibly repair it when I know so much less than they do?

Unnaturally quiet night. Windless. Becalmed. As if the sky is sucking up everything deep in its throat before spitting it back out. Eko may have been sharing a bit of the truth with me. Feels like bad weather is indeed coming our way.

A hurricane brewing far out in the tropical North Atlantic? Gathering strength. Heading slowly, inexorably, ineluctably for Jack Danielson in the Graveyard of the Atlantic?

Look those words up, my friend, but not now. Now I feel uneasy. Marshes are not supposed to be silent. Insects and frogs are oddly muted. They know something's coming. Finding shelter. Mudholes to crawl in. Logs to burrow under.

I'm exposed. No mudhole. No log. Just this three-story house for Jack to hide in and a blue cube to warn us.

Of what? Who's coming, and when? What will I do when they find me?

I climb out of bed. Peer through window. There. On a rock, fifty feet away. Traitorous dog. If I had a gun I could shoot him from here. Cloud covers moon. When it passes, he's gone.

I glance the other way. Human gargoyle on roof. Eko. Motionless. Facing bay.

I lean out window. Find handholds. Pull myself up.

Climb toward her. Arms out for balance. Steep slope. Careful, Jack. My steps are silent, but she knows I'm coming. "You should be asleep," she says as I get close.

"Not tired. Can I join you?"

She doesn't say no. For Ninja Girl, that's a warm invitation.

I sit next to her. Apex of roof. Highest vantage point. Moon casting glow. Patchwork of silver marsh channels threading into glass-smooth bay. A million reflected stars captured by the shallow water like a swarm of bright-winged insects entombed in an endless sheet of amber.

"I saw that lying dog," I mutter. "Gisco. What's he doing snooping around?"

"Why are you still angry at him? He just did his job. He brought you to me. Why do you care if his methods were a little dishonest?"

"I don't know if you can understand this," I tell her, "but when you're all alone and you start to be friends with someone and trust them, it's awful when they betray you."

"Don't pity yourself," she responds. "From the moment we're born to the moment we die, we're all completely alone." Her voice quivers, and she stops talking.

I glance at her face and she turns away. "What happened to your parents?" I ask.

Eko remains silent for such a long time that I'm sure she's not going to answer. Then she surprises me, and says softly, "They're both gone. I have no memory of my father at all. But I remember my mother. Searching for a hideout with her last energy. A hut. A cave. Someone she could trust. She turned me over to the Caretakers. Then she died."

An owl hoots, far off. Strange hunting call. Inchoate. Primeval. We listen to its echoes fade.

"I'm sorry," I say. "Now I understand why all my questions about my parents must have been painful for you."

"You don't understand anything," she snaps. "Don't ever feel sorry for me."

I glance over at her. Short black hair framing her features, an ebony shawl. Fingers cupped, as if the moonlight is nectar she has collected in her upturned palms. Lips slightly parted. Eyes wandering over the night sky.

"Eko, will I hurt your feelings if I tell you the truth?"

No answer. Is she listening to me, or is she far away?

"Sometimes I think you're the most heartless and mean psycho bitch imaginable," I say, "and, frankly, I hate your guts.

Other times I think you're the saddest person I've ever met in my life, and something of a soul mate."

Eko gives a slight nod, as if both descriptions fit. "It's very hard not to give in to the sadness," she admits, her voice so soft it seems almost like a confession. "They tried to prepare me for it. Warned me how hard it would be coming back this close to the Turning Point. But the irony is brutal and the guilt is crushing."

"What turning point?" I ask. "Don't talk in riddles. Just tell me what happened. You said this morning that humans ruined everything. How did we screw it all up?"

Eko slithers out of her lotus position and I remember the eel emerging from its hole. I sense that meditation is her way of hiding in herself, sheltering from the world. Now she's exposed and vulnerable.

She pulls her knees in to her chest. For a minute she doesn't look like a ninja or a yogi. She looks like a girl at a campfire about to tell a scary story that she knows will end up frightening her, too.

"If you really want to understand what I'm saying, remember that I'm looking backward," she says. "As we sit here on this roof tonight, it's a thousand years in front of us. But forget that. Pretend it's all already happened and now we have to deal with the result."

"Okay," I said, "take me to your world and let's look backward. Where are we ten centuries from this night?"

Eko looks up at the stars. Inhales a deep breath through slightly parted lips. And then she does the last thing I would ever expect her to do. She starts quoting Scripture. Not just a line of it, but a whole ponderous chunk.

My parents weren't exactly churchgoing types, but I know what she's reciting is famous, and I sort of recognize it.

"One generation passeth away, and another generation

cometh: but the earth abideth for ever," Eko whispers. "The sun also ariseth, and the sun goeth down, and hasteth to his place where he arose. The wind goeth toward the south, and turneth about unto the north; it whirleth about continually, and the wind returneth again according to his circuits. All the rivers run into the sea; yet the sea is not full; unto the place from whence the rivers come, thither they return again. All things are full of labour; man cannot utter it: the eye is not satisfied with seeing, nor the ear filled with hearing. The thing that hath been, it is that which shall be; and that which is done is that which shall be done: and there is no new thing under the sun."

"That's beautiful," I tell her, "but awfully depressing. It's from the Bible, isn't it?"

"Ecclesiastes. You find it depressing?"

"Yeah. What it's saying is that there's no point to doing anything, because nothing really changes."

"To me, that's so comforting," she responds. "How lucky people were to have had that to believe in. You're born, you live, you struggle, you die, and the earth goes on and on. The winds blow and the rivers run and nothing a man does in life can possibly change a jot of it. And if you think you can leave a permanent mark or change the world, then you're vain and deluded because that's the biggest vanity of vanities."

Eko falls silent and we sit side by side looking out at the endless Milky Way reflected in the inky bay. For a minute the stars seem to swirl and assume a ghostly shape. I see an old man, looking back at me. He looks like Merlin the magician, with long white hair and a shaggy beard. But his features are somehow familiar. And not in a creepy way. A comforting way.

My features. He looks a lot like me. But so sad. And bone-weary. Mournful. Like the weight of the world has been pressing on his shoulders for decades.

He looks right at me. Into me. Through me.

Is it my father? My real father?

How can it be?

And then he's gone and I'm sitting there watching the reflected stars again, and somehow I now understand what happened.

29

W e changed it?" I ask softly. "That's why you say we're an appalling species? We damaged the world?"

"Permanently." She nods. "Irreparably."

"Pollution?" I guess. "The ozone layer?"

"Sure. Pollution. The destruction of the ozone layer. And a hundred other big and small ways all taken together. Hunted out the jungles. Fished out the rivers and the lakes and finally the deepest oceans. Cut down the rain forests. Destroyed the coral reefs. Defoliated the edges of the deserts. Changed climate patterns. Manipulated the genetics of plants and animals. Body blows to nature. One after the other. Each one undoing millions of years of evolution and development. And do you know why we did it?"

"No," I admit softly. "Why?"

"Because we're human," Eko tells me, and there's a ring of disdain and self-loathing in her voice. "That's the reason. That's what humans do. That's what sets us apart from the rest of the animals. We think. We create. We try to control. And for a bunch of good reasons, like trying to create more farmland and feed more people and have insect-resistant crops and better weather, we played God more and more. And we couldn't do it. We weren't up to it."

For days she's been stingy with her words. Getting her to say anything has been such an effort. Now the truth spills out of her in an angry torrent. "We mucked it up," she says bitterly. "So, instead of there being no new thing under heaven, suddenly everything was new. Instead of nothing ever changing, everything was different. A thousand years of hothouse changes at an ever-accelerating pace."

"And those changes were not for the better?" I guess.

"Not at all," she agrees, and shudders. She closes her eyes and presses her knees to her chest, and I get the strong vibe that the future world is not a pretty or a happy place. "Most of them were horrible. The earth stripped of beauty. Barren and desiccated. Water holes and pockets of green like oases in an endless desert. People fighting over food, energy, and resources. And not just people but . . . things! We created our own nightmare and now it's swallowing us up."

So that was it. That was the mess a thousand years in the future. And the ironic thing was, that was my messed-up world she was talking about, even though it was a world I didn't know. And this world of blue skies and herons and wild horses was not my world, even though it was the beautiful planet Earth I had always taken for granted.

"Didn't anyone see what was happening and try to stop it?" I ask, my own voice now sounding a bit sad.

"Yes," she nods. "Even today a few people see. They're regarded as fanatics or alarmists now, but in the far future they're looked upon as visionaries. As things got worse, and we approached and passed the Turning Point, more and more people saw what was happening. Movements sprang up, all over the world, trying to prevent what was seen with increasing clarity as mass suicide—our species dooming itself. Over centuries the movements merged into one coalition, one"—she searches for a word—"global effort to save the earth."

"Did this movement have a name or a leader?" I ask.

Something in Eko's voice I haven't heard before. Respect. Even reverence. "Its founder was a great man, a philosopher-scientist named Dann. People who followed him came to be called the Caretakers or the People of Dann, and his descendants, the House of Dann, led the struggle to save the world."

My whisper comes very low. "My name's Jack Danielson."

"You are of the House of Dann," she tells me. "A great legacy. And a tremendous responsibility. Your ancestors saw that the earth could be saved only if people changed every destructive and indulgent habit. We had to stop being consumers and cor-rupters, and start being caretakers and restorers. It was an all-consuming way to live, to act, to think. I myself have followed it since my mother left me with the People of Dann. That was her parting gift to me."

"At least she had a good reason for leaving you," I mutter. "Mira wasn't dying. How could she just send me away?"

Eko smiles. Third smile. This one affectionate and tinged with sadness. "How indeed?" She lets her question hang in the night air. "Enough questions for one night."

"Just one more. You still haven't told me what the Turning Point is," I remind her.

Eko is clearly tired, but she gathers her strength. "It's the name we gave to the moment when the damage to our earth could still be reversed," she explains. "It's impossible to pinpoint a day or a week or even a year. But there was a time up until which all this beauty could have been preserved. The damage could have been contained and rolled back. And then there was a Turning Point, when things spiraled wildly out of control. After that, it be-came much more difficult. We still tried. We fought. But it was too late. It's hard to come back so close to the Turning Point. To see it when it could have been reversed. To think what might have been."

She falls silent. I am silent also.

The night has become even more calm. There is not the slightest puff of breeze or ripple of wave. We are far from any big city and there are zillions of stars overhead. Time and all human folly and toil seem to shrink beneath the cold vastness of the night sky.

Eko is not finished with her surprises. She reaches out and takes my hand. Her fingers are warm and soft. "Thank you for swimming back and saving me from that shark," she whispers. "Even if you think I'm a psycho bitch. It was a brave thing to do."

"I'm sorry you're so sad," I tell her. "But now I understand why."

We sit there holding hands. Sharing a moment. I consider kissing her. I think she wants me to. But I can't. This is the Ninja Babe, after all. This is the drill sergeant who's been kicking my butt in basic training. Built like a fire hydrant. Mean as a rattlesnake.

"Do you know Basho's last haiku?" Eko asks softly.

"I don't even know who Basho is," I confess.

"A Japanese poet," she tells me. "The master of the haiku. He was born into samurai nobility. Rejected social rank and all worldly possessions. He became a wanderer. Wrote the most beautiful haiku. In his last years, he made many long journeys. He became ill on a trip, and as he lay dying in Osaka he wrote his last poem." Eko whispers it slowly:

> *"Fallen ill on a journey,*
> *In dreams I run wildly*
> *Over a withered moor."*

She shudders.

It's the first time in my life a girl has ever quoted a poem to me. "It's very sad," I whisper.

"Yes," Eko agrees, "and it keeps running through my mind. Strange that such a short poem should have such power."

This time it's not just a shudder. Her body trembles. I let go of her hand. Put my arm around her. Eko leans in. We turn our heads to look at each other.

Her gray eyes are sparkling. Our lips brush.

And then I stand up so abruptly I almost fall off the roof. "Well, I guess I should be turning in," I stammer. "Good night."

"Good night," she says softly.

I climb down the slant of roof, and glance up only when I reach my window.

Eko is sitting in the lotus position again, shrouded in silence and sadness, a gargoyle contemplating her own destroyed world.

30

Basic training out of whack. How can there be military discipline when you sat on a roof holding hands with your drill sergeant the night before? No wonder the military has an anti-fraternization policy.

Pre-sunrise jog. Don't have to blunder along after Eko now. We run side by side. I sense spiderwebs and duck just in time. Avoid holes and sharp rocks. Don't ask me how, but I know they're there. We run at same pace in identical rhythm. Sometimes our hands brush as we pump our arms.

Kayak trip. Skimming through eerie fog. Sky and water the same copper-gray. Storm coming. Twists of marsh channel wrapped in morning mist. Eko doesn't have to point out birds and animals to me. Now I know where they're hiding.

White-tailed deer behind bayberry cluster. Copperhead on slate pebbles in shallows. Frog motionless beneath low-hanging grapevine. All perfectly camouflaged. Expertly concealed. But I know they're there.

We both cease paddling at the same moment to watch osprey swoop down from folds of mist to snatch small fish. The swoop, the splash, the struggle, the soaring back up and away with the silver fish thrashing in the razor-sharp talons. We look at each other, thrilled.

Cattle egret circling dunes. Not trailing a family of wild horses this time. Just one old stallion.

He clambers over the dune ridge and saunters down the sand to the water's edge. Noble animal. Aged but still formidable. I remember Eko's warning. Keep back. "How come he's alone?"

"Look at the scars on his neck and back," she tells me.

Thought they were part of his coloring. Now I can see that they're welts running from nose to tail. "He fought hard for his family," Eko whispers. "Didn't want a younger stallion to take his wives and children. Fought and got beat and fought again. Nothing he could do about it. Too old."

Shed stallion stands in surf gazing out to sea. So large. So noble. Once so powerful. Now completely defeated and alone. "What will happen to him?" I ask.

"Once they're alone and their spirit is broken they give up. Lie down in the sand and die. Stay here."

Eko walks toward stallion. He sees her coming. Turns to face her. New angle allows me to see the deep scars more closely. Boy, did he fight, and boy, did he suffer. Wounded, cast-off, vengeful beast. What the heck is Eko doing? In his solitary rage he will kick her head off her shoulders.

Sure enough, stallion bares his teeth as she approaches. Rears up. Hooves slice the air like scythes.

Eko doesn't even slow. Walks up to him. Palms raised. Exuding calm. Puts her hands on his scarred flank. Stallion slowly lowers his head. She leans her cheek against him. I watch, fascinated.

Horse and Ninja Babe stand motionless. She is holding his

great head in her hands. Then, as if reaching some understanding, the great horse turns and ambles off.

Eko walks back to me. Her eyes are wet, and it's not from the cold or the mist. I don't say anything to her.

Convincing display of sympathy on Ninja Babe's part. She is warm after all. Does have a heart. At least when it comes to wild horses.

Fighting practice. Hard to spar with somebody you're feeling close to. Each strike, each block, each step of the dance has a new second meaning. Throws and holds seem intimate. Arms wrapped around each other. Legs entwined.

I understand now that Eko's fighting power doesn't come from her muscles. Every kick, every strike, every leap has a thought component. A kind of energy I have to tap into. Then I can knock someone twenty feet away. Then I can jump through the air and land in a tree branch.

I ask her point-blank. "This fighting is more mental than physical, right? Your real power comes from your mind."

"All of the martial arts are based on mental discipline and achieving a greater awareness," she tells me. "Kung fu was practiced by monks in mountaintop monasteries for centuries."

"Yeah, but this isn't kung fu. What is it? You told me last night about my ancestor Dann, and how he started a movement to try to save the world. Was it a religion?"

"No, it's not about God or an afterlife," she tells me. "Dann taught us that no one can save us if we don't save ourselves. So it's a way of living. Understanding the world and our place in it. I can't explain it any better."

"Who taught you how to fight so well?"

Eko looks at me. "Your father," she finally says. "So, in a way, he's teaching you."

It's by far the most powerful punch she's landed in hours of combat drill. Her answer nearly knocks me off my feet. What? There's that close a connection between Eko and my dad? When did he teach her? What's he like? How do they know each other, and where do I fit in?

She takes off running, so I can't follow up with more questions. But I'll find out the answers soon enough.

31

Meditation drill. I sit in lotus position. Eko draws line in sand. I attempt to bend it. No success.

My mind drifts. To the osprey. The stallion. The morning's fighting drill, and Eko's big revelation.

My first direct connection with my birth father. He instructed the woman who beat the tar out of me. Showed her the punches that knocked me across the barn. Thanks, Dad.

We sit looking out at a desolate beach, swathed in mist. It's hard to tell where sand ends and clouds begin. Eko tangled up in a knot of a yoga position, legs folded like origami paper, body inverted in a headstand, mind no doubt empty as a mirror.

I sit next to her trying to bend the line in the sand and not think about my father in the far future, who I have never known but have started to dislike. This mess I find myself in is his fault. He sent me back in time. He constructed the artifice of my childhood in Hadley. And he sent Eko, his student in causing pain, to bang me out like a piece of iron.

Concentrate on the sand. Home in on it. Grain by grain. That tiny brown sand pebble with the ungainly shape. Move it, Jack. I can't. Focus. Come on. You don't have to slide it across the beach or make it spin. Just stir it a jot.

No dice. Can't do it. I bore in, trying my best. Use all that I've learned in the Outer Banks. I feel my mind coming out of my body. Sinking slowly into the sand.

Now I'm among the pebbles, as if I lost my balance on a ski slope and tumbled down and started seeing the moguls from ground level as I slid past.

The texture of the sand motes.

The way they stack together at odd angles.

One grain in particular. White. Round. Soft-looking.

A pillow. A sugar doughnut. A face.

Blurry. Merlin the magician. Bushy eyebrows. Beard. Shock of white hair. Familiar features because I've seen them in the mirror. The contours of my own face, but sagging with fatigue and deep-lined with suffering. Captivity. Torture. Pain on a scale I have never known. Dad?

"Son."

A single word from a great distance. Not spoken. Not telepathy. Don't ask me what it is or how it comes to me. The lips on the face I am staring at never move. But I know he sees me. I sense he's calling me. Urgency. Love.

Dad, what is it? Tell me. What should I do? What are you reaching across a thousand years to tell me?

The face blurring. Another word. I can't make it out. "Fee"? No, "Free." Free what? Free him? Free myself?

Snap. I lose the connection.

I'm lost and terribly cold. Not down among the grains of sand anymore. Not back in my body either. Don't ask me where I am. Adrift. Cast loose. Drowning in a cold, swirling miasma.

Words reaching out to me. "Jack? Come back, Jack."

A blanket covering me. No, not a blanket. Arms. Tightly around me.

I'm shivering uncontrollably. Eko hugging me. Holding me. Whispering in my ear. "It's okay. You're back."

I look at her. "I saw my father."

Eko's turn to look shocked. "Where? What happened?"

"In the grains of sand. He said something to me. Free."

"Free what?" she asks. "Free who?"

"I don't know. He faded. He was too far away. And he looked so tired. And like he was in terrible pain."

"Yes." She nods. "Your father is a great man, Jack. A brave fighter. He's sacrificed everything to give you this chance. To give us this one and only chance."

"If he's such a brave fighter, who's he fighting with?" I ask her. "You said last night that this was all about a struggle in the far future to try to save the earth. But it's not just a race against time, or a battle with our own worst impulses, is it? There's an enemy, right?"

"Yes," she acknowledges. "There is an enemy."

"The people chasing me?" I press. "Trying to kill me and stop us at all costs from doing whatever it is that I'm supposed to do?"

"They'll do anything to stop you," Eko agrees. "As I will do anything to help you."

"Who are they? Do they have a name?"

"We call them the Dark Army," she whispers.

32

Deserted beach. Storm definitely coming.

Now I know my enemies. The Dark Army.

"Not a very nice name," I whisper back. "Why do they want to stop us from saving the world? Isn't it in everybody's interest to protect the planet?"

"No," she says. "As the earth deteriorated, they thrived. They believe in doing whatever it takes to adjust, to gain power, to prevail. Two competing philosophies, Jack, that have no compromise. A thousand years from now they are hunting us down and killing us."

"And they're also chasing me?" I recall the tall man in the Hadley Diner whose eyes flashed, and the bat creatures, and the Gorm. "They don't seem human."

"Some of them are," she says. "But the Dark Army believes in tampering with nature in every possible way, to gain an advantage in the battle for survival."

"So they're genetic mutants?"

"Many of them are genetically engineered," Eko says. "Others are constructed. Do you know what cyborgs are?"

I'm not much for science fiction movies, but I've seen a few over the years. "Part man, part machine. That became a reality?"

"A hideous reality," she whispers. "Mary Shelley could never have imagined a world of Frankensteins with a common cause. We want to save the earth. They thrive as conditions worsen. We believe in what is natural. They were created by the unnatural. It's a battle to the death, Jack. It has been for centuries. And it's nearing a conclusion."

"It doesn't sound like the good guys are doing so well."

Eko doesn't answer. She's staring at the ground. "Look," she whispers.

The line she traced in the sand is no longer straight. It's been bent and curved into a perfect oval.

I look back up at her. "Did I do that? No way. I can't bend sand."

"You can do anything you put your mind to," she whispers. "You are our beacon of hope." She's still hugging me. She lets me go. Stands. "Come," she says.

"Sorry, but I don't think I can run or swim right now. Whatever my father did to reach out to me, it tired me out."

"We're not going to run or swim," she promises. "It's time to fly."

33

Standing in crevice between dunes. Day is calm no longer. Breeze stiffening. Sky darkening ominously.

Storm wading in from Atlantic like an angry sea monster. Godzilla's still a few hundred miles offshore, but I can feel his steamy breath. Hear his echoing footsteps.

Eko has me run through wind tunnel with my arms spread to full wingspan. Nothing could make me feel sillier. I put up with it for a few minutes. "Don't just use your arms," she calls. "Steer with your whole body. That's better."

"No, it's not better." I stop running. Lower my arms. "This is preposterous. I quit. Let's go home. There's a big storm coming, if you hadn't noticed."

She gazes up at the darkening sky. "Yes," she agrees. "That's why we can fly soon. No one will see us."

"Eko, about flying. I don't know if you noticed, but I wasn't born with wings."

She unzips small backpack. Takes two shirts out. No, not shirts. Thick, like life jackets. But form-fitted, like wet suits. And they glow, as if made from phosphorescent material. "Put this on and forget about wings," she says.

I'm tempted to ask if she's kidding. But Eko isn't a kidder. I tug on wet suit. Snug. Rubbery. Warm as fleece.

Glance up at stormy sky. Then look down at my wet suit.

Same angry shade of gray. Camouflage? Why does one need to look like the sky?

Unless one is really going up in the sky! I'm getting excited now. Heart's flitting around in my chest like a moth near a klieg light. I force myself to keep calm. Be real, Jack. No way. "Eko," I ask, "what is this thing exactly?"

She's pulling off her clothes and tugging on her own gray wet suit. "Do you remember the apple that fell on Newton's head?"

I flash to Hadley High School. Brick building on hill with view of Hudson River. Mr. Zimmerman's honors physics class. Dreaded by most students. Not me. Oddball Jack. I loved it from the first formula that popped out of his mouth.

"Isaac Newton, Law of Universal Gravitation," I spit back at Eko. "1666. He observed an apple falling off a tree and theorized that the same invisible force must be holding heavenly bodies like the earth and moon in orbit."

Eko stares back at me. Hard to impress the Ninja Babe, but maybe I just did. "This shirt would make Newton's apple jump back onto the tree," Eko informs me.

My heart's no longer a flitting moth. Now it's a barn owl bashing its great wings together. "It's some kind of antigravity device?" I guess.

"Listen to me carefully," Eko says, her wet suit now on. "We don't want an Icarus moment here. Stay close—one cloud bank looks pretty much like another. If you lose track of up and down, spit. The way your spit falls is down. Stay away from populated areas. We're camouflaged, but you never know who's looking up with a telescope. If you hear a helicopter or a plane, head for the nearest bank of clouds. Got it?"

Can't believe I'm about to do this! I've been a passenger in a few jumbo jets, but never flown in a small plane or a helicopter. It's always been a dream of mine to be some kind of aviator one day, in a small craft, at the controls, climbing through the sky.

Never imagined I wouldn't need wings or a propeller. "Okay, Eko, how do we go up?"

She gives me a funny look. "You are up."

I look back at her. Then I look down. We're ten feet off the ground! How did that happen? How does this work?

Weren't you thinking about flying?

Yes, but . . .

That's how it works. Steer, Jack. Not just with your arms. With your whole body. There you go.

Effortless! Gentler and more magical than deep-sea diving. Like daydreaming on the most comfortable bed ever designed, and suddenly you find the bed is sweeping you along like a magic carpet.

The Atlantic below. Skimming over waves. Turning inland and soaring over sand. The great dunes of Kitty Hawk somewhere close. Did the Wright brothers feel this same thrill when they lifted off the sand?

We go yet higher! Mother Earth releasing her tenacious grip. Marshes, beaches, and ocean dwindling to patterns of blue and brown, glimpsed through cracks in cloud.

The sun warm and close. No wonder Icarus pushed the envelope. How could he turn back? I whirl on a wind current. Eko nearby, whirling also. No longer earthbound. Freer than I've ever been. A son of sky, a creature of cloud.

A stanza of Shelley's "To a Skylark" flashes through my mind:

> *Higher still and higher*
> *From the earth thou springest*
> *Like a cloud of fire;*
> *The blue deep thou wingest,*
> *And singing still dost soar, and soaring ever singest.*

And I am hearing birds. Two of them. Flying near us. Calling out to us. Whirling as we whirl. Climbing as we climb. Birds of prey, but they are not hunting now. They are exulting. Ospreys. A couple. Eko told me they mate for life and travel together.

Something enormous rolls around in the sky. Thunder? Never heard it that way before. As if it is being stirred up in a kettle with an iron spoon, just above my head.

Blinding flash of lightning. I can feel the sizzle. Eko, are we in danger?

The suits will keep the lightning from striking us. Does it scare you?

Of course, but it's also glorious. The ospreys don't seem to mind it, so why should I?

You can really feel the storm up here. A dangerous, hulking creature. Its plodding progress. Its unfathomable outrage. This hurricane has a hammering pulse, a musky smell, a palpable intent to destroy.

Our flight is no longer playful, light, and merry. Now we are witnessing the landfall of an enraged behemoth. Dark clouds are wind-twisted into the haggard profile of a sky-shattering monstrosity. We comb our way through the locks of the storm. Rain and lightning are the snaking hair and flashing eyes of a mile-tall Medusa.

Thunder rolls right through us, and we both laugh and shout with the sheer insanity of it. I've been chased too long, mournful too long. I needed this release and I sense Eko needs it also.

She soars right along with me, reckless and joyful.

And then we are diving back down and down, down toward the water, and out over the sand, toward the misty dunes.

Watch out, Jack. You're coming in too fast.

You didn't tell me how to land.

Don't hit the bushes! Pull up!

What bushes? Too late!

Legs bent to absorb shock. Can't stop myself from toppling forward. Crash landing. Spinning and somersaulting through prickly thorns. Finally come to a stop. Ouch.

Eko right there next to me. How did she land so smoothly?

She must have done this lots of times. "Are you okay? You're bleeding?"

I register the sincere concern on her face. Stand up and dust myself off. "It's nothing. Just a few scratches."

"You hurt yourself. Why are you laughing?"

"Because that was great. Better than great. Amazing! Stupendous! When can we go up again?"

Eko tries to contain her own exuberance, and then gives up and laughs with me. "Yes, it was fun, wasn't it? Let's get you patched up."

34

My cuts and bruises are not serious, but there sure are a lot of them. I've stripped off wet suit. Stand in Eko's second-floor bedroom a bit self-consciously in just my briefs.

Eko fusses over cuts. Afraid they'll get infected. Or maybe, since she was the flight instructor, she feels responsible. Insists on administering first aid right away. First time we've ever come home when she didn't run right up to the living room to check the blue cube.

Instead she led me here. First-aid kit in closet near her bed. A yellow flashlight that makes each skin puncture glow. Vacuum tongs that suck out sticker needles.

But nothing high-tech about the disinfectant. Comes in an ugly green bottle, and Eko squirts it out onto a swab of cotton. "This is going to sting," she promises.

She's still wearing her gray wet suit. Form-fitting. As she touches my bare chest with the cotton swab, I look down and see the swells of her breasts.

"Does it hurt?"

"You're killing me and you know it."

"Think of something else," she advises.

I look around bedroom. First time I've ever been here.

Her bed is a futon floor mattress. On her bookshelf I see books in English. Japanese. And Russian.

An easel is set up to catch the best light. On the easel is a minimalist Asian-style nature painting. Swirling river. Heron in flight. Cottony clouds. It's not detailed, but the masterful brushwork suggests nuances of mood and tone.

P.J., you're lucky Eko didn't enter that art contest back in Hadley.

Makes me feel weird to think about P.J. right now.

A finished painting hangs on a wall. Shocking. Exquisite. A couple making love standing up. A big man. A shorter woman. He's holding her off the ground. She has her legs around his back. Her face is flushed.

Eko notices where I'm staring. I look away quickly. "So you liked flying?" she asks, turning me so that she can get at the prickers on my back.

"One of the best things I've ever tried."

"Almost as good as sex," Eko says, extracting a thorn.

"Uh, yeah," I grunt noncommittally. "Sure. Ouch."

"I have to admit, you picked it up faster than I expected," she says. Teasing chuckle in her voice. "You had good form. Superb stamina. Not much fear. You got a little too excited at the end, but that's normal for a beginner. The important thing is to relax and enjoy it."

I'm not sure exactly what we're talking about. I try to stay on a safe track. "You didn't tell me how to land."

"Do I have to teach you everything?" Eko turns me again, so we're facing each other. "Now I need to check your legs."

She bends. Cleans tiny cuts on my knees. Her light fingers brushing over my kneecap. Moving up my thigh.

I'm breathing harder. Getting excited. The briefs don't hide much. I'm embarrassed. Turn away. "Sorry."

"Don't be silly. It's natural. You're a healthy boy."

"Man."

"Young man," Eko says. "It's hot in here. Don't move, I'm not done yet." She tugs off her gray wet suit. Not wearing much under it. Sports bra and panties.

I fight to stay calm. Think of baseball, Jack. Leading home run hitters. Hank Aaron. Babe Ruth. Barry Bonds.

"You look kind of exposed," Eko observes. "Here."

She takes off her bead necklace and drapes it over my neck. "A little gift. It looks good on you." The red beads smell faintly of jasmine. "Men should wear more jewelry. It gives them a sensual dimension."

She bends back to her task. Disinfects cuts on my thigh. Each dab with the cotton stings. Concert of storm outside. Trombone slides of wind. Cymbal crashes of thunder. Violin pizzicato of rain.

"Now let me check your buttocks," she says as if it's the most normal thing in the world.

"Eko, that's okay."

Too late. She's turned me and tugged down my briefs.

"Be a good patient. Just try to hold still."

She cleans and disinfects. My heart does NASCAR in my chest. I try to quiet the engines. Where was I? Oh yeah, Barry Bonds. But does he count, because of possible steroid use? Who's next? Willie Mays. Then Frank Robinson.

Can't stop myself from glancing at Eko's futon. At the sexy painting on the wall. My mind flashes again to P.J.

Always thought she would be my first, and me hers. That I would be the initiator of the encounter. That we would discover this mysterious part of life together. In my car. Or in her bedroom. Used to fantasize about it all the time.

This is pretty far from my fantasy. Of course, nothing may happen. A medical emergency brought us here, after all. First-aid kit was in Eko's bedroom. She had to disinfect my cuts. This moment of intimacy could be just the end product of a coincidental chain of events. May lead nowhere.

"So," Eko says as she finishes extracting a thorn from my right buttock, "our time together is almost over. There's one more thing I think I need to teach you, Jack."

I gulp air and tug my briefs back up. "Uh, yeah?"

Eko stands. Looks at me. I remember her eyes as I first saw them, glinting coldly from inside the black Ninja death mask. Now they're alive. Warm. Inviting.

"I taught you how to fight," she says. "To dive. And to fly. What does that leave?"

"I'm not sure," I admit, my mouth dry. "I don't know the curriculum. Eko, maybe I'd better go."

She grabs the red bead necklace and pulls me closer with it. "Vulnerability is your enemy," she whispers.

"What does that mean?"

"They're chasing you. They'll use every weakness you have to trip you up, to destroy you. You must be expert in every area. There must be no chink in your armor." Her hot breath glazes my cheeks. "No dullness to your sword."

I need space. Stall for time. "Why are they chasing me?" I whisper back. "How do they know I can find Firestorm and change the future?"

"It was prophesied when you were born, a thousand years from now," Eko whispers. "The last hope of a dying planet. That's why you were sent back by your father and hidden by those he trusted. That's why you were flushed out by the Dark Army. And that's why you are now being chased."

"But how can I save a world I don't even know? Where am I supposed to go and what exactly am I supposed to do?"

"Find Firestorm," Eko replies. "And use it to change the world. Halt the damage and prevent the Turning Point, and the long, awful decline into darkness."

"How will I use Firestorm? Where will I find it?"

"No one knows," she says. "The Dark Army are searching for it right now, to destroy it and protect the dark future they are close to owning. But even with all their energy and evil science, they will fail. The prophecy says that you and you alone can find it. I have prepared you as best I can. But you still have one great weakness."

"I'm actually feeling pretty strong," I rasp, my throat suddenly as dry as a sand dune. "You did a great job training me. I'm in tip-top fighting shape now."

Eko reaches out gently with her right hand. Her warm fingertips descend the steps of my abs. "The male human animal, no matter how tough and fit, is made vulnerable by his sex drive," she says, looking into my eyes. "This is especially true during his teenage years, when his hormones are strongest but he is not very good at satisfying his urges."

"Thanks for your concern—" I begin to interrupt.

"This is an even more serious problem when the young man is a virgin," Eko continues. "Lack of experience creates fantasies and misconceptions. It's a grave weakness that can be easily exploited."

I think of Reilly in her New York apartment, and Jinny on the train. Maybe what Eko's saying is true, but . . .

She steps even closer. Our bodies touch. "When I first met you, Jack, I knew how much we had to accomplish, and how little time we had. Friendship would hold us back. I forced myself to be stern and demanding. Even cruel."

"You did a great job," I tell her.

"But I've learned to respect you," Eko whispers. "You attacked a shark to save me. Now time is running out."

She leans forward. Our bodies are pressed together. We're

slow-dancing, except that we're not really moving. Or maybe we are. Swaying very slightly.

"Sexuality is like any other part of life," Eko informs me softly. "Like fighting or diving. It can be a weakness or strength, a source of fear or of pleasure. You just need a good teacher—"

I react without thinking. Push her away. Can't believe I just did that. I really do like her. Do desire her.

But not this way. I was willing to learn a lot of things from Eko, but not this. No matter what she says, this isn't the same as learning to fight or dive. I don't want basic training in this personal realm of attaining manhood.

And then there's P.J., wherever she is. I keep flashing to her. And all she represents.

Not that it has to be her. But I want my first time to be with someone I love. Someone I choose. When I choose.

"Sorry," I tell Eko. "Don't take this personally."

She looks back at me. Not quite a pout. But close. "I'm not attractive to you?"

"You are. Truly. In many ways. You're a very admirable person. Girl. Woman."

"But you don't want me for a sexual partner?"

"No," I tell her. "Sorry, but I don't. Let's just be friends."

Eko turns away from me and walks to a closet. Pulls on a blue silk robe. When she turns back, she's smiling. She chuckles. And then she bursts into a peal of laughter.

Uh-oh. Women are at their most dangerous when you don't understand them.

"Did I miss something?" I ask. "What's so funny?"

"It's just that most men find me attractive and very desirable," she says.

Wounded pride? I look back at her. Strong, athletic body, but built like a mailbox. Brilliant mind but quirky, moody, and often sadistic. "I'm sure that's true."

"Of course, it might have something to do with the way I appear to you," Eko suggests softly. "This is my fighting guise. As you've probably figured out, in the future there have been many advances in the ways we use our minds. Telepathy. Telekinesis. And shape-changing, too."

"Shape-changing?" I'm intrigued. "Can you really do that? Why didn't you teach me how?"

"Only women can do it," Eko says, "and it takes years to learn. Here, Jack. This is the way I really look."

✳

35

Saw this once before. Reilly in her bedroom on Central Park West. Except this time girl is not turning into Gorm. Mailbox seems to be tapering to hourglass. It's impossible for me to tell if Eko is really transforming, or if it's just my perception of her that's changing.

Legs seem to be lengthening. Hips curving. Ample, perky breasts nearly squirm out of blue silk robe. Luxurious jet black hair. A surpassingly lovely face, strong yet delicate, sexy but re-fined. Lips now red and soft as rose petals. Dancing, provocative black eyes.

Forget about beauty pageants on TV. Forget about the *Sports Illustrated* Swimsuit Issue. Eko seems far and away the most beautiful woman I've ever set eyes on.

"You see?" she whispers. "Now, good night, Jack. Sleep well." She extends her hand for a goodbye shake.

Something tells me I won't sleep well after this. "Wait a minute," I whisper back. "You may be right. What I have to do is so crucially important I can't afford to take any chances. We have to make sure I don't have any weaknesses or vulnerabilities that could be exploited."

Eko smiles. "No, Jack," she says. "If you changed your mind now, I would think you were only interested in me because of my shape-shift, and you're so much deeper than that. So as you said, let's just be friends."

She nods toward the door. I don't go. Instead, I glance down at her futon. "I thought you were sent here to help me," I remind her, a note of pleading in my voice. "That the fate of the world was at stake. That no one could deny the beacon of hope."

"Only in this area," she responds with a smile. "Sorry, beacon . . ."

Has she rejected me? Are we still flirting? I try to think of something playful to say . . .

Suddenly her smile vanishes. "What was that?"

"I didn't hear anything."

She stands very still. Senses on full alert. "That."

I hear a distant thudding. It stops. "Just the wind. Probably blew something over outside. But if you're scared, I think I should stay and comfort you—"

"They're coming!" Not joking anymore. Hourglass transforming quickly back into mailbox.

"Are you sure?"

Before Eko can answer, her bedroom door flies open and a seven-foot-tall man steps in and points a gun at me. Eko dives at my knees, knocking me out of the way of the laser beam. A section of her bedroom wall ignites.

He re-aims quickly, before I can stand up. I dodge around on floor like a roach, desperately crawling for my life.

The tall man's focus is entirely on me. Trying to get the shot that will take me out. So he loses track of Eko.

Big mistake.

She flies through the air and kicks his head off. Literally. Right leg strikes with the full weight of her body behind it. Ball of her foot explodes into his chin. For a moment I think she has de-capitated him.

Then I see that it's not a head. He's part man, part machine. Head is still attached to body by cables. Eyes flashing the way the tall man's eyes flashed at me back in the diner in Hadley-by-Hudson. Could even be the same tall man. Strike that. Not man. Cyborg! These eyes are not flashing to mark me. They're short-circuiting!

Footsteps climbing stairs. Eko leads me to hallway. Two bat creatures. She takes one out with open-hand strike to throat. I kick the other one back down the steps.

But there are other dark forms on their way up. Slower but tougher-looking. Gleaming teeth, eyes strobing like searchlights, and long serpentine tongues.

"No chance to go down. Up the stairs," Eko shouts.

I take her advice. Make it to the third floor before I realize she's not coming up with me.

She's stayed behind to take them on. King Leonidas at Ther-mopylae. Holding the pass so that I can escape.

I look down. Eko's in the center of the hallway, blocking the stairs. To climb after me, they'll have to go through her. That won't be easy. Never seen anyone fight so desperately, savagely, and expertly. They're swarming her, and she's lashing out at them in all directions.

I start to run back down, and she yells, *"No. Get away!"*

This time it's not one pissed-off shark. It's a whole blood-thirsty army. She's sacrificing herself so that I can escape. No choice, Jack. If you go down, you both die.

So I go up. Third floor. But where can I hide? I run into kitchen. Look around for a weapon. Problem with vegan diet. No big cleavers or steak knives. Grab first thing that comes to hand. Big serving plate.

Uh-oh. Footsteps. On this floor. Someone was waiting here for me. Man runs into kitchen. Barely fits through door. Almost as wide as he is tall. And it's not fat. Sheer muscle. Whatever he is, he's a killer.

He raises an enormous arm. Throws something at me. Red paralysis dart. Been hit by one of those before. Don't want to try my luck twice.

I vault over countertop. Hurl serving plate at him like discus. It spins into him and shatters. Buys me a second or two.

But there's no way out of this kitchen.

More attackers thundering up stairs.

Eko! They've gotten around her. Or through her. And now they're coming for me.

Blue firecracker explosion. Plasma net. Spreading out through kitchen. Only one place to go.

I kick out window. Jump through.

Dive-roll onto sloping roof. Dark outside. Cold rain splashing down in sheets. But I know this roof well. Three stories to ground. Much too far to jump.

Big man squeezes through kitchen window after me.

I clamber away across slanted roof. Heading for the spot above the nearest of the marsh channels.

Roof surface wet. Slippery. Big man is gaining on me. Moves hunched over but fast, like a mountain gorilla. Ten feet behind me. Five. He grabs at me—

I reach the roof's edge and dive off! It's thirty feet to the nearest marsh channel. Impossibly far.

I open my arms to full wingspan. Steer with my whole body. Remember Eko's lessons. How she jumped to the high tree branch. At a certain point it's all mental and even spiritual. If I can move sand, I can glide thirty feet.

Mountain gorilla of a man has leaped out after me. I can hear his desperate, blood-curdling bellow as he flies through the air.

I force my mind clear. Disappear inside myself. I am a beam of light moving through darkness.

My fingertips feel cold. Damp. Water! The marsh channel. I

hit it hard, a shallow-water dive that knocks the air from my body. I lie in the channel, in fifteen inches of water, stunned.

CRUNCH. Behind me. No, not a crunch. More of a thump. Sound revives me. I blink. Twist around to see.

The big man has landed on mud and rocks five feet from the bank. Like an asteroid coming down in a parking lot. Visible crater. He groans and lies there.

Tough luck, gorilla man. No more chasing Jack for a while.

That's the good news. The bad news is a pack of shadows are streaming out of the beach house toward me.

Bat creatures. Tall men. Something on four legs that looks like an overgrown jackal. Yellow eyes. Sharp, flashing canines. Genetically altered hounds from a hell a thousand years in the future. Boy, can they move fast.

I get to my feet. If they catch me, they'll rip me apart. I take off through the dark, storm-battered marsh, sprinting for my life.

That was what my dad was trying to tell me. Not free. Flee.

36

Sprinting through marsh in pitch darkness. Lashed by rain. Whipped by wind. Lightning zapping overhead.

Pursued by menagerie of horrors. I can hear them behind me. Every fifty feet or so I glance back and see them coming on.

I head for wildest marsh channel. Bottom pocked by holes. Sharp rocks. Vines and branches overhang water.

I couldn't have even walked through this treacherous passage two weeks ago. But Eko has taught me well.

Can hear bat creature gaining on me. I'll have to turn and fight before I reach the bay. But then the rest of them will catch up, and I won't have a prayer.

Sense an overhanging branch. Duck just in time.

Bat creature tries to pounce on me, and instead his head WHAPS into branch. He sinks beneath marsh water.

Bend in channel. I round corner and they're out of sight for just a second. My chance! I scamper up the steep bank.

Plow through underbrush like a runaway tractor. Thorns rip at me, roots trip me, and branches grab at my arms. I forge my own trail, and then dive back down into . . .

Another, deeper marsh channel. Swim underwater the other way, heading toward the dunes and the Atlantic Ocean.

Stay under for two minutes. Pop up to reconnoiter.

As soon as I surface I see a large bird circling. Bigger than the blue heron. Orange eyes glowing like searchlights. It wheels toward me. No doubt about it. Bird serves as spotter plane. Communicating with the shadowy creatures. Letting them know where I am.

I find a round stone. Always had a good right arm. Center fielder for the Hadley Tigers. Once threw out two guys at the plate in one game.

Step and throw. Rock nails circling recon bird. Feather-ripping beak-shattering impact. Bird zigzags to the ground like a helicopter hit by a ground-fired missile.

I run along edge of channel, heading for dunes.

The storm has grown even more furious. Wind blows the rain sideways in gusts that slap against my face.

Reach end of channel. Stumble up sandy hillocks that separate marsh from dunes. Feel exposed. Look back.

Shadowy shapes less than a half mile away and coming on fast. Bird thing must have alerted them.

I slide down hillock to dunes. Sprint across wet sand. Murder on the legs, but I'm in superb condition. Thanks, Eko. Most interesting, not to mention beautiful, woman I ever met. Sorry I pushed you away. You sacrificed yourself for me, and I'll never forget you for as long as I live.

Which will probably be less than ten minutes.

Because they're gaining on me. I glance back and see them cresting the hill and streaming down onto the dunes.

No place to hide. Just an angry ocean pummeling an expanse of gently sloping sand.

I reach the water's edge and look back. They're halfway down the dunes, angling to cut me off. When they catch me, they'll probably rip me apart on this beach. But I won't go easily. Eko's seen to that.

I stop running. No point. Stand there, waiting for them. It's not a bad place to die, this beach in this storm.

Humans! You're pathetic sometimes. Especially young male humans of warrior age. Such a weakness for melodrama. It leads to a unique ability to convince yourselves that defeat is actually some kind of victory. As if there's anything good about being torn apart on a beach by one's enemies! Please. Get over it.

A familiar telepathic voice. Insulting, condescending, and completely unhelpful at the same time.

Wherever you are, fur ball, get lost. I don't want a traitor distracting me as I prepare to make my final stand.

You can't just give up and die, fool. You are our beacon of hope.

Watch me.

You don't know who's chasing you. They'll eat you alive!

And maybe they'll have dog for dessert.

I'm saying all this as bravely as I can, but the truth is I don't want to be torn apart on this beach by the Dark Army if there's a way out. But what choices do I have?

Mutt brain hasn't dared to show himself. That's exactly the kind of cowardly behavior I've come to expect from an overeducated canine with a thousand years' worth of insults but no moral convictions. Man's best friend? Hah!

Still, I'm running out of options fast. I scan the dunes in all directions. Lightning flashes, and I see my shadowy pursuers less than a hundred feet away and closing. Still no sign of Gisco.

Over here, blockhead.

Where?

In the water. I need help with this.

Turn toward waves. See it. Small boat. Forty feet out. Foundering. Buffeted. Nearly capsizing. No one on board. No sign of dog. When you're about to be torn apart on a beach, a small boat in a storm is better than nothing.

I run into surf and dive low into breaker. Fifteen-foot wave slams me against sand bottom as it crashes down over me. Backwash sucks me out. I keep my bearings and try to swim. Make it back to surface. Boat now closer. Still no one on board. I swim to it. Grab side. Start to pull myself up.

No. We'll get washed into shore. You have to help me.

I spot traitorous dog. Mooring rope in his teeth. A thrashing canine tugboat trying to pull the boat out to sea.

I jump back into water. Push boat with my hands, shove with my shoulders, butt with my head. Kick legs and fight for every watery inch. I'm pushing. Gisco's pulling.

Giant waves toy with us. Smash us down. Sweep us in. Yank us out. Hard to tell if we're making much progress.

I lose track of time. The struggle to push the boat out becomes my life. Got to win this one. Our only chance. Must move us beyond the breakers.

Swallow seawater. Choking. Exhausted. Arms and legs waterlogged. I start to sink. Grab boat. Pull myself up and over the side. Kneel, retching.

Glance back. Lightning strobes beach. Dunes a half mile away. Shadowy forms on sand watching us sail away. We moved the small boat into a riptide. It's yanking us out to sea.

Scratching against side of boat. Desperate canine telepathic SOS. *Help me in, Jack. I'm drowning.*

Climb in yourself.

Dogs can't climb.

Whose fault is that?

I just saved your life.

Thanks. I appreciate it.

Much weaker. *Help me. Jack. Please.*

He did say "please." I roll to side of boat. See what looks like a submerged shag rug with ears and a snout. Reach into foaming brine. Grab two handholds of fur. Try to lift.

I'm in tip-top shape, but it's a Herculean task. Gisco is not exactly a lightweight, even on his dry days. I grunt and strain and he scrabbles with giant paws on the side of the boat. Just when I'm ready to give up and let him drown, a swell tips the boat and he tumbles in on top of me.

Yuck. Buried under several hundred pounds of sopping, mangy, fetid, and macerated mongrel. Get off me.

Shag rug untangles itself. Large dog peers back at distant beach and then turns toward open ocean and strikes preposterous nautical pose. As if he's Nelson at Trafalgar. *I've got good news and bad news.*

I'm afraid to ask. What's the good news?

There's no way they can follow us. By the time this blows through, we'll be safely away.

I should quit while I'm ahead. Okay, snout face, what's the bad news?

We're in a small, open boat, sailing right into the teeth of the most ferocious hurricane I've ever seen.

37

Don't let anyone ever tell you a hurricane is just wind and rain. It's alive, strange as that may seem. A great howling beast. And I'm riding in a peanut shell on its back.

Shall we talk about waves for a second? You know those six-footers that are fun to boogie-board on in summer sunlight? Towering ten-footers stirred up by strong winds? Freakish fifteen- and twenty-footers that provide photo ops in surfing documentaries?

Forget those. Unimpressive. Totally irrelevant in my current situation.

Try to conceive of moving mountain ranges of water. Think slip-sliding Alps. Roiling Andes. Glaciers of tipping spume and avalanches of tumbling froth. Towering gray-green peaks and yawning fuliginous valleys.

Look that one up, my friend, but not right now. Now there's an angry mountain range marching toward me heart-stoppingly quickly. Ka-thump, ka-thump.

You see it rolling in at you and you think oh my God, nothing could be that big and move that fast. And then it's under you and around you and you are pitched up on its back, higher and higher, till it seems you are being raised in slow motion to the threshold of the sky.

Poised there for an instant. Hanging. Suspended. You know what's coming. Just waiting for it to begin. Knowing that it will. It must. Because what goes this far up has to come . . . down, down, down, you are skidding and plummeting into its inky trough-craters, and you can't believe the boat didn't capsize or crack in half.

But it didn't.

It made it.

Before you can take a breath and celebrate the fact that you're still alive, you glance out. Not much visibility in a hurricane. But enough. Joy vanishes. Euphoria evaporates. Because an even bigger mountain range is surging out of the mist. Growing and swelling as it gets closer.

You're looking up at it from a small boat, miles from shore. The Himalayas of the Atlantic. Everest itself. Bearing down on you. Under you. Around you. Up you go again, skyward. Higher than before. Higher than anyone has ever been in any ship in any storm. And the only two things you can do are hold on and pray.

Actually, we can't hold on. We gave up on that long ago, when the first giant waves slammed us down and washed over us, nearly knocking us loose. So we took whatever ropes there were on board, and lashed ourselves to the boat. If it sinks, we sink. But as long as it stays afloat, we have a chance.

Prayer is a funny thing. If you put a gun to my head I couldn't tell you if I believe in God or not. I certainly don't have the kind of relationship with a divine being where we communicate frequently. So now, even though I'm helpless and scared for my life, it feels hypocritical to pray.

Do I even have a right to ask God for help? If there's no God, I'm wasting my time. And if there is a God, won't he or she see me for a fake, who only pretends to believe in moments of danger? If I clasp my hands together and promise to be a better person if he intervenes now, won't God see through my flattering words and feeble promises?

On the other hand, I'm in a small boat in the middle of the Atlantic, surrounded by a force-five hurricane. If you can't turn to God in such a situation, who can you turn to?

While I'm wrestling with these doubts, I hear a telepathic barrage going out on all channels. *O Great Dog God, you magnificent, sublime, unparalleled specimen of canine perfection, I, Gisco, your humble servant, I who am not fit to walk in your shadow, I who grovel in the mud under your four paws, beg for your help. Save me, anointed Hound of Heaven, and I will spend the rest of my miserable life worshipping your gloriousness . . .*

Gisco, what are you doing?

Praying, fool.

It's pathetic to hear you grovel that way. If there really is a Great Dog God, which I very much doubt, what must he be thinking?

Hopefully, he's thinking of saving us.

If we're gonna die, we're gonna die. Stop making promises you'll never keep.

O Great Dog God, forgive my feeble-minded human companion his mocking words. Truly my fate is linked to a race of fools. Save us, and I will show him the error of his ways, and we will both light a thousand candles to your canine beneficence. Save us, and from this day forth I will be a loyal and true dog, a humble and meek dog. I will stop overeating, and feed the stray puppies and the widowed bitches . . .

At this moment, we reach the crest of the Mount Everest of water that has reared up beneath us. I look down over the side of the boat and see a bottomless, churning chasm waiting to engulf us.

We hang for a moment between sea and sky, and then start the long tumble from pinnacle to abyss. The roaring of the maelstrom is deafening. The tiny boat slams and whirls, nearly ripping my body free from the ropes.

My hands come together, even though I don't remember willing them to move. Words escape my lips unbidden. O dear God, this is Jack Danielson, in the middle of an Atlantic hurricane. I know I haven't prayed to you often. I realize I am a sinner in all kinds of ways. I lie. I think about sex too much. I didn't love my parents enough or appreciate how much they did for me when they were alive. And I myself have done very little that is good in this world.

But ever since that tall stranger appeared in the Hadley Diner, I've been living in mortal danger. And I have noticed that time and again I've been uncannily lucky. Perhaps you're the reason—maybe, just maybe, you've been saving my life, preserving me for a higher purpose.

O God, if you save me again, I promise I'll find a way to do better. I can't change the past, but I'll do what I can to achieve that mysterious higher purpose, and to change the future.

When my moment comes, I'll take it.

I'm so scared, God. I don't want to drown. There's nothing more I can say except please, God, save me.

38

We are drifting. Where? I don't know. Will anyone find us before we die of thirst and starvation? I doubt it.

Stomach empty.

Two days since the storm passed. Forty-six hours with no food and no water, trapped on small boat with traitorous dog.

He's tried a few conversational salvos. I shot him down. Sorry, Rover. When a friend betrays me, I don't take him back. No need to talk. Let's suffer in silence.

Throat dry. Tongue parched. Every cell in my body crying out for liquid refreshment. Nothing available. Stupid dog forgot to take provisions when he stole this boat.

I didn't steal it. I borrowed it without a clear intention of returning it. There is a distinction. Anyway, you seemed pretty happy to climb on board when those fiends were about to rip you apart on the beach. And you can stay silent and morose if you want, but if you're going to think nasty things about me, I wish you'd screen your thoughts.

Cowardly mongrel promised Great Dog God that if we were saved he would eat less. So perhaps he's to blame for this slow death. Perhaps the Great Dog God is taking him up on the dietary offer, and me too, since I'm along for the ride.

My prayers were private.

You broadcast them on all channels.

I wanted to make sure they were heard, but not by you. And you can be assured the Great Dog God didn't save us from that horrible storm only to starve us to death.

How do I know that?

Dogs are not cruel by nature. They are merciful and kind. So it follows that Dog gods must be wonderfully merciful and tremendously kind.

Maybe so, but right now no one is showing us any mercy.

The sun is a red fireball overhead. Not broiling us or frying us. Toasting us excruciatingly slowly.

The worst part of it is that all around us is water.

I recall two stanzas from Coleridge's "Rime of the Ancient Mariner":

> *Day after day, day after day,*
> *We stuck, nor breath, nor motion;*
> *As idle as a painted ship*
> *Upon a painted ocean.*
>
> *Water, water everywhere,*
> *And all the boards did shrink;*
> *Water, water, everywhere,*
> *Nor any drop to drink.*

And there is indeed water all around our little boat, in every direction, as far as we can see. It's tempting to just lower my hands into the cold Atlantic, pull up a draft of seawater, and swallow it down.

But I know this won't work. I've read about shipwrecks, and the tortures suffered by people who drink seawater.

Better to slowly thirst and starve to death. I can feel my stomach digesting itself.

Can't stop myself from thinking about pitchers of iced tea. Plump, greasy cheeseburgers. Curly french fries dipped in sweet, creamy catsup.

Dog food without end. Hard lamb-flavored nuggets and soft pudding-smooth porridges of chicken and liver encased in circular golden cans. Boxes of turkey-flavored niblets. Tins of mixed grill with shimmering salty-gold globules of congealed beef fat that melt on the tongue—

Okay. Yuck. Enough dog food fantasies.

What else can I do but daydream? Since you won't even talk to me.

Okay, I give in. We have to talk, even if it's just to keep our sanity. What shall we talk about? How about a nice chicken-and-egg game? Isn't that your specialty?

Sorry about that. I was just doing my job.

Betraying me was your job?

Saving you, actually, old bean.

Thanks for all your help. Right now I really feel safe.

This was hardly my fault.

Nothing's ever your fault, is it?

You're really quite hostile.

I'm much nicer when I'm not dying of dehydration.

For what it's worth, I felt very guilty when I had to leave you in that barn. Maybe I didn't handle it the best way I could have. I knew you were emotionally vulnerable, and you trusted me. I took unfair advantage of that, and I apologize.

You're just apologizing because we're dying and you don't want to die a guilty dog.

We're not dying. Not even close. We've got lots of fight left in us. Do you accept my apology or not?

No.

Truly a race of stubborn fools.

✳

39

Three days in open boat in hot sun.

All my anger toward traitorous dog long gone. Everything else gone, too. Last reserves of strength. Hope. Even prayer. We've accepted our fates. Now we're just drifting on a painted ocean, waiting for the inevitable.

Okay, now we're dying.

I thought it would be more painful.

It's not exactly pleasant.

Anyway, it will be over very soon. Gisco?

What?

I accept your apology for betraying me at the barn.

I'm glad. Let's end this trip as friends.

The end comes very slowly. But death is settling around our boat like a sail of lightest gauze. I can feel its first spidery strands brushing my shoulders, enmeshing me.

Wish it would hurry. The storm must have blown us southward. It's brutally hot. We're no longer being toasted. Now we're being charbroiled.

I've chewed my nails down to the nub. Gisco has done the same. If you've never seen a rotund dog trying to gnaw at the nails on his hind paws, you've missed something. I almost smiled at the ridiculous sight.

But there is not much smiling going on in this boat. Dying of thirst is no fun. Your mind drifts, and you think wild thoughts about your life and how you can hold on just a little bit longer. I even consider drinking my own urine. I read somewhere that survivors of shipwrecks have done that.

But there comes a time to go gracefully. I'm not a quitter, but further struggle seems futile. I'm weak. Blistered. Tongue swollen. Can barely keep my eyes open. So I've given up. Gisco, too.

He's not taking it well.

Who would have thought sweet little Gisco would come to such an ignominious end? There were so many puppies I wanted to sire. So many meals I wanted to eat. Did you know that I was a cute puppy? The pick of the litter, my mom always said.

I'm sure you were, I respond graciously, although I seriously doubt this could possibly have been true. If so, it must have been one hell of a disappointing litter. But this is not the time for insults.

And my father always said I was destined for great things.

At least you knew your true father.

I knew yours, too. Met him once. Greatest honor of my life. It was just before he was taken prisoner.

My father is a prisoner?

When he sent you back in time, with your two guardians, the energy pulse revealed his presence to his enemies. No way to shield it. He knew it would happen. But he had no choice. He had to send you back, to save the world.

I haven't saved anything. He sent me back so that I could live a lie my whole life, be chased and beaten, and die in this boat on this stinking, sweltering ocean. If he was so great, why didn't he come back and save the world himself?

His heart was weak. The journey through time is arduous.

You made it. Eko did. The Gorm. All those fiends.

The crossing got easier as the technology improved. But you and your guardians were the first ever to be sent back. It was prophesied that only you could change the world. The Dark Army was closing in on you. So your father saved you the only way he could. He knew others would come after you, to try to hunt you down and kill you. So he sent you back with two trusted guardians. Their mission was to hide you, to shield you, to conceal your presence for as long as they could. The only way to do that was to bring you up thinking that you were a normal kid, born of this world.

As I lie on my floating deathbed, I think back to my birth certificate, kept in a packet with the other Danielson family papers. High-quality fake, right down to the state of New York seal.

Bogus baby pictures in the family album. Mom in a green hospital delivery room. Looking exhausted from labor, holding me in a blue blanket on her lap. Dad puffing on a cigar.

All of it false, sham, artifice. Lying in a small boat, waiting for death, I see that they were creating an identity. Inventing a baby boy who was supposedly born into this world.

And once that baby's identity was hatched, the falsehood had to be shaped. It wasn't just that my parents didn't want me to stand out. Looking back at it from this final vantage point, I can see how my whole life was a calculated lie.

The clothes Mom picked out for me were exactly what the other boys at school were wearing. The haircuts they gave me, the friends they encouraged me to make, the sports they directed me toward—all were dictated by a single strategy: the more I blended in, the less chance I would be discovered.

None of it was really about me, or unique to me. It was all an elaborate masquerade.

I will die out here in an hour or two, unmarked and unmourned. Worst of all, I never really lived.

From start to finish, Jack Danielson, pea in the Hadley-by-Hudson pod, was a person who I'm not and never really was.

Who am I really? Who would I have been friends with? What might I have accomplished? They never let me find out, because they had their own agenda. Now I'll never know.

My father sent me back a thousand years to live a lie, and now I'll die a mystery to myself.

I shut my eyes. Feel so weak.

All a waste. I didn't save that future world. Couldn't do it. Didn't save anyone. Dad. Mom. Eko. Now Gisco. And Jack. All as dead as the dust. And for no good reason.

So what was I supposed to do? I ask Gisco. Even my thoughts are fainter. Telepathic whispers.

He doesn't quite get it the first time. *What was that, old bean? Turn up the dial a little.*

My last request is the truth. What was all the fuss about, anyway? What is Firestorm?

40

*F*irestorm? Dog feebly repeats the word back to me with awe. *Nobody knows exactly. That's the great mystery you were supposed to clear up.*

Come on. My father sent me back a thousand years. He must have known something concrete.

Firestorm is a weapon, a mysterious force. Everything about it is shrouded in legend, but a thousand years from now we documented that it really existed, and that it could have been used to halt the destruction of the earth.

When did it first appear?

Now. Right before the Turning Point. As if someone was offering us a way out. And then, just as mysteriously, it disappeared when the Turning Point was past. The People of Dann searched for it for centuries, but it was gone. And the chance it offered was gone, too.

So I was sent back a thousand years to go on a quest for this legendary weapon that no one understands?

Quest is a good word, the dog agrees. *It's not the first time in history, at key turning points, that mysterious forces appeared which people tried to find and use to change the world. When the Roman knights in Britain were trying to stave off the Dark Ages, the legend of King Arthur's sword was born. And many of the Crusades were launched to find the Holy Grail. The difference is that you were sent back to find something whose existence has been scientifically documented. If you could find it and use it, all would be different.*

Eko told me that a thousand years from now we're losing the battle.

She was putting a positive spin on it. We've lost. You were our last hope. Our final shot. That's why I came back. And Eko, too. The High Dog and the High Priestess of Dann. To try to assist you. The whole future depends on your success.

Great. Thanks. Now I can die in peace.

You'll die, I'll die, and the Dark Army will prevail.

So where did Firestorm come from?

No one knows. Some say it was created by a wizard, or dropped off by space travelers. Others say it was fashioned by the forces of technological destruction—smelted into being in a nuclear conflagration. Still others point to the fact that Firestorm has a mysterious connection to the seas. They maintain it was dredged up from the heart of the ocean.

So fate may have led us to this boat? We may actually have come close to finding Firestorm?

It's possible, Gisco agrees. *Or the whole thing may have been a miscalculation. Listen, I think I'm going to sleep. The kind of sleep I won't wake up from, if you get my gist.*

I understand, old fellow. Me too. It's over.

Not quite. Once I'm gone, my corporeal remains will furnish you with a source of sustenance for a while longer.

Meaning?

It's repugnant to speak of such things, but I'm referring to cannibalism, or rather, canineabalism.

I appreciate the offer. It's very generous. Don't take this the wrong way, but no thanks.

Why not? You don't think I'd be palatable?

Frankly, no. And there's no mustard on this boat.

The expiring hound is not deterred by my attempt at humor. He says, with pricked dignity, *Survivors of shipwrecks have a long history of eating the remains of those less fortunate. It's one of the lasting traditions of the seas.*

Count me out. I draw the line at canineabalism.

You have a solemn responsibility to the future to cling to life as long as you can.

No! The future deprived me of my past. Now I say screw it. Screw my father. Screw Eko. Screw all of you.

I can't argue with you. I'm too weak.

Me too.

Goodbye, old bean. Into the care of the Great Dog God I commend my soul.

Farewell, jabber jaws. Au revoir, or perhaps adieu.

What's that?

French. You said it to me in the Outer Banks. It means—

No, that! Can't you see it?

My eyes are closed.

Well, open them! There!

I see it. A half mile away, a giant water bug crawling across the water. No, not a water bug, some kind of weird ship.

Maybe there's still hope. Wave to it. Shout at it.

I drag myself up. Manage one feeble wave. Collapse back into boat. Sorry. Couldn't do more. It's passed us now. It's sailing away.

So close and yet so far. What's that buzzing?

I also hear it. And feel it.

My arm. My wrist. Dad's watch. Glowing. Tingling. Feels almost electric.

A lightning bolt zigzags down out of the clear sky and strikes the water just behind our boat.

Whatever you just did, old bean, it worked. They've seen us. They're turning! You really are the beacon of hope!

41

Iron monster of a ship. Angular bow. What looks like a soccer goal near the front. Behind it, a white cottage rises two stories above the deck. Tall mast. Not built for holding a sail but for communication. It bristles with antennas. An enormous flat area in the rear. Soccer field?

Crew gathered along rail, shouting down at us. Trying to figure out if we're alive. Twenty men. Mixed heights, colors, races. White, black, Asian. Shorts. T-shirts and bare chests. Variety of hats.

Two men standing apart. One tall, with eye patch. Nasty-looking. Modern-day pirate.

Next to him, an older man. Better dressed. Stooped posture. Bald head that glitters in the sunlight.

For a minute his inquisitive eyes meet mine. Somehow I know he's the captain, and I can also guess what he's thinking: Should I save them or not? Is it worth the trouble? What will I get out of it?

I'm groggy. Can't shout up to plead my case.

Captain mutters something to First Mate Eye Patch, who nods and walks away.

I'm losing it. Can barely keep my eyes open. Dimly aware that a dinghy is being lowered. Men paddling to us.

Voices asking me questions. English. Spanish. Russian. I open my mouth. Too weak to answer back.

Someone with an Irish accent says, "Forget about the dog. Just take the lad."

I crack my eyes open. Force my head up. Try to croak out a few words. Raspy whisper: "No. The dog, too."

One of them hears me. "Ronan, he's trying to talk to you. He said something about the dog."

Broad-shouldered sailor looks down at me. Tall. Freckles. Friendly face. Shock of red hair. "Got a name, lad? Where are you from, then?"

I look back up at him. "Please. The dog."

"No use. He's dying."

I manage, "My friend." Can't say more.

Muttered conversation. Hands grab me. Pass me over the side. To other hands in the dinghy.

Then I'm hoisted up and up. Weak. Light-headed. The motion makes my world spin. I faint.

Splash. I'm in the storm again. Down in a dark trough. A great, freezing wave washes over me.

I gag and open my eyes.

No storm. Not a wave. Just the world spinning and pinwheeling and blurry. I'm on my back on the vast, open rear deck of some sort of boat.

My vision clears for a moment. Orange netting comes into sharp focus. Hung up to dry. Fish stench. This is some kind of deep-sea trawler.

A fat man with tattoos on his arms has just thrown a pail of cold water on me. He grins as I choke and blink. Other men stand around smoking cigarettes and laughing.

"That woke him up."

"The kid needed a bath."

"Hit him again, Jacques."

The fat man obliges, throwing another pail of icy water over me. Some of the water runs up my nose.

I snort and retch it back out.

Why are they treating me this way? They're my rescuers. Can't they see how weak and sick I am?

I roll over and try to curl into fetal position. Go away. All of you. Leave me in my misery.

A boot kicks me onto my back and pins me there. First Mate Eye Patch towers over me, surveying me like an unusually ugly specimen of fish his nets have dragged up.

He kneels. "Who are you?" Accent I can't place. German? French? Maybe Dutch. Voice used to issuing orders.

I shake my head. Sorry. Conversation postponed.

He reaches down and pries my right eye open. Sunlight spills in, but I can't shut the lid. Helpless as a rag doll.

Next he feels my carotid artery. "He'll live," he says without enthusiasm. "But he stinks. Clean him up."

"The dog smells even worse," the fat man they call Jacques observes. "We should throw him back. Nothing smells worse than a dead dog."

So they rescued Gisco, too! I can't even turn my head to look for my canine friend. Is he really dying?

Another sailor says, "You're not one to talk, Jacques. The way you smell, maybe we should throw you back."

Shouts of agreement. Rough laughter.

Jacques's pocked, unshaven face goes from pouting to pissed off in nothing flat. "That's the thanks I get for all the wonderful meals I've cooked you?"

Hoots of derisive laughter and insults from the crew:

"What wonderful meals?"

"He cooks worse than he smells."

"No, he smells worse than he cooks."

"One more word and I'll poison all of you," Jacques promises, his face growing red. "Don't think I won't. I've done it before."

"You nearly killed us with breakfast," some wit calls out. "And you weren't even trying." More loud laughter.

Jacques scowls and looks down at me. "Let's clean you up. And then I'll fix you some food."

42

Rough hands carry me belowdecks, to a cool, dark place. A blanket is draped over me. "Go to sleep, lad," Ronan's voice advises. "You've had a close call."

I spiral down into a deep, inky pit.

Dream of my father—my real father, who lives in the far future and looks like Merlin having a really bad hair day. I see him lying on a bed in a stone chamber, his face as pale as his white beard. Is this where he's being held prisoner? There are no chains on his wrists or ankles.

I'm seated in the room. He's watching me.

Eyes weary with suffering yet still vibrantly alive.

His lips don't move, but I hear two faint syllables, as if whispered across a thousand years. "Beware."

Even asleep, I know enough to ask, "Beware of what?"

His voice is so faint I can't hear his words clearly. It sounds like he gasps, "Cinema." Could movies really be so dangerous? "Cameras," he tries again. No, that's closer, but he's not warning me about photographs, either. He whispers a final time, "Chimeras. Beware of chimeras."

Then he shrinks into himself, and a ferocious monster blooms from his breastbone. It flies around the stone chamber and ends up hovering above me. I can smell its rancid breath, feel its sharp talons as they dig into my face.

I wake up fighting back. A powerful thumb and index finger dig into my jaw, forcing my teeth apart.

I open my eyes. It's Jacques, the fat cook with the illustrated arms. I can see his tattoos more clearly now. Coiled sea monsters. He pours something down my throat.

It scalds. My tongue on fire. Poison!

I try to cough it back up. Claw at my throat.

"That Canadian piss you drink woke him up," Ronan's voice says.

"It's good stuff," Jacques answers.

"For stripping paint off a wall," Ronan suggests.

"He likes it," Jacques says. He holds up a green bottle with a family of elk on it. "Want another one?"

Not poison. Cheap whiskey. I shake my head.

Ronan steps into view. Twentyish. Looks genuinely concerned. "How are you? Can you talk?"

I open my mouth experimentally. My voice comes out stronger than I expected. "Did you save the dog?"

Ronan smiles. "He's on board. Whether he'll live or not I can't say. You were both in bad shape. You've been out for nearly two days."

"Where am I?"

"The fishing trawler *Lizabetta*. In the mid-Atlantic, heading for the Azores—"

"Enough," Jacques cuts him off sharply.

"He's one of us now," Ronan points out.

"That's for the captain to decide," Jacques replies, a warning in his voice. He looks back at me. "Captain wants to see you. I'll find you some food." He walks off.

I sit up. I'm on a mattress on the floor of some kind of dingy sleeping quarters.

Two dozen iron-frame bunk beds are arranged in rows. Each frame holds an upper and a lower sleeping berth, narrow as a coffin. The compartments have curtains for privacy.

Most of the curtains are open, and I see photos of family members and sexy pinup girls from magazines.

The reek of the place! A nauseating smell of body odor with a few other unpleasant odors mixed in. Unclean bedding. Dirty laundry. Stale food. Spilled alcohol.

"Can you stand up?" Ronan asks. "I found some clothes for you."

I struggle to my feet. Weak, but I can move around. "Why didn't he want me to know where we are?" I ask Ronan as I struggle to pull on some shorts and a T-shirt.

The Irishman shrugs. "He's a fat fool. But don't be too curious when you talk to the captain. Just ask him what you can do to pay him back for saving your life."

I ponder that advice as Jacques returns. "I made you some lunch. Eat fast. The captain doesn't like to be kept waiting."

A wooden table is bolted to the floor in a small space between the beds. I sit on a worn bench. Gobble down the worst meal of my life, but it tastes wonderful.

Dark mush. Somewhere between stew and porridge. Rice, potatoes, and a few chunks of greasy meat. Washed down by lukewarm water. A piece of stale bread.

"He likes my cooking," Jacques says with pride.

"He was starving to death," Ronan reminds him.

"Then my food saved his life."

"He might've been better off dead."

"What does an Irishman know about good food?"

"I know this ain't it, ya Canadian slob."

"Keep talking. See what happens."

"Anytime you say, Fat Man. Goodbye, lad. Good luck."

A few minutes later Jacques leads me through the bowels of

the ship to the officers' quarters. We reach a small door. Jacques knocks softly.

A voice from inside grunts a command to enter.

Jacques looks at me. "Just don't ask how he lost his arm," he whispers. Then he opens the door and shoves me in.

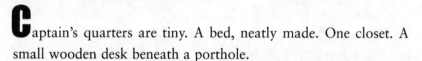

43

Captain's quarters are tiny. A bed, neatly made. One closet. A small wooden desk beneath a porthole.

Seated at the desk is the bald man I glimpsed standing on the deck trying to decide if he should save my life. He's looking at me now as if he's not sure he did the right thing.

Not a cruel face, but a tough one. Time-tested. Weathered. Ledger book open before him. A page filled with numbers. Without looking down, he inserts a mark and closes it.

A decorative crest on the book's leather cover. The letter "D" written with a florid swirl, like a coiled snake, but with ornamental wings. Sea monster?

I remember my father's warning in the dream to beware of chimeras. Years ago I went through a phase when I read a lot of Greek mythology. I recall that the chimera was some sort of fire-breathing monster with a serpent's long tail. Could this captain and his ornate ledger be the danger my father reached back through the centuries to warn me about?

The captain doesn't speak. Silence wielded as a weapon. Eko also used this technique. The best response is silence right back at you.

I stand straight, staring down at him. At the million interlocking wrinkles on his neck, face, and forehead. Like reptilian scales. At his hands, folded on his desk. He wears a white glove on his left hand, and I can see that the limb is a prosthetic.

I sense that he's felt my glance dart down to his gloved hand. I look up quickly, awkwardly, and our eyes meet.

"You speak English?" he asks. Unexpectedly gentle voice. Russian accent.

"Yes, sir."

"American?"

"Yes."

"What happened to you?"

"I ran away from home."

He frowns. "So the police are looking for you?"

"Not anymore. I've been on the road for a while."

"Where did you get the boat?"

Careful, Jack. They may have already traced it and learned that it was stolen. I lower my eyes, as if ashamed, and mumble, "I stole it."

"So you're a thief?"

"Someone was chasing me and I needed to get away."

The captain doesn't like this. His shrewd eyes narrow. "If you steal from me, I will punish you severely. Do you have any useful skills?"

"I've never been on a ship before."

"I will find you work. You must work twice as hard as everyone else. Because your dog is going to eat food."

"I'll do whatever you say, sir."

"Yes, you will." The icy blue eyes glitter with authority. He leans forward. "What's your name?"

"Jack."

"Why did you run away from home, Jack?"

"There was an accident." I swallow. "My parents died. I didn't want to stick around."

His gloved left hand drums once, hard, on the desk. "Why are you lying to me?"

"I'm not lying, sir."

"Then you must be a very unlucky boy."

"Yes, sir."

"I don't like unlucky people on my boat." It's an unmistakable threat. "Work hard. Keep your mouth shut. Don't give me any reason to regret saving you."

"I won't, sir."

His voice stays soft, but it's no longer gentle. "Because this boat is in the business of death." The captain's whisper sharpens till it's as pointed and lethal as a marlinespike. "We are a factory of death."

I look back at him. Don't be curious, Ronan advised. So I nod and keep my face expressionless, even though several questions spring to mind. Is the "D" on his ledger for "death"? Where *did* he lose his arm? And what exactly will my role be on this floating factory of death?

The captain waves me toward the door with a dismissive flick of his good hand.

*

44

Hard work. Joint-aching. Bone-numbing.

Scrubbing the deck. Stem to stern. Bow to aft. Do you appreciate the nautical lingo? I'm learning.

What looks like a soccer goal is called a superstructure. The two-story cottage is the wheelhouse. And the flat rear deck is the work area. I wonder if anyone ever cleaned it before I was hoisted aboard.

We're between fishing grounds, so no one else on board seems to be doing much of anything. Crew members hang out in the bunkroom. Read. Play cards. Catch up on sleep.

Meanwhile, Jack is working for two stomachs. Mine and a missing canine's. Sweeping and mopping and scrubbing.

I still haven't spotted Gisco. Keep asking sailors. Where's my dog? Is he alive? Did you throw him back?

Should have, they say. Bad luck to kill a dog. Worse luck to keep him. Get back to work. You missed a spot.

They're teasing me. Having fun at my expense.

And the captain is testing me with all this backbreaking work. But the truth is, I'm kind of enjoying it.

Read a lot of seafaring books since I was a kid, starting with *Treasure Island*. But never really been at sea before.

I like the feel of it. Like the roll of the waves. The salt tang. The open ocean all around. Watching the sea-birds circling above. Sunrise and morning mist. Sunset and evening stars.

I like having other guys around. It was a bit kooky and claustrophobic cooped up with Eko on the Outer Banks. And besides that, since I left Hadley, I'd just been with Gisco, fleeing for my life on trains and motorcycles.

Nice to be with normal people again, who don't dress up in ninja outfits or ask you to bend sand or tell you that your world is about to end.

These sailors are hard, but they're fair. They argue. They play practical jokes. They insult each other and bait Jacques about his cooking, which I have to admit is abysmal. But their games—even the cruel ones—are understandable and familiar, and at least the food is filling.

The crew is secretive about where we're going, but some of the guys are starting to open up a bit. They're proud of being fishermen. They're excited because we're about to let down our nets in a new spot. They tell me that if we rake in a good catch, everyone will get rewarded.

High noon now. I'm on my knees, shirtless, with the sun beating down on my back, as I scrub the deck. Ronan taps me on the shoulder. "Do you play football, lad?"

Football? I squint up at him. Decide not to mention that I once rushed for three hundred and forty yards in one game. New league record. "A bit," I mutter.

"Fancy a game?"

"Here? Will they let us?"

"It's a tradition. We always play before we fish. And you're on my team, so I hope you're decent." The ball he tosses me is not a football. It's round and looks like it's been whipped around the fleet. Or kicked around. Soccer ball. Ragged. Torn. But still playable.

A few minutes later I find myself in a soccer game with a dozen other guys. Goals set up on the big work deck. "Kick it in the water and you go get it," Ronan warns me. Crewmen who are not playing stand around cheering and shouting advice.

Soccer's not my game, and some of these guys are real good. I'd never appreciated just how international soccer is. The African players have their own free-flowing style. The South Americans are wonderfully skilled. The Europeans like Ronan play a more disciplined game.

And then there's me. An American. The wild card. I've played a bit of soccer in my time, though I don't have their technique. But they can't match my speed. Jack Danielson. Fastest runner in my school. In my town. In my county. And on this trawler, too.

The game swings back and forth. I kick two goals. They match us. Game tied. Next goal wins. "If I kick the winner, you have to tell me where my dog is," I say.

"Deal, lad," Ronan agrees. "But be careful. They'll take you down before they let you beat them."

A big German named Rudolf, who is the fishing master, whatever that means, feeds me a long, high pass.

I chest it down, and cut sharply past two defenders. There's only one more guy to beat, and then the goalie.

Guys on the side shout that he should tackle me. Take me down. I'm loving this. Just having fun in the sun.

I fake one way, then break the other. He can't match my pace, so he tries a desperate tackle. I hop right over him and blast the ball past the goalie.

GOAL! High fives. Congratulations in six languages.

"Well done, lad," Ronan says.

"Where is he?"

"Two levels down, the refrigeration control room."

45

More a closet than a room. Tiny. Windowless. Cool. Machines humming. Something to do with refrigeration. Smell of damp fur.

Moldy rug on the floor. No, not a rug. Decaying seal carcass. Scratch that. Seal carcasses don't move and groan. That you, mutt face?

No. I'm dead. Gisco has perished. In the act of dying but still hungry. They're feeding me scraps. Scraps! You don't have any food with you?

I'm not room service. It's time for you to stop dying, get up, and help out. We're on some kind of mysterious fishing trawler and I'm doing all the work while you're having a siesta in your stateroom.

There's nothing for a dog to do on a ship. Anyway, I can't even stand up. How can I get my strength back when they're not feeding me anything?

Physical exercise might help, I suggest.

Foolish is the dying dog who expects sympathy from humans. Leave me to my final woe.

Your final woe seems pretty comfortable compared to my busting my butt. Listen, the sailors are friendly enough, but no one will tell me where we're going. And I'm picking up weird vibes from the captain and first mate.

What kind of weird vibes?

I don't think they trust me or believe my story about how we ended up in that little boat. They're working me, testing me, and watching me all the time.

Work harder to win their trust.

That's easy for you to say. And there's something else. I dreamed of my father. He warned me to beware of chimeras.

Chimeras? Are you sure you heard him correctly?

Yes, and it's making me nervous. The chimera was a monster and a portent of disaster at sea, and we are in the mid-Atlantic.

It was a "mythic" monster, who supposedly mothered the Sphinx, the dog corrects me with a professional air. *It never really lived. Even the myths are vague. Some say it had the head of a lion, the body of a goat, and the tail of a serpent. Others describe it as a monstrous jumble of different animals. Anyway, it's just a silly old legend. I wouldn't lose sleep over it.*

Jacques, the cook, has sea monsters tattooed onto his arms, I inform Gisco. And the captain has a ledger book with what looks like a serpent on it.

Interesting but probably coincidental. Any sign of Firestorm?

No, not yet. But then I don't know what it is, so how will I know if I'm close to it?

You are the beacon of hope. You'll know it when you see it. I wish I could help, but I don't think I'm up to it.

I have to admit, you don't look so good. Maybe I can find you a little more food.

Gisco perks up noticeably. *Not fish. Upsets my stomach. And tinned meat gives me gas. Beef or lamb would be acceptable. Also fresh water. Cool but not cold.*

Uh-oh. Something happening. Boat slowing and turning.

Cacophony of sounds from outside. Loud voices. People climbing. Running at full speed.

Ronan pounding at the door. "C'mon, lad, there's work to be done. We're going fishing! Don't make the captain come looking for you."

Right. I know good advice when I hear it.

Gotta go, I tell Gisco. I'll see if I can get you a bit more food.

Thanks, old bean. Be careful. If this is a bottom trawler, you're about to see the horror of horrors.

Actually, I've been looking forward to the fishing.

Dog turns away and lowers his snout to floor in contempt.

I sprint out the door and up the stairs. Maybe now I'll get some answers.

46

Reach the deck and pop out into hot sun.

Trawler buzzing with activity. Shirtless men rushing about connecting cables. Manning winches and cranes. Laying out an enormous orange nylon net on the work deck.

Jacques stands with a few of his cronies in the shade of the wheelhouse. "What's going on?" I ask him.

"We're about to lower the nets," he says, and then turns and spits off the side. "For good luck. Your turn."

I follow his example and spit over the rail. Wind catches my saliva and blows it back into my face.

Jacques bursts into a throaty laugh and his friends chuckle. Then they suddenly look very serious.

First Mate Eye Patch has walked up. "What's so funny?"

"Nothing, sir."

Eye Patch barks out orders. "Freddy and Eduardo, slime line. Scotty, starboard winch. Alex, cable crew. Jacques, when the catch comes in, try to find us something decent to eat. We've had enough of the crap you serve." His gaze turns to me. "You. By-catch disposal."

"Sorry, but I don't know what that is," I confess.

He shrugs disgustedly. "Not a high-skill job. Here's your equipment." Hands me a shovel and walks away.

The other men hurry off to their tasks. Jacques lingers, still smarting from the insult to his cooking.

"What's bycatch?" I ask him.

"All we're likely to snag in this fished-out reef," he grumbles and then looks around quickly to see if anyone heard him complain. Satisfied that no one did, he stomps away.

I watch the crew prepare the net, connecting its different sections to hooks and cables. I can see that they're laying the sections out in a very careful order.

A tight bundle of netting is hoisted to the top of the stern ramp, so that it can be rolled down the chute first.

I spot Ronan crouching on the work area, sweating in the hot sun. He finishes hooking up a cable and wipes his forehead. He sees me and calls out, "How's your dog?"

"Alive but hungry."

"*Cod end away!*" the first mate bellows. The packed bundle of netting is pitched down the chute.

I follow it with my eyes as it splashes into the water. Ronan walks up and smiles. "This all new to you?"

"Yes," I answer. "What's a cod end?"

"The back of the net," he explains. "Where the fish get trapped during the trawl."

We stand together, watching the cod end bob in the trawler's frothy wake.

"If it's the back of the net, why does it go out first?" I ask.

He grins. "That curiosity of yours is gonna get you into trouble, lad. But I guess it won't hurt to teach you to fish. We let the net out backward. Pull it up forward. See how the cod end drags the rest of the net out?"

I watch as the packed bundle of netting is washed backward by the motion of the boat. As it's swept farther away, its weight tugs the body of the netting toward the stern ramp. Ronan and the other men make sure the orange nylon doesn't get hung up as it slides over the work deck toward the water. Now that it's all spread out, the body of the net seems incredibly large. You could catch whales in it, or even snag a submarine.

"What are we fishing for?" I ask.

"Orange roughy. Beautiful fish, lad. And it fetches a good price, too. What are you doing with that shovel?"

"Bycatch disposal," I tell him. "What's bycatch?"

"Everything that's not orange roughy," Ronan informs me. For a moment, his cheerful face darkens. "Which may be pretty much all we get today." He glances around warily.

His prediction of failure and his fear of being overheard remind me of Jacques's grumblings. Clearly, something's wrong. Has the fishing been so disappointing? Is it considered bad luck to complain? Or are they afraid of something else? Or someone else?

The orange netting is now all played out into the water. Ronan grabs my arm and tugs me to one side as the arm of a crane swings past, lifting a length of heavy cable to the edge of the stern ramp. The cable has wheel-like bobbins strung through it that are weighted—they grind loudly as they roll across the deck.

"Rock hoppers. Don't let them roll over your foot," Ronan cautions.

"Why are they so heavy?"

"See that cable they're attached to? That's the footrope. It keeps the mouth of the net touching the bottom. Those wheels are called rock hoppers 'cause they can hop over boulders. They knock pretty much everything else down."

Pulverize it is more like it.

I glance over, surprised. Gisco has dragged himself out on deck, and is now standing next to me, watching, with a strange expression on his face.

I thought you were dying.

I had to see this. Although I don't know if I can bear to watch.

47

*F*ootrope away!" the first mate shouts. The heavy cable with its weighted bobbins slides down the stern ramp and hits the water, sending up geysers of spray.

Gisco winces.

You have a soft spot for orange roughy?

It's one thing to study something horrible when you're a thousand years removed from it. It's another to see it happen.

Lighten up. It's just a big fishing net.

"*Final check on otter boards,*" the first mate calls. "*Disengage on ten.*" There's a sudden frenzy of activity.

"Better keep your dog away from the cables," Ronan warns.

"Don't worry. He's more intelligent than he looks."

A backhanded compliment if I ever heard one.

"What are otter boards?" I ask Ronan.

"The big doors that hold the mouth of the net open," he explains. He points to two immense steel plates, mounted on either side of the back of the trawler. "When they're open, they funnel the fish into the net, down the chute, to the cod end. They could swallow two 747s at once."

Or just about anything else for that matter, Gisco adds for my benefit. The big dog looks truly miserable. And I sense that it's not from weakness or hunger, either.

His eyes range over the work deck. He's watching the winches and the cranes, and following the netting as it floats away. I'm picking up something from him, telepathically, that I've never felt before. A burning anger, but it's not personal, not directed at me or at Ronan.

The first mate finishes his count and shouts, *"Ten! Otter boards away!"* and the vast "doors" are disengaged from their notched mounts and splash down into the ocean.

The captain walks out onto the bridge, looking tense. Rudolf, the fishing master, begins to call out precise orders to the winch operators. "Bring the net starboard. Give me another two hundred feet." Crew members carefully lower and position the net with hydraulic winches.

Gisco's eyes shut tight. *Fortitude, Gisco. It's your duty to watch this.* He forces them back open.

Chill, Purina breath. We're just casting a net out.

Gisco swivels his head to look at me. *You may be the beacon of hope, but you're as blind as they are.*

Blind about what? We're just going fishing.

There's a deep sadness in his face that makes me recall Eko, on the roof of the beach house. I remember how she sat silently, her fingers cupped, her eyes wandering over the night sky, as she contemplated the imminent loss of all the beauty that she knew would soon be gone forever.

Now I'm getting the same combination of fury and futility from Gisco. The only difference is that Eko also felt guilty, perhaps because she was a human.

Gisco has no such burden. He's angry and terribly sad. But he's also, oddly, a bit curious.

His eyes sweep the trawler from stem to stern, staring at the faces of crewmen. *It was always my biggest question about the Turning Point. The one thing I could never quite understand. What were they thinking? Your species is, after all, intelligent and capable of deep compassion.*

Dog eyes can be unexpectedly expressive. Gisco's are wide and wet with sadness. *Now that I see it, I'm starting to understand.*

I stand next to him and watch the positioning of the nets. There's the smell of the engine, and a fume of lube oil. I ask him: What do you understand now?

He's watching the men who are doing the work of lowering the nets. Crew members of every race and color, stripped to the waist and sweating in the hot sun. Their muscles, straining. Their serious faces. Eyes intent on their tasks. None of them look like bad or evil men. *As they scraped the floor of the oceans bare reef by reef and acre by acre, they were just too busy to care. It was a hard job on a sunny day. They were just going fishing.*

48

The big boat slows as its net is lowered.

"You'll feel the otter boards hit the seamount," Ronan promises.

"I didn't know there were mountains in the sea," I tell him.

"There's a whole range of them called the Mid-Atlantic Ridge. Coral grows on them and fish just love them."

And trawlers love to destroy them, Gisco contributes darkly.

"Your dog doesn't look so good," Ronan notes. "Is he seasick?"

It's heartache, carrot top, Gisco mutters telepathically, and walks off, shaking his head.

The big trawler judders all along its length, as if it's struck a small iceberg.

"That's the otter boards hitting bottom," Ronan tells me, excited. "Now we'll start to fish."

The crew finishes positioning the net and opening the great doors.

The next three hours pass very quickly.

Anticipation builds. The increasing drag of the trawl net pumps the crew's excitement up and up.

I share the adrenaline rush. Like a big-game hunter, seeing a bush move near a watering hole. Will it be a rhino? Lion? Wildebeest? You grip your gun and you wait.

Or, in my case, I grip the handle of my shovel and join the crew at the starboard rail, peering down into the water.

I can tell they're imagining the catch. I also try to picture what's going on more than a thousand feet below us.

In my mind's eye I imagine a vast school of orange roughy teeming above the cold and shadowy seamount.

Our net sweeps forward, anchored to the bottom by the footrope, skipping merrily along on its weighted wheels.

The rock hoppers jitterbug up boulders. Shimmy through coral. The great steel doors are spread wide, zeroing in on the school of bottom-feeding fish we've located from above.

Orange roughy channel in through those huge otter board doors. Are caught in the net. Swim in circles trying to find a way out, but are funneled to the back, till they end up packed into the cod end.

Then the mouth will close and the net will be hoisted up. I imagine a victorious cheer from the crew. The fish will be deposited on the deck in a flopping reddish heap.

The orange roughy will go to the slime line to be filleted. I'll shovel the small, unwanted bycatch back into the ocean, and everyone on the boat will celebrate.

That's what I imagine. What's Gisco's problem? Men have been fishing for thousands of years. People have to eat. Fish is a good source of protein. The ocean covers three quarters of the earth's surface, and we're just trawling one tiny swath of it.

Perhaps coming from an awful future skews your judgment. Eko was full of gloom and doom, too. Vegan meals. Rooftop ruminations. Since the future is so messed up, maybe my canine companion is just a bit too sensitive.

The trawler moves very slowly now, just two or three knots. Chugging along, pulling a laden trawl net. I can feel the load of orange roughy a thousand feet down.

Maybe when our catch comes up, the captain will relax and I'll be able to play a little more soccer and do a little less scrubbing. Maybe they'll pass around rum and dance the hornpipe, or whatever the modern equivalent is.

"That's it, boys," Rudolf, the fishing master, finally shouts. "Haul it up."

The winches grind as the cables are brought in, wound around huge spools by hydraulic motors. It's painstaking progress—the reverse of when the nets were let out, except now tons of fish are being dragged up from the depths.

I gather with other crew members on the starboard side of the work deck, waiting expectantly.

Ronan stands near me. "Ready with your shovel, lad?"

I shrug, unsure. "How will I know an orange roughy when I see one?"

"Can't miss 'em," he assures me. "Reddish orange. Bony

heads. Big eyes. Fillets are great, broiled with a little white wine. Real distinctive taste."

Maybe it's 'cause they grow so slowly, Gisco suggests, padding up to join us. *Orange roughy live to a hundred and fifty years. The fillet you're thinking of cooking is probably older than your grandmother.*

"If we're lucky we could hit the jackpot," Ronan adds, peering down into the water. "When they spawn they gather in huge schools."

Since they live so long, they don't start breeding till they're twenty-five. So when you wipe out a school of breeders, it takes three decades to replace.

"Oh, stop being so negative," I admonish Gisco. By mistake I utter the words out loud.

"What, lad? Who's being negative?"

"No, not negative. Nets. I said here come the nets."

They are brought on board in reverse order. First the giant steel doors are remounted on the sides of the trawler and locked back into position. Then the footrope is hoisted aboard and lifted to the back of the work deck by a derrick.

The body of the net is tugged up and moved to one side, where it will not get in the way. The cod end is now visible, just off the stern ramp. It's not a small bundle anymore. It's become a giant orange bag, ten feet wide and long as a school bus, cinched up with white ropes.

I hear a few of the crew members curse, but I don't understand why yet.

Hooks are placed in the cod end, and a crane is used to drag it up the ramp and onto the work deck. It instantly becomes the center of activity as a dozen men surround it. I stand back, trying to get a glimpse of exactly what is taking place.

Angry curses are ringing out more frequently now, as different sections of the cod end are unstitched and the catch is dumped onto the deck.

Curiosity gets the better of me. I creep forward for a closer look. Worm my way between two burly sailors. And then I, too, see it, and I catch my breath.

✸

49

There must be some mistake. The net is orange, but the fish in it are not. Nor do they have bony heads or big eyes. Sure, a few of them do. Here and there I see flecks of bright orange in the vast, dark trawl net. But it looks like just a smattering of orange roughy.

It's a catch of bycatch. A school bus of bycatch. Tons of other fish, squid, octopus, crustaceans, corals, and anemones that are breathtaking for their variety and diversity. In fact, the mountain of sea organisms dumped gleaming on the work deck have only one thing in common: they're all dead or dying.

Eko tried to teach me how to communicate telepathically with wild creatures, but I could never seem to make the connection.

Now, for a split second, a previously unknown little trapdoor in my mind blows open. And I hear it. And feel it. Don't ask me how you can feel a sound, or a thought, but I sure do, just the way you can feel thunder. What I hear makes me tremble and drop my shovel on the deck.

A cold HOWLLLLLL of pure, primordial pain sweeps across the deck like an icy wind. I've never heard anything like it in my life, and yet somehow I know exactly what it is: the final agonies of a million life forms, hauled up from their reef, crushed during the trawl, and now slowly dying from the radical change in pressure.

As quickly as it opened, the trapdoor in my mind whips shut and I pivot.

This is Eko's training, too. The anticipation of a blow that I do not see. The fist comes from behind me, and by turning my body at the last second, I dodge the worst of the punch. It's First Mate Eye Patch, in a foul mood. "Stop gaping, pick up that shovel, and get to it."

So I get to work. And it's not fun.

The sun is directly overhead, beating down on the tons of bycatch that I'm trying to shovel back into the water as quickly as I can. The mountain of sea life seems to be moving and melting and moldering all at the same time.

Heaviest and most dangerous are the branches of coral that the rock hoppers cracked apart and pulverized. All of the coral is sharp to step on, but some that crew members call fire coral burns my skin on contact.

I weave and sidestep around the deck, digging into the heap of bycatch with my shovel. A dozen times, and then a hundred, and then a thousand, I carry twenty-pound loads to the edge of the deck and dump them back into the ocean.

I try not to look down into my shovel, to see what's stirring there, alive and in pain. But sometimes that's impossible. I often have to pry apart things that have gotten tangled up with each other or enmeshed in the netting.

And to do that, I have to look.

I pull apart branches of broken coral trees that have been wedged together like stacks of firewood. Octopus and eels are stuck deep inside the stacks, as creatures that spent their lives in caves sought some familiar hiding place from the unknown force yanking them skyward.

Anemones, starfish, mussels, and sponges have to be sliced from the mesh by the shovel's blade so they can be tossed overboard in dying clusters.

Then there are the deep-sea lobsters and crabs. Some still grip the orange nylon with their claws as if continuing to fight against a baffling enemy.

The small catch of orange roughy is taken belowdecks to be processed by the slime line. The fillets are frozen, while their heads, tails, bones, and guts are fed into drainage systems that scramble them and shoot them out in red flumes behind the boat. The sailors call this vapor of fish paste gurry, and there's a tail of seabirds a quarter mile long that follows our boat, cawing loudly as they snack on the bloody mist.

Listening to the hungry calls of the feasting seabirds, as I bend to my grim task, I start to understand why the captain said this was a floating factory of death.

Most of the fish we hauled up, however, are not orange roughy. There are thousands of them, their scales flashing all the colors of the rainbow as they lie on the deck. Their eyes are bugged out and their bellies have exploded from the change in pressure. Their protruding guts are the first things to stink in the sun.

Last, and most horrible, are the larger fish and sea animals. There's a dead dolphin. Dolphins breathe air, so I guess that this one must have been snagged while diving and drowned when the trawl net took him to the bottom. As I haul him by his rear fin over to the side, I touch his skin—soft as the most luxurious leather—and remember the dolphins that saved me when Eko and I were menaced by the bull shark.

A giant sea turtle lies upside down on the deck, flailing with its legs, bleeding gobs of red blood from a cracked carapace. I grab its tail and with another crewman drag it the length of the work deck to the stern ramp.

The cracked shell makes a *pap, pap, pap* sound as we haul the turtle along. Blood stains my shirt and pants. I make the mistake of glancing into its eyes.

I know sea turtles grow slowly, to great ages. How old is this Methuselah of the deep? Two hundred years? Three hundred?

How many times has it circled the earth, only to be entangled in the nylon net of the *Lizabetta* and cracked apart by the weight of the trawl? It looks back at me and seems to be asking, If you weren't going to keep me, or eat me, why did you do this?

I have no answer for the dying giant, so I shove it down the ramp and it sinks out of sight.

An eternity later, I toss the last shovel of bycatch into the ocean and drop my shovel.

Are you okay? Gisco walks up next to me. *You don't look so good.*

I'm not so good.

What's the matter?

Instead of answering, I vomit over the rail.

50

Grumbling during dinner.

Unhappy fishermen. Paid partly by how much they catch. Disappointed. Fearful that they may be blamed or even fired for the day's orange roughy debacle.

By whom? I don't know. Not the captain.

Someone above and behind the captain, pulling the strings. Someone they're too scared of to name directly.

They allude to him in whispers as the Boss.

"A friend of mine was on a skunked boat," one sailor says, between reluctant spoonfuls of Jacques's odious fish stew. "The Boss radioed the captain and had him sack the whole crew. Left them stranded in Nouakchott."

"Where the hell's that?"

"Mauritania. A thousand miles from nowhere."

"Aye, the Boss'll breathe fire when he hears about this," another fisherman agrees in a nervous whisper.

I wonder who this mysterious Boss is, who sacks whole crews and breathes fire. Could this be the monster my father warned me of?

The men start drinking. Beer, whiskey, rum. They chug the beers and slug the hard stuff down straight. Their voices get louder, and tempers start to flare.

I've never seen fishermen drink before. Bottles sprout like a glass forest on the table, and empties soon spill out of a trash can.

"If we were going after orange roughy we should be off New Zealand," an African sailor complains.

"You know the limits there have been taken," Ronan points out.

"So what? Russian boats still go in."

"That's true enough." Ronan lowers his spoon and spits on the floor. "What is this crap anyway?"

"The finest fish stew you'll ever eat," Jacques announces proudly. "I gave it the special family flavoring."

"Does that mean you pissed in it?" Ronan asks.

Jacques grabs a cleaver. "One more word and I'll cut your tongue out."

"Then at least I won't have to taste your swill." Ronan stands. "And don't you ever pull a knife on me."

"It's not a knife, it's a cleaver. Would you like to see how it feels?"

In answer, Ronan swings a rum bottle against a table leg. The bottom shatters into a crown of jagged glass.

The other crewmen back up fast, scurrying out of the way as the fat cook and the tall Irishman square off and begin to feint and swipe.

"I'll cut your lying throat open," Jacques promises.

"Come on, then, Fat Man. I'll gut you like a fish."

Jacques is surprisingly nimble on his feet, but Ronan is

younger and quicker, and has a longer reach. He swipes suddenly and the jagged glass rakes the cook's shoulder.

Jacques trumpets like a wounded elephant as red blood stands out against his blue tattoos. He picks up one of the benches, which must weigh two hundred pounds, and charges forward with it. The bench becomes a bulky battering ram that knocks Ronan off his feet.

The big cook is on him in a second, swinging his cleaver in lethal arcs. Ronan desperately rolls under a bunk.

Jacques squats and circles, trying to get at him, slicing and dicing the air. When that doesn't work, he shoulders the bed sideways, and the heavy iron frame tips. It falls to the floor with a resounding crash, depriving the Irishman of his cover. Ronan tries to roll away, but Jacques corners him against a wall. The cleaver begins to descend . . .

A gunshot rings out and everything stops.

Jacques's arm literally freezes in midair.

We all turn.

First Mate Eye Patch stands there, gun in hand, ferocious look on face. "Drop the knife."

"The bastard cut me . . ." Jacques protests.

The first mate's pistol swings toward the cook. "If anyone's killed on this boat, the captain or I will be the one doing the killing. Last chance. Drop it."

With a salty curse, Jacques lets the cleaver fall. "Later on, I'll finish you for sure," he promises Ronan.

"No you won't," the first mate snaps. "Don't you fools know it's bad luck to spill blood on a fishing boat?"

Superstitious crew members murmur their agreement.

"Now all of you go to bed," the first mate tells them. "Tomorrow we're going to be trawling a virgin reef."

The crew likes the sound of this. Men shout out, "Finally," and "That's the stuff."

But First Mate Eye Patch isn't done yet. "Mark my words," he warns from the doorway. "If there's any more fighting, I'll sack the lot of you and hire a new crew that likes to fish. Do you all understand that? Ronan?"

"I'm going to sleep, sir."

"Jacques?"

"I'm a peaceful man," the big Canadian growls. "Except when some fool insults my bouillabaisse."

"Is that what it was?" a sailor calls out. "I thought it was raw sewage."

Jacques climbs into a top bunk, insults all of our mothers in French-English, and pulls the curtain closed.

51

Semidark bunkroom, still thrumming with the bloody energy of the knife fight.

Poker game revolving endlessly around dining table. Small change and large insults exchanged. No more fights, though. Everyone's taking the first mate's warning seriously.

I'm in bed, exhausted from shoveling bycatch in the hot sun. Gisco is stretched out on the floor beneath my bottom bunk. Jacques lies in the bed directly above me. I'm starting to figure out why my bunk just happened to be vacant.

The fat cook's been drinking Canadian whiskey for over an hour, and is blustering and raving out loud. Sometimes he shouts down to me, to make sure he has an audience. "Insult my bouilla-baisse, will he? And didn't my grandfather serve the very same to the King of England? A shame that Cyclops with the pistol stopped me. I would have cut the heart out of the leprechaun. You down there listening, boy?"

"Still here, trying to sleep," I call up.

"Ah, but he didn't know who he was dealing with. Never mess with a Newfoundland cook. Proud of our secret recipes, we are. Did you know my grandfather cooked for a giant cod boat? Seventy men freezing on the Grand Banks, and only my grandpa to keep them warm and fed."

He falls silent, and Gisco chimes in from beneath: *Don't tell me that buffoon is going to brag about his family's part in the annihilation of the North Atlantic cod.*

I'm pretty confused about how I feel. There didn't seem to be anything wrong with doing a little fishing and lowering one net. But the sight of the bycatch, and the smell of it, and the needless death toll, literally made me sick. So I ask Gisco: What's wrong with catching a few cod?

A few cod? he thunders. Dog has his dander up. Must have been the trawling. *Let me spell it out for you, beacon of ignorance. When the Grand Banks were first discovered, fishermen didn't even need hooks. They just hauled the cod up in buckets. Even after they had been fished relentlessly for five centuries, the schools were still so great that the best scientists of the time believed they were inexhaustible.*

"Grandpa was lucky!" Jacques rumbles. "Cod made Newfoundland. Men got rich from it! Wars were fought over it."

So what happened to the schools of cod? I ask Gisco.

Human ingenuity is what happened. Great factory ships set out from Europe that could catch a hundred tons of cod in an hour. In the blink of an eye the schools were gone for good and tens of thousands of Newfoundland fishermen like the grandfather of this boozing blowhard were out of work.

The bed heaves as Jacques rolls over and continues his drunken rant. "The cod ran out, so my father became a whaler! It was man against the leviathan, boy, and man had to be fed. My pa cooked bouillabaisse for hungry crews as they fought noble battles with the gargantuans of the deep!"

Noble battles? Gisco sputters. *Now he's bragging about his father's role in the extinction of the great whales!*

As if in response to this accusation, Jacques farts loudly. Then, inspired by the musical qualities of his own flatulence, he breaks into a drunken whaling chantey:

> *"Come all you brave fellows that's bound after sperm,*
> *Come all you bold seamen that's rounded the Horn.*
> *Our captain has told us and I hope he says true,*
> *That there's plenty of sperm whale on the coast of Peru."*

He pauses for another swig of whiskey.

Listen to him crow about it, like it was something glorious! Gisco is outraged. *The Annals of Dann have no more brutal example of one highly intelligent and far-flung species trying to completely wipe out another than the thousand-year war* Homo sapiens *waged against cetaceans.*

Jacques's throat wetted, he pipes up again, with gusto:

> *"Oh, we gave him one iron and the whale he went down,*
> *But as he came up, boys, our captain bent on,*
> *And the next harpoon struck, and the line sped away,*
> *But whatever that whale done, he gave us fair play."*

This is appalling. I can't bear it.

Actually, I think his voice is pretty good.

Listen to the words! Celebrating a vicious slaughter.

No, he's celebrating a battle, I point out. And you have to admit, there is something heroic about men with harpoons setting out on wooden boats to hunt the biggest animals that ever lived on this earth. Think of Ahab and Moby Dick.

Gisco kicks my bunk with his paws. *The tendency of your species to dramatize and extol when it should be apologizing and cringing! There was nothing noble about the slaughter of the whales from start to finish. The smaller ones were the first to be hunted to the point of extinction, the right whales, the bowheads, and the humpbacks with their lovely songs— so much better than this harmonic hash.*

As if on cue, Jacques launches into another stanza:

> *"Oh, he raced and he sounded, he twist and he spin,*
> *But we fought him alongside and got our lance in,*
> *Which caused him to vomit, and the blood for to spout,*
> *And in ten minutes' time, me boys, he rolled both fins out."*

I can't help enjoying this old saga of the sea. I tell Gisco, His song makes it sound like a heroic battle—

It was sheer butchery, the maddened mastiff insists. *Ships followed the whales to their breeding grounds and wiped out whole populations, including mothers and calves. When one type of whale was finished off, the whalers just moved on to the next.*

Other crewmen shout from their bunks for Jacques to quiet down. His voice defiantly swells even louder:

> *"We towed him alongside, and with many a shout.*
> *We soon cut him in and begun to try out.*
> *Now the blubber is rendered and likewise stowed down,*
> *And it's better to us, me boys, than five hundred pound."*

I hear scrabbling—Gisco is trying to cover his ears with his paws. *Will someone please stick a harpoon into that caterwauling creator of culinary catastrophes.*

Jacques takes an enormous swig of whiskey. When he speaks again he slurs his words. "Then there was my Uncle Leo, boy. Loaded Leo! Made his fortune on tuna boats, catching bluefin for the Japanese. Gold that swims, Leo called it."

One of the two or three fastest and most beautiful fish, Gisco contributes. *The Japanese called it* honmaguro. *They thought it was so delicious that they ate it into extinction. The last piece of bluefin tuna will be picked up by chopsticks and popped into a mouth about five years from now.*

"Now it's just me and my brother, Mitch. He's a proud longliner! Braves the waters of the Antarctic for Chilean sea bass."

Patagonian toothfish. Became a fad delicacy in restaurants and within three decades was fished to extinction. I can't believe this! Gisco shudders. *This nitwit's family deserve to be flensed! The longlines were hideous! Miles of baited and unbreakable lines, floating in darkness, catching and tangling and drowning anything that swims.*

"Yo ho, ye brave swordfishermen!" Jacques blurts out, and for a second I'm afraid he's going to break into song again. "Taught me how to cook, Mitch did. Stewed up the family bouillabaisse as they hauled in the fierce swordfish!"

Till the swordfish were gone. Not to mention the albatross and other seabirds that dived for the baited hooks and drowned, and the endangered sea turtles that got tangled in the lines and died by the thousands.

"But I was a trawler man, from the day I could stand to piss. It's a fine life, boy, bottom trawling. Been all around the world. Trawled for shrimp off Florida."

The beautiful Lophelia *reefs, gone for good.*

"You name it, I've been there when they've scooped it up. Bottom trawling is fishing's finest miracle, boy! We can reach anything! That's the tradition I come from, that's the salty seed I sprout from, and if any Irish potato farmer wants to pick a scrap with a proud outport cook, I'll cleave him into ribbons, just as my pa and grandpa would have done! Now it's time for some shuteye. Tomorrow we're on to a virgin reef! What could be better?"

52

Middle of the night. Crew members asleep. Jacques snoring drunkenly above me. Each time he exhales, it sounds like a lumberjack sawing down a thick tree with a blunt blade.

Okay, Gisco. Let me have it.

What?

Why are we here?

Because the storm blew us here.

You stole the small boat. You have a major thing against trawlers. And you say Firestorm is linked to the oceans. Are you manipulating this whole situation? Is this another chicken-and-egg game?

You're giving me too much credit. How could I know we'd survive the storm? How could I predict this trawler would pick us up?

I don't know, but I don't trust you.

Maybe fate brought you here. The prophecies say that only you can save the future. Nothing was as damaging to the oceans right before the Turning Point as bottom trawling. So it makes sense that fate would send you to a bottom trawler.

Why not a longliner? Or a whaling ship? I just listened to you condemn all kinds of different fishing boats. What was so especially horrible about trawlers?

Aren't you the boy who threw up after shoveling bycatch?

I admit today wasn't pleasant. But people need to eat. You seem to think that all fishing is evil.

No. Wrong. The problem lies in the methods.

Forgive me, High Dog, I'm trying to open my mind up to your futuristic wisdom, but it's hard for me to believe a little human ingenuity directed at catching fish really doomed the world. Bigger nets? Longer lines? Better fish finders? Was that really such a big deal in the grand scheme of things?

There's nothing wrong with fishing. For thousands of years people fished. In the back of their minds was the notion that the oceans were bottomless and the fish were limitless. When primitive methods were used, that was true. But the methods got better and better. The lines got longer and the nets bigger, and the fish finders more sophisticated. But the fish didn't get smarter or more elusive and the oceans didn't get any deeper. The "earth" is a misnomer—seen from space, we live on a blue planet of oceans. The Turning Point hinged on the emptying of those oceans.

I lie there and try to take this all in. The way Gisco says it— proclaims it—with the ring of doomsday. The way his big, wet, agonized eyes ranged around the deck during the trawl. Eko's face on the rooftop in moonlight. The eyes of the sea turtle as I dragged it down the deck.

I start to feel deeply guilty, even though I haven't done anything wrong. Like I'm complicit in something horrible that I do not approve of.

But what can I do?

Bunkroom full of sleeping fishermen. From all different countries. None of them bent on world destruction. Just earning a living. Jacques snoring above me. Third-generation cook on fishing boats. Not a nice guy, but not exactly a destroyer of worlds either.

Yet Gisco says it's their fault. It's our fault. It's my fault. And Eko, in her own way, believed the same thing. I remember her sadness. Her guilt. Her anger.

Directed at us. At now. At me and mine.

That's why they left their world and came back right now. That's why I was sent back eighteen years ago. To prepare for this moment. This Turning Point. And I'm starting to grasp that the crucial thing about a turning point is that it can be used to tilt fate one way or the other.

I get quietly out of bed.

Where are you going?

I don't know exactly.

Come back. They'll catch you. If you don't know where you're going—
if you don't have a smart plan—get back into bed now. That's an order!

Screw you. I can't listen to this anymore. Humans did this, humans did that. If you're right, and fate has brought me here, then I'm supposed to accomplish something. Let's find out exactly where we're headed and what's going on. Are you in or out? Or are you just like Cassandra, from Greek mythology, who could warn of calamities but could do nothing to prevent them?

I would like to help, the big dog declares, *but I'm weak, not to mention underfed. And it's so warm and comfortable here.*

Being comfortable is overrated. I'm gonna go do something. *Hasta la vista*, hound.

Okay. Just wait a minute. I still think this is a rotten idea, but you guilted me into it. The big dog crawls out from under the bed. *Let's not take any risks. If that first mate with the pistol catches us skulking around, he'll probably feed us into the fillet machine.*

53

We creep upstairs to dark and deserted deck.

Where are we going?

The wheelhouse. That's where they keep the charts.

It's also where the night watch is likely to be.

Don't sweat it. We'll crawl in through a rear window. Even if someone's at the wheel, they won't hear us or see us.

That's your plan?

Got a better one?

Why don't we set a fire? When they run to put it out, we can take a quick look around inside.

Only an idiot would set fire to his own boat.

Your plan's not exactly brilliant either. I don't know if you noticed, but dogs are not great at climbing.

So wait outside and keep watch for me. There's the window. Let me climb on your back. Hold still.

Unlike simple beasts of burden like the burro, the canine does not have a spine designed to support extra weight. Ouch! Your heels! You're crippling me!

I've almost got it open. Just a few more seconds . . .

That window's locked. Get down. Give up.

No, it's just stuck. There, got it open. Now I'm just going to bounce on you like a trampoline . . .

You're cracking my vertebrae like walnuts!

Made it! All that weight makes you a good springboard. Stay there in case I need you to break my fall.

Dog steps quickly away from window. *I am not a leaf pile.*

I peer around tiny chart room. In the moonlight that filters through the grimy window I can barely make out a desk.

What do you see? Gisco asks anxiously from outside.

Nothing. Too dark. I'm going to turn on a light.

No! There's someone in the front. He may be asleep.

I walk to the door. Open it a crack and peer out at the helm controls. Sure enough, a crewman sits snoozing in front of the steering wheel, his head slouched to one side.

I pull the door closed again. Find the desk lamp. Hold my breath and switch it on. Look down at maps.

Do you see anything useful? Gisco wants to know.

Charts of the ocean, with underwater topography.

Are there points of reference? Landmasses? Islands?

Just something labeled Great Meteor.

That's one of the most famous seamounts, near the Azores! You must be looking at a map of the reefs of the Mid-Atlantic Ridge. Who prepared the chart?

I see a five-letter acronym near the bottom. ICCAF.

Oh my God! That's it!

What?

Jack! No time. Someone's coming! The captain and the first mate! Get out now!

Footsteps thump up the steps to the wheelhouse. I start to clamber out the window. Stop myself. Hang there for a moment. And then climb back inside the tiny room.

What are you doing?

We need to know what's going on, right? Who better to hear it from than the two guys running this ship.

You're crazy! They'll catch you and flense you alive.

They'll hear me if I try to climb out now.

What choice do you have? Get out!

Chill, dog. They just probably want to make sure we're on course.

Voices ring out from the helm.

I tiptoe to the door. The crewman who was napping is now trying to defend himself. "I swear I wasn't asleep, sir. I have a bad neck, so I sit with it tilted to one side—"

"Shut up, fool," the first mate's voice snaps, and I hear what I think is a punch.

The crewman cries out in pain.

"This'll cost you five hundred dollars," the captain says. "If I catch you napping again, you're fired, and that won't be the worst of it."

"Yes, sir," the crewman responds miserably.

"Now keep a sharp lookout," the captain orders. "We're going to look at some charts. And what we have to say is private."

I edge to the window. Too late! The doorknob is turning!

I dive beneath the desk as the captain and first mate enter. The first mate closes the door behind them and latches it with a hook.

"The fog will help us," the captain says in his gentle voice. "Visibility should be less than ten meters."

"Do we really need to worry?" the first mate asks. "We'll slip in, fish it out, and be gone in less than a day. What are the odds that a spotter plane will see us?"

"True, but Dargon doesn't want any trouble." There's something strange about the way the captain whispers the name. His soft voice is almost immune to inflections of weakness or fear. It's the voice of a man who is scared of nothing. Yet his voice trembles as he whispers "Dargon."

"Then let's not get into any trouble," the first mate agrees. "The fog will serve our purpose well."

They walk over to the desk. I scrunch back as far as I can, so that my back is pressed to the wall. My heart starts kettledrumming in my chest. Will they hear me breathe?

"Some fool left the window open," the captain says.

The first mate steps to the sill and closes it. "That boy, probably," he guesses. "I told him to mop up in here."

"I don't trust that kid," the old captain mutters. "And there's something strange about his dog, too."

"We had to save him," the first mate points out. "The crew saw him in the boat. But there could be an accident."

"We'll see if that's necessary." The desk shakes as the captain thumps it with his titanium hand. "Here's the chart. We'll trawl the reef in fog and we'll sail away in fog. We can't come in with another lousy catch."

"That's for sure," the first mate agrees.

The captain's heavy hand traces the route. "According to this chart, we should be reaching the reef in less than an hour. We'll lower the net as soon as the crew wakes."

"With the rock hoppers?"

"Of course. I don't care what we have to smash. We go in, we get a rich catch of fish, and we get the hell out. Once we're gone, no one will be able to pin it on us. Agreed?"

"Dargon will be happy. Surely he will reward us."

I watch the captain's polished shoes step toward the door. He unlatches the hook. Then he turns. "Be careful when it comes to Dargon," the old voice cautions. "A flame knows neither gratitude nor mercy. Only how to scorch and consume."

✷

54

Raise window. Squeeze outside. Hang by hands. Jump down to deck. Gisco? You still here?

You don't really think I'd run away? How little you understand the loyalty and bravery of dogs. Didn't Odysseus' faithful hound, Argos, await his master's return to Ithaca lo those many years? Didn't Themistocles' brave dog refuse to be left behind when Athens was evacuated, and swim behind his master's boat all the way to Salamis, where he fainted and died from exhaustion on the beach? Didn't the great sled dog Balto prevent a diphtheria epidemic in Nome by heroically—

Okay, I get it. Then where exactly are you?

Hiding behind the derrick.

I join the cowardly canine, cowering in the farthest night shadows. I tell him what I overheard, and see the horror on his face at the prospect of soon trawling a virgin reef. So what's the ICCAF? I ask him. Why did you nearly jump out of your pelt when I mentioned it?

It's an acronym for the International Committee to Control Atlantic Fisheries. It was a group formed right before the Turning Point, chartered by the United Nations. Its crucial mission was to protect all the remaining undestroyed reefs outside territorial waters.

Like the one we're about to fish?

Right. Those unprotected reefs lay in what was called the global common, meaning they were not close enough to any single country to be protected by that country. So they were supposed to be protected by all countries, working together. What it really meant was that all countries exploited them.

But if the ICCAF was supposed to protect the reefs, how does it figure that this trawler is using an ICCAF chart?

Future historians of the destruction of the seas speculated that the International Committee to Control Atlantic Fisheries was corrupt. They dubbed it the International Conspiracy to Catch All Fish. The ICCAF used international conservation funds to survey all the still-uncharted floors of the world's oceans. Someone in the committee must have sold the maps of virgin reefs to this trawler company.

The ship is dark and silent. We must be over the reef now. I can feel the trawler cutting its engines. The fogbanks are thick around us. When the crew wakes, in a few hours, the net will be lowered.

I'm starting to understand what I should do. But I'm afraid of it. Is it absolutely necessary?

One question, dog. The ocean is so vast. We're just going to trawl one reef today. Is that really so damaging? Won't it grow back?

That's what's so special about reefs, Gisco answers. *Coral grows slowly. A deep-sea reef takes thousands of years to form. But a trawler can pulverize it in a single day. Bottom trawling with rock hoppers destroyed all the world's reefs in less than two decades. And that took away the last chance.*

The last chance to do what?

Deep-sea reefs and trenches were the incubators of ocean life. Life first began there. Fish spawn there. Overfished species recover there. Fish down a single species, and it might recover in the deep-sea reefs over time. Rip apart the incubators of life, and you deprive the ocean of its only way of healing itself. So yes, ripping up a virgin deep-sea reef is a big deal. What are you doing now?

I need to see it for myself.

What?

The reef.

Are you crazy?

I hesitate for a second. Am I? Why exactly am I doing this? My father's second warning has been haunting me. I'm aware that there is another, very different meaning of the word "chimera." It was the fire-breathing monster of Greek legend, but it also means an illusion or fabrication of the mind. The deep-sea reefs that Gisco described sound fantastical. Can meaningful life really exist so far down, so removed from sunlight? I need to see it for myself, with my own eyes. I need to make sure that my father wasn't warning me about risking my life for an illusion. I start to climb over the rail. Ask dog: Do you want the good news or the bad news?

The good news, please.

I'm going to dive down and check out the reef. I should be back up in less than an hour, if I don't get eaten by a shark or squeezed to pulp by a giant squid.

That's the good news?

No, the good news is that one of us should stay behind. So you don't have to come.

The dog cheers up. *Yes, that makes sense. I'll remain here, watching over everything. What's the bad news?*

If I'm not up in an hour, it means the beacon of hope has been extinguished. So then it'll be up to you to find Firestorm on your own, and figure out how to use it, with the weight of the whole future on your back.

Hold on a minute! I told you that the canine spine was not designed to support weight. Come back here!

In one smooth motion I dive over the side. Glide easily down

five feet, seven feet, ten feet into the dark, cool water. Gisco's telepathic warnings begin to fade as the pressure builds in my ears.

55

Can't take this for long. Pitch darkness. Numbing cold. Roaring
pressure.

Feel my arm, my wrist, the dark metal band with the old-
fashioned watch face. Sure enough, the band grows warmer. The
watch begins to glow. A million points of light surround me.

Goodbye, cold. *Adios*, pressure. My watch is now like a high-
beam spotlight, shining a tunnel-path downward.

I fumble with the beads around my neck. What was it Eko
said when she put the necklace on me? "Men should wear more
jewelry. It gives them a sensual dimension."

Jewelry wasn't the approved accessory for Hadley jocks. I
never wore a chain or even an earring. But I'll keep Eko's necklace
as long as I live. It's all I have left from the woman who took me
beneath the waves and flew with me among the clouds.

I swallow a bead. Feel it breaking apart inside me. Okay, I'm
ready. Can I really swim down to a seamount? Only one way to
find out.

Seems like I swim downward for an hour. I don't have Eko to
show me the way and point out the dangers. Will I end up as
shark bait? Do I have enough oxygen? Am I on course or am I
lost at sea, or rather lost far under the sea?

Just when I'm convinced I must have missed the seamount
and be headed down to the empty Atlantic floor, I'm suddenly
surrounded by orange roughy.

Thousands of them. Mingling and swirling like kids in a playground during recess. They swim around me and brush up to me, fearless or oblivious. I imagine the gaping maw of the trawler net sweeping through this cloud of orange. It could scoop up the whole school in a matter of minutes.

Then I'm through the orange roughy, diving down alone. I miss their bright color and companionship. Nothing else down here. Maybe I should turn back.

Wait, something looms ahead, shimmering like the mirage of an oasis in a desert. I stop swimming and stare.

It's not a mirage. Not a chimera. It's real! More than a thousand feet beneath the Atlantic, an unspoiled Garden of Eden blooms up at me out of the cold darkness.

A virgin reef. Thousands of years in the making. This is not a shipwreck that has been taken over by fish and coral. This is in no way a work of man.

This is pure ocean.

Imagine a vast tabletop, protruding up from darkness. As I swim down toward it, I can see where the edge of the table ends and massive black boulders slope away into the uncharted depths.

But the plateau of the seamount is aflame with vibrant colors, teeming with fish, and crawling with sea creatures.

Here's the strange part. I've never seen anything like it before. It's the most exotic, otherworldly place I've ever been. But at the same time, it feels strangely familiar.

Can there be such a thing as ancestral memory stretching back millions of years? It doesn't seem likely—I can't even remember what I had for breakfast. Yet, swimming toward this oasis of life, I'm overcome with wonderment and odd nostalgia.

The seamount is a garden, a secret, magical garden, hidden from the world! The kind you imagine in childhood games, tended by fairies in the woods.

My mom kept a small garden in Hadley-by-Hudson. When I was a baby she used to lay me on a grassy spot in the center of the planting beds. Summer breezes stirred the ferns and flowers, and bees and crickets buzzed and chirped around my head.

That's what I think of now. A country garden. Bees and crickets, worms and centipedes, pollinating flowers and stirring soil. The bustling magic of it comes back to me.

Yesterday I saw coral pulled up in the nets, pulverized. Here it's intact, the way it's been growing for centuries. A thicket of it near me is rosy red and wide-branched, with yellow anemones glinting from its folds, like an orchard of scarlet apple trees hung with ripe yellow fruit.

Next to it bristles a grove of what looks like bamboo—thin tapering coral fronds in a brown and yellow thicket.

Uh-oh, I've disturbed an octopus convention. No, wait, they're not animals. It's a patch of green and brown corals, each of which have eight armlike tentacles reaching upward.

I gingerly set down on the seamount and wander past giant sponges and tendril-twitching anemones. The sponges are comically similar to shapes I know from my own life—they look like elephant heads and Christmas trees and baseball mitts. The pink and red and rainbow-spackled anemones flutter in the deep-sea current, like petals in a rose garden.

A shadow roves silently over rock and coral. It's a ray skimming effortlessly, like a square Frisbee. There's a funky flounder watching me from all three green eyes on top of its flat head. A spindly eel pokes out of a coral formation to take a look. No, he's not looking at me, but at a white arrow shooting past. It's a three-foot-long albino squid propelled in sudden bursts.

There are mussels that look like turkey wings. Tiny luminescent jellyfish with scarlet tentacles. And almost transparent sea spiders crawl by, like moving flakes of ice.

I have no idea how long I've stayed down. Twenty minutes? A half hour? An hour? I can't say. I have no desire to return to the trawler.

It seems so much safer here.

And more beautiful.

But soon it will all be gone. That's the thought that makes me kick regretfully off the seamount floor and head up into darkness.

In a few hours the trawler net will sweep down and the rock hoppers will pulverize this coral, and the fish and the sponges will be netted and yanked skyward.

Somebody has to do something about that.

56

I emerge from cold ocean into warm soup. That's how thick the fog is. I'm lucky I surface near the trawler, or I might miss it in this gray miasma.

Gisco? Are you there?

I thought you were reef roadkill.

How do I get back up on deck?

Here's a rope. Did you learn anything useful?

I grab hold of rope and clamber back up to deck of trawler. Yes, I can't let them do it.

What?

Trawl the virgin reef. It's too beautiful.

Beautiful or not, the crew will be waking up in less than an hour. The net will soon be on its way down.

No it won't.

Who's going to stop it?

We are.

We meaning?

You and me.

Impossible.

Possible. We've seen how they lower the nets. It shouldn't be hard to wreck the equipment.

Even if you succeed, they'll figure out it was you.

Is that a reason not to do it?

They'll punish you in some painful and permanent way. And they probably won't have mercy on your dog, either. Then we won't be around when we're really needed, to save the future. So, whatever scheme you're concocting, please abandon it. We need to be patient. Where are you going?

I saw a fire ax hanging near the wheelhouse.

Haven't you been listening to my sage counsel? We need to take a long-range view here.

No, I tell him, halfway to the wheelhouse. It's time to act. I can't control the whole world, but I can do one very specific thing to prevent the atrocity that's about to happen. Let's boogie.

Gisco looks a little shocked. *The words of Dann! You echo them perfectly!*

Which words? "Let's boogie"?

No. Dann wrote: Do not waste time seeking to save the whole earth. Try to preserve one tiny pebble. And by doing that, you can, in fact, save the planet.

Well said. Dann and I are on the same page. And here's the fire ax. Damn, it's heavy.

Your intentions are noble, but your priorities are wrong.

Meaning? I head back across the deck toward the starboard winch, lugging the fire ax.

Dann was trying to inspire the general population. His words were not addressed to the beacon of hope at the critical moment just before the Turning Point. If he were here, he would tell you to put that ax back and play ball.

No, if he were here, he'd say "Strike hard and true."

Nonsense. I've studied his philosophy all my life.

He's my ancestor.

And you can be certain that if he were here he would say, "My brave descendant, listen to wise Gisco. Be guided by his caution and superior intellect. See the big picture." There's a time for heroics and a time for cowardice. Sometimes cowardice can actually be heroic . . .

The fire ax is big and red and heavy in my hands. I step up to one of the two main winches. Spot the cable and the hydraulic controls. Raise the ax over my head.

Don't do this. I'm begging you. I'm pretty sure the captain isn't fond of dogs.

I summon every iota of strength I have and bring the ax down with a CRASH. And AGAIN! And yet a third CRASH! Cable split. Controls wrecked. Dials dangling. This is one winch that won't be lowering nets anytime soon.

Okay. You did it. Now throw the ax in the sea and let's go hide in some dark spot. I know the perfect closet . . .

I walk across the deck to the winch on the port side. Raise the ax. CRASH.

Oh no. They've heard you. They're coming!

Voices approach rapidly through the fog.

I strike one last fierce blow with the ax. CRASH! Cable severed. Port winch also inoperable.

Half a dozen crewmen surround me. The first mate's there, too. Holding a pistol.

The old captain walks up. His shrewd eyes survey the damage. Then they flick toward me and lock onto my own eyes for a long second.

He whispers gently to the first mate, "Tie him up. And his ugly dog, too."

57

Dog and boy bound together, hand to paw, to the steel cable of the aft winch—the only one still functioning. Fog lifting a bit. Morning sun burning through.

Crew assembled on deck. Many of them look furious at us, but also deeply apprehensive.

The first mate addresses them: "Less than a week ago we saved this boy and his dog. They rewarded us by sabotaging our ship. Instead of fishing today, we're on our way to a dockyard. Repairs will take weeks. Some of you may be fired because of the delay. So it's time to punish those who are responsible."

The captain steps to the winch controls. He's going to do this himself! Lower us slowly down into the depths. I destroyed his winches, so he's going to use the sole remaining one to destroy me. Slowly drown us. Let the pressure crush us. Let the bottom feeders nibble on us.

He looks right at me for a second. Tough old guy. Unblinking, purposeful stare. You screwed with me and now you're going to pay the price. He glances at Gisco, who snivels pathetically.

Unmoved, the captain looks back at his angry crew and announces, "This boy is a runaway and a confessed thief. No one will miss him. No one will mourn him. From this moment forward, he never existed. We never picked him up. He died on that small boat in the hurricane. Does anyone have anything to say?"

No one does. I spot Ronan, in the second row of crew members. He wets his lips with his tongue, but remains silent. His face is pale. For a moment our eyes meet, and then he looks away.

I try to move my wrists. To pry the knots loose to at least create a tiny bit of slack. Forget about it. Sailors know how to tie knots, and they've done their job expertly. There's no escape for me. Nor for Gisco, who has stopped sniveling and begun to shed big dog tears. They gush out of his eyes and splash onto the deck, like the sudden onset of a monsoon.

Oh, woe is me. Who would have ever thought Gisco would come to such an end? Surely they'll have mercy on an old dog who's much too young to die.

There's no point in blubbering, I tell him. They're not the merciful sort. Death is coming, so let's take it with a stiff upper lip and show them what we're made of.

I'm made out of pure fear, Gisco admits, trembling. *I told you to put down that fire ax. The whole future depended on you, and you let it down. Oh, woe is me.*

I did what I thought was right, I tell him. I saved the reef. If I was really destined to find Firestorm and save the future, then they shouldn't be able to kill us now. But they are, so I guess I wasn't.

Yes, that doesn't make sense to me either, the miserable mongrel admits.

A sad-faced crewman with a Bible begins intoning a passage that I think is used for burials at sea. Strange that they should introduce religion into what is essentially a double murder. But maybe the captain is trying to make the crew feel better about the whole thing.

Another crewman checks the knots that bind us.

The prophecies about you finding and using Firestorm were pretty definite, Gisco says. *We came so far and got so close. They shouldn't be able to stop us now.*

I don't really believe in prophecies, I admit.

They are not of your world. But over hundreds of years, as life on earth changed and darkened, the powers of the mind deepened. You your-self as a descendant of Dann have some of these abilities. You mastered telepathy. You've seen shape-changing. There are other powers that to you might seem magical, but that I fully accept.

Such as?

Curses and spells. And by far the rarest power is prophecy. The greatest seer of the future, the Mysterious Kidah himself, divined that you were the one who could find Firestorm and change things. If he said it, it must be so. And yet it cannot be so if they drown us, which they seem very intent on doing. Oh, woe is me.

Why didn't you get the Mysterious Kidah to save my father and pinpoint Firestorm?

Because Kidah is gone. He disappeared. Vanished.

Is that what made him so mysterious?

How can you joke at a moment like this?

It'll all be over soon. Here they come to finish us off.

The captain steps close. "You have no one to blame for this but yourself," he whispers. "Do you have any last words?"

"A last question," I tell him. "Exactly how did you lose your arm?"

He doesn't like that. "I forgot my place," he answers, "and it cost me very dearly. As it will now cost you."

He steps to the winch and begins to work the controls.

Goodbye, Gisco.

Farewell, old bean. You did well to save the reef. It was a brave act. I'll show them what Gisco is made of.

The big dog looks right at the captain and lets loose a ferocious growl.

For a moment, even the tough old captain is thrown. Then he recovers his poise and pushes a button. There's a whirring sound.

The steel cable begins to move slowly downward. I look away from the captain and the crew and fix my eyes on the farthest sweep of azure ocean.

There are banks of fog, white wisps on the water, but we are in a clear patch, showered with sunshine.

I feel that sunshine on my neck, my hair, my face. Such a bright, sweet world to leave forever.

I try to remember P.J.'s eyes. They merge into Eko's eyes. Did either of them really love me? I hope so.

Wait! I see something. Far out on the rim of azimuth, where sea meets sky.

A black dot. A ship!

No, not a ship. Not like this trawler, anyway. It's under sail. The sails are black and billowed with morning breeze. It sweeps forward, swift and beautiful.

Heading our way!

They've seen it on deck, too. Men shout and point.

A crewman runs from the wheelhouse. "Sir, it's Dargon! We let him know what happened, as you ordered. He was cruising nearby. He wants to take care of this himself."

The black yacht races closer. Tall masts. Ebony sails. Lovely yet ominous.

Gisco and I are winched back up to the deck, where we await our fate.

I can see a man stride out onto the prow of the yacht. He's tall and has the build of a weightlifter, but he moves with the grace of a ballet dancer. Even from this distance I can tell he's movie-star handsome. There's something familiar and unsettling about him.

"Dargon," the captain murmurs near me, and crosses himself. Then he looks away from the man on the yacht, and his old eyes meet mine. "I was right," he whispers. "You are an unlucky boy. I was going to kill you quickly. Now you belong to him."

A crewman finishes cutting me loose, and I rub my wrists to restore circulation.

"When you meet Dargon's pets," the captain whispers, "you can ask them what happened to my arm."

58

A ladder is lowered, and Dargon comes aboard.

He inspects the wrecked winches, while I strain to get a good look at him between the bodies of the assembled crewmen, who stand straight and silent.

I can tell that he's quite a specimen. Big. Colorful. Somewhere between pirate king and male model.

Mid-thirties. At least two inches taller than I am. Sandy brown hair hanging down to broad shoulders. Bird with bright plumage perched on right shoulder.

Dargon's dressed like a seafaring dandy. White linen shorts. Gold-chain-link belt. Black silk shirt, tight enough to show off muscles. Abundant abs. Precipitous pecs. Bulging biceps.

Don't mess with this guy, Jack. Underneath the silk and linen, he's hard as a mountainside.

For ten long minutes he doesn't give Gisco or me so much as a glance.

He's the Boss. We'll do this his way. First check out the damage. Then punish the culprits.

He discusses repairs with the captain and first mate. Where to go. What to do. How much time it will take.

He's clearly not pleased by the delay.

Dargon finally turns toward the crew, who all but salute as he walks past. Tough men of the sea, now hushed, fearful.

Gisco and I are shoved forward, into his presence.

Careful, Jack.

Don't worry, I'm planning to be on my best behavior.

I am worried. He likes birds, but he may not understand the joys and rewards of friendship with dogs.

Probably not too fond of beacons of hope, either.

There's something oddly familiar about this guy.

Yeah, I feel it, too.

Strange. We don't know many people in common.

Suddenly I'm face to face with Dargon. Realize what was so unsettling. It's not just that he's got plucked eyebrows. Not his perfect teeth—dental wonders. Nor even his manicured toenails, painted gold.

It's the leonine shape of his face. And the aura of it. A shape and an aura that I've seen somewhere before.

Visions of my own death. Nightmares of being hunted.

Jumping between buildings in Manhattan. The same face watching me from windows, all the way down.

Aristocratic. Handsome yet sad features. Strong jaw. Aquiline nose. Perfect teeth. White hair. Raptor-like eyes. The wise and knowing visage of death.

Again, on my first night in the Outer Banks beach house. A lion's roar of a voice sounding through my nightmare. "Jack. Jack." The same fine-boned face, with demonic red eyes. "Jack. You can't hide. Give up."

And here, on the deck of the trawler *Lizabetta*, is a younger version of that death face. Just as handsome, as assuredly aristocratic, with the same strong jaw and refined cheekbones. But the hair is sandy brown instead of white, and the eyes are soft and liquid gray.

"Who damaged my ship?" Dargon asks. Rich bass voice. Could probably sing the hell out of a whaling chantey.

"That would be me," I answer.

He smiles. Understands that I'm the only one on the *Lizabetta* who's not afraid of him. "Why did you do it?"

"Because they were getting ready to trawl a virgin reef," I tell him honestly. "I couldn't let that happen."

He shrugs. "Your personal feelings are irrelevant. It wasn't your ship. It was my ship."

"Your ship," I agree, looking right back into those liquid gray eyes. "But not your reef."

The moment of silence stretches as he decides my fate. Trawler sails slowly into a fogbank. Morning sun is dimmed, filtered. Dargon's gray eyes darken to a majestic purple-black flecked with tiny seeds of blood red.

The parrot on his shoulder shrieks unexpectedly, breaking the silence. A shrill whistle: "Kill the dog."

Shut up, tweezer beak.

Easy, Gisco.

Did I ever mention that I hate birds?

No, you never did.

This feathered fathead in particular belongs in a nice roasting pan with some rosemary potatoes.

"Kill the dog," the parrot repeats in a loud trill. "Cut him up. Kill the boy, but butcher the dog first."

"No, Apollo," Dargon says, "but there does need to be punishment here. Bring the boy to that flensing table."

The first mate is strong, but no way he can drag me there by himself. So he has a few thuggish sailors help. In seconds I'm dragged to the table and forced to my knees.

"Press his hand flat and hold him still."

I fight like hell, but my right hand is pulled onto the table. They dig into the pressure points between my knuckles, and my clenched fist flattens on the tabletop.

"Look at me, boy," Dargon says.

I look up at him. He opens his mouth wide.

I hear the crew gasp before I see it for myself. Red and orange flames shoot out through his mouth. The heat from the flames singes my forehead and hair.

The flames subside and he's holding something in his right hand that glints in the sunlight. A knife.

He bends till our faces are level, six inches apart. "You ruined something of mine, and now I'm going to ruin something of yours," he whispers. "Pain for pain. Don't fight, or it will be worse."

I try to fight, to rear up and break the grip of the men who hold me. No chance. Too many of them.

The sharp blade slides over the back of my right hand. He moves it to my pinkie and probes for the knuckle joint. When he finds it, Dargon presses down with all his weight and saws off half of my little finger as I watch helplessly from a few inches away.

Hear myself scream. Start to faint from the shock of seeing it happen, and then the sudden searing pain.

Deck tilts and swirls.

Vaguely aware of blood spurting.

Ronan cursing, and being restrained.

Crewman clumsily tying on a tourniquet.

Does the inch-long piece of my severed pinkie end up in the parrot's beak, or is that my imagination?

The last thing I hear is Dargon telling the captain, "I'll take them both with me. They're mine now."

59

Hoisted aboard yacht. Still woozy from shock and pain.

Gisco is leashed and led away. *Where are they taking me? Do you think they'll feed me or kill me? I hope they at least believe a condemned dog should get a last meal.*

I try to focus for a second. If they wanted to kill us, they would have done it on the trawler.

Good point, old bean. And it's close to lunchtime. Let's hope for the best. Take care of that hand.

I assume he'll be locked in some kind of nautical dog cage while I'll be thrown in the brig.

Wrong.

A very tall black man in a flowing African robe hurries up. "I am Femi, the butler," he says with a British accent. "I will show you to your room. Can you walk or do you need assistance?"

I take an experimental step. Light-headed, but fairly steady. "I can make it."

"Good. This way, please."

He leads me down a flight of stairs to a small, bright room, elegantly furnished. Wood paneling. Leather-bound books on shelves. Tiny but functional bathroom. Porthole.

Much nicer than the captain's room on the *Lizabetta*.

"There are clothes that will fit you in the closet," Femi says. "Let me see your hand, please."

One of the sailors on the *Lizabetta* had packed my hand in ice and wrapped it in a white towel. The towel is now crimson with seeped blood.

Femi unwraps the bloody package. Doesn't seem at all fazed that half my pinkie was just hacked off. They must have warned him. In fact, he's come prepared, with a small medical kit.

He cleans what remains of the finger with antiseptic. "Neat cut," he says. "No bone fragments." Expertly bandages it and puts on a small plaster cast. "Leave this on for one week." Gives me some blue pills. "Take two with water. They'll help the pain."

"Where's my dog?"

"Safe," he says. "Dinner will be at six. My master requests that you join him." Femi stands. He must be almost seven feet tall, and he has to bow his head to avoid knocking it against the sloped ceiling of my room. "Someone will come to fetch you. Please be dressed and ready. My master values promptness."

"Well, I value my fingers," I shoot back. "Tell your master if he cares so much about good manners, he might want to go easy on the forced amputations."

Femi looks back at me inscrutably. "Rather than remain bitter at your loss, it might be more profitable to learn a lesson from your punishment and move forward."

"Easy for you to say," I mutter, feeling the throbbing in my bandaged hand.

In answer, Femi draws his right foot out of his slipper. He's missing two toes. Inserts his foot back in the slipper and walks away.

My door is locked from the outside.

I decide not to take the pills. Who knows what's in them? My situation is bad enough without my being drugged.

I last about five minutes. Each throb of the finger is a separate agony. Give up, and swallow two pills.

Pain subsides a bit. Not totally. But tolerable.

I explore the room. Comfortable, but there's no escape. Just a sealed porthole. Nothing I can use as a weapon.

No clues about Dargon.

Who is he? Why did he bring me back here? Is it possible that he knows about my mission? How could he? Why didn't he kill me on the trawler? Does he have something slower and more painful in mind?

No answers to my questions, so I end up checking out the books. They have something in common. History. Ancient history. Ancient military history. Hannibal.

That's right, they're all about Hannibal Barca, perhaps the greatest general who ever lived. In the third century B.C. he did what no one else had ever even thought possible. Led a huge army and elephants over the Pyrenees and then the Alps. Descended into Italy, won battle after brilliant battle, and brought the Roman Empire to its knees.

Don't ask me why this is Dargon's favorite reading material.

I try to forget about my throbbing hand by losing myself in the books. Five-thirty rolls around. I take a shower, and dress in the clothes that have been left for me. They fit perfectly.

Five to six. Three soft knocks on door. *Bap, bap, bap.* I open it.

Babe-a-licious blonde standing there, unsteadily on one leg, as she scratches her freckled ankle with her other foot. Looks nineteen. Dressed, if you can call it that, in micro bikini. Sipping tropical drink complete with cherry and tiny umbrella. Smiles at me and then giggles. "He didn't tell me you were so cute."

Even Hannibal would have slipped off his elephant at this. Who is she and what the heck is she doing on Dargon's yacht? Besides flirting with me? "I beg your pardon?"

Perky, playful, shamelessly sexy smile. "What's your name, sailor boy?" she asks in a soft purr.

"Jack."

"I'm Kylie," she whispers back, sways, and grabs the doorknob for support. She giggles again, and it's the kind of frolicsome laugh that makes her whole body jiggle so that the top of her bikini almost pops off. "That's what I get for drinking in the sun. I know better. I really, really do."

"I believe you," I tell her, trying not to stare at her breasts, which is virtually impossible.

"Mistake, Jack," she warns mischievously. "Never, ever believe anything I say." She fishes the cherry out of her drink and pops it in her mouth, watching me all the while. She teases it with her soft lips for a second, and then, as if remembering something important, glances at her watch. Snaps to attention with mock seriousness. "Follow me, sailor hunk. Dargon's a grouch when he's kept waiting. You can believe that for sure."

60

"How kind of you to join us for dinner," Dargon says with a mocking smile.

He's seated at the head of a polished teak table in a little jewel box of a ship's dining room. China and crystal place settings. Floor-to-ceiling windows with views of an ocean sunset spreading itself like a magician's cloak over endless small waves. Changing light coaxes a fireworks display of sparkles from the chandelier overhead.

Dargon has traded his white shorts and muscle shirt for a flowing purple robe. Gold crest on back—ferocious serpent devouring helpless crane. Am I the crane? The charisma of the man is startling. The strength and definition of his features. The vibrancy of his physique. His grace of movement as he helps Kylie into a chair and then bows to me. "Welcome."

"Don't try to shake my hand," I warn him. "It's still sore where you hacked off my finger today."

"Yes, it would be." Dargon nods, as if this is polite table conversation. "Did you take some of Femi's pills? By tomorrow it should feel better."

"Great. Maybe tomorrow you can cut off one of my feet."

"I'm sure that won't be necessary," Dargon says. "Doesn't Kylie look radiant in this light? Please be seated."

We sit. Look at each other. Mad tea party atmosphere.

"Shall I say grace?" Dargon offers.

Didn't exactly see him as the pious sort. I shrug. "Say whatever you want."

He folds his hands, throws me a look of thinly veiled menace, and says, "Lord, help us to enjoy each day as if it is our last." His gaze shifts to Kylie, and unmasked lust flashes in the gray eyes. "And may we always remember that beauty exists so that it can be consumed by the bold and relished by the strong."

Strange prayer. I don't say amen. But I also glance at Kylie. Can't help it. With the sunset behind her and the chandelier sparkling above her blond hair like a diamond tiara, she does look radiant.

She feels my glance, smiles, and turns her head as if to offer me the very best viewing angle.

Femi pours wine and sets out a first course of what looks like slivers of raw fish. "Bluefin tuna crudo on ruby grapefruit," the tall butler announces.

"Isn't the bluefin tuna endangered?" I ask, recalling Gisco's environmental harangue.

Dargon shrugs. "It's too late for this one anyway." He devours a heaping forkful. "Endangered but delicious."

Since I'm starving, and nothing will bring this poor bluefin back, I follow suit. The raw fish has a meltingly delicate taste, set off by the sour grapefruit.

Dargon nods approvingly. "You're willing to break your own rules. I like that. Your room is comfortable?"

"Fine."

"I trust you found something interesting to read?"

"A hundred books about the same man seems like a waste of shelf space."

"Not when the man is interesting enough," Dargon says. "Hannibal is a role model for me."

"Because you're both sadists?"

"Don't believe the Roman propaganda about Hannibal," he cautions. "As for me, we're just getting to know each other."

"I got to know you this morning, on the wrong end of a knife."

"You must know you left me no choice. Ships run on discipline," Dargon points out. "The crew saw what you did, and they also needed to see that a price would be paid. They're simple men, so it had to be blood. I gave them what they needed and what the situation demanded. Now, as far as I'm concerned, it's over and done with."

"As far as you're concerned," I repeat softly.

Femi serves the main course. "Chilean sea bass with lobster and black truffles," he announces.

"It's actually Patagonian toothfish," I correct him. "In a few decades it'll be extinct."

"How can you know what's going to happen in a few decades?" Kylie asks.

It's a good question. Dargon answers for me. "My dear, those who don't study the future are doomed to repeat its mistakes. And I believe that our guest is a budding scholar of the future. Of course, that's a risky field of study. One must be very sure of one's teachers."

I'm not sure exactly what he's talking about, so I taste the sea bass. It's buttery and melts in my mouth.

"I'm sorry we couldn't have your dog to dinner," Dargon says. "I have a firm rule against birds or animals at the table. Though, of course, he's obviously not a normal dog. Is he?"

"Your parrot's not exactly from Parrots of the World dot com, either," I point out.

Dargon won't be diverted. "We were talking about your dog. Where did you get him, I wonder?"

"New York," I grunt as I swallow down another forkful of fish. Watch it, Jack. He's after something.

The gray eyes are locked on me now. The voice is demanding. "Did you find him or did he find you?"

I half stand, holding my dinner knife loosely in my right hand. "Is this a dinner party or an interrogation? Because if it's a dinner, then I don't choose to answer your questions. And if it's an interrogation, you might want to get four of your henchmen to hold me down before you try messing with me again, you craven bastard."

Kylie lowers her fork. "Wow, nobody ever talks to Dargon that way." She looks from him to me to him again. "Are you guys gonna fight or something? Can I be the prize?"

Dargon's eyes flick down to the knife in my hand. "Just for the record, so we understand each other," he says in a calm voice, "I spent years mastering a variety of deadly fighting skills. If you're ever foolish enough to take me on, you won't last more than twenty seconds."

"That must be why you needed five sailors to hold me down today," I fire back, watching him so that if he even twitches, I'll be able to dodge and counter.

But he doesn't move a muscle. "To answer your fair question, this is a dinner and you are my guest. Perhaps, in my eagerness, I was too hasty and direct. Food first, and we'll leave business to the end of our journey."

I lower my knife to the table. "What journey?"

"My island," Dargon says. "We should arrive early tomorrow morning. I'm sure you'll like it. It's quite beautiful. Wouldn't you say, Kylie?"

"Dreamy," she agrees. "You'll never want to leave."

"What business can we possibly have to discuss?" I ask Dargon, watching the gray eyes carefully.

"Fishing, of course," he replies. "Jack, I might want to go into business with you."

"Why?"

"I've been waiting a long time for a suitable partner to come along. We could do wonderful things together."

"And why would I ever trust you when I despise you?"

He leans forward. The power of those eyes! "Poor confused fellow. Raised by strangers, among strangers. The answer to your question will blow your mind. You see, Jack, the simple fact is that you and I have more in common than anyone you've ever met before in your entire life."

I'm trembling, scared, fascinated. I sense that the reason his words have power is that they're rooted in truth.

Dargon reaches out. Touches my arm. Grasps it lightly. Establishing a connection. "We're cousins, Jack," he whispers. "I'm the first family member you've ever met. Sleep well, cuz."

61

Restless night. Yacht rises and falls with the night swells. Hand throbs. I pop Femi's blue pills.

Sink into uneasy sleep. Feverish dreams. Dargon's words. "We're family." His touch. The way he breathed fire. Holding the knife. Cutting into my finger.

I wake before sunrise. Shower and dress. Find that my door is not locked, or rather has been unlocked during the night. Nothing on this yacht happens by chance.

An invitation. I climb stairs to deck.

Dargon and Kylie standing at prow, holding hands. First dawn sparking far to the east. In that kindling glow, a green spot unfolds itself from the night shadows.

An island!

Small. Mysterious. Green with forests. Ominous with jagged mountains.

Dargon waves me over. "Did you sleep well?"

"No," I tell him. "Bad dreams. Mostly of you."

"Get over it," he says. "Here comes paradise. And the good

news is I own it hook, line, and sinker. So there are no laws or rules and you can do whatever you like here."

"As long as the King of the Island agrees," I mutter.

"Of course," he says, and walks off to check on something.

"Don't worry, Dargon's cool," Kylie assures me. She's wearing short, short blue jean cutoffs and a tight, tight leather top. Her body has more mountains and valleys than Dargon's island.

"You know him better than I do," I tell her.

"I don't know him at all," she says. "We've only been together a little while. But he's cool to just about anything."

"Is that a good thing?" I ask.

"To me it is," she says. And then that mischievous, sexy smile. "I'm looking forward to getting to know you much better, Jack. On the island we'll have lots of time to get lost together. And who knows what else . . ."

Before I can answer, Dargon returns. "Everything is ready for us. How nice to be coming home."

We sail in. Men and women waiting at the dock. Dressed in the same "uniform" of khaki shorts and white T-shirts. Everyone trained, polite, subservient to Dargon.

We tie up at the dock. I walk across gangplank. Easy to disembark here. Something tells me it won't be quite as easy to leave.

I stroll down the dock and set foot for the first time on the volcanic rock of the island.

Feel it instantly. Don't ask me how, but I know. It's here. On this island. Firestorm! Whatever it is, wherever it's hidden, I can sense its steady pulse. Like the insistent beating of a heart, hidden deep inside a body, yet pumping, vital, the wellspring of aliveness.

Gisco is led off the yacht on a leash.

It's here! I tell him.

What's here? How are you, by the way? That was an unexpectedly pleasant interlude in our gastronomically deprived travels. Whoever cooks the cheeseburgers on that yacht sure knows what they're doing. Now, where are we and what were you saying?

We're on Dargon's island.

Which we came to for what reason, exactly?

We were brought here, cheeseburger brain. I don't know why. But Firestorm's here, too. I can feel it.

Dog becomes agitated. *Are you sure? Where is it?*

I don't know. But this is a small island. It can't be too hard to find.

Dargon's parrot is brought to him, finds a comfortable perch on his thickly muscled shoulder, and throws a nasty yellow-eyed look at Gisco. "Dog needs a bath!" he trills.

And you need to be plucked.

"Bathe him in acid. Boil him in oil."

I'd like to curry you with ginger and tomato.

Dog bares his teeth. Parrot pecks the air. For a moment it looks like pooch and perching bird are going to battle it out right there on the dock. "Come now, Apollo, that's no way to treat our guests," Dargon says. "And here come the welcome wagons."

A convoy of Jeeps arrives. We are soon twisting our way up a winding road to an imposing gate.

I spot a familiar crest on the wrought iron: a serpent devouring a crane. It's vividly rendered, so that you can feel the crane's agony.

Atop the gate is a single silver letter—the ornate "D" I saw on the ledger in the captain of the *Lizabetta*'s room, with scaly, serpentine wings as part of its design.

Didn't your father warn you to beware of fire-breathing monsters? Gisco reminds me.

Yup, I agree as the big gate slowly opens.

It looks like we're heading right into the chimera's lair.

And there's nothing we can do about it, I point out as the Jeeps head in. Do you really think my father was warning me about Dargon?

I'm not sure, Gisco admits, *but our host does remind me of some nightmares of the far future. The Dark Army was willing to do anything to adapt and gain an advantage.*

Yes, Eko told me. They created cyborgs.

And they experimented wildly with genetic material. A chimera in Greek mythology had a lion's head, a goat's body, and a serpent's tail. But in genetics, a chimera is a creature with DNA from more than one source.

You're saying that Dargon may not be human?

He may be more than human.

"Welcome to my humble home," Dargon says with an expansive sweep of his hand, as the gate swings shut behind us.

His mountain villa lies before us.

The compound itself is a graceful sprawl of interconnected white buildings that glisten in morning light. They've been architecturally stitched into the hills so that in form and scale they fit the mountainside that frames them. Crystal swimming pools, gardens aflame with tropical flowers, and foaming fountains spill down the slope in terraced steps from the compound to the silvery sands of a beach that arcs around a magically beautiful, crescent-shaped bay.

"Isn't it loverly?" Kylie asks.

"Okay," I grunt, as if I've seen better billionaires' compounds on nicer private islands.

"Femi will take you to your room and give you a chance to freshen up," Dargon says. "And then I'll give you a private tour. We have business to discuss, and time is short." The veiled threat in those gray eyes is almost palpable. "Also, I have some pets I'd like to introduce you to."

62

Gisco is led off on a leash to the dog quarters.

Jack is escorted by Femi to the guests-who-may-be-maimed-at-any-moment wing.

Not bad digs. Large, bright room with marble bath and stunning ocean views from every window.

"I'll come back in an hour to take you to Dargon," Femi says. "Is there anything else you need?"

"A life insurance policy."

The inscrutable Femi doesn't crack a smile.

I take steamy needle shower. Put on the shorts and T-shirt that have been laid out for me. They fit me perfectly.

Study myself for a moment in full-length mirror. Hard to believe it's the same Jack Danielson who cared so much about a football game in Hadley-by-Hudson a month ago.

But there he is—that same strapping young fellow with straw-colored hair and piercing blue eyes smiling back at me. All-American grin. Six feet two inches tall. Hobbies: chicks, flicks, and fast cars.

Same boy, same arms and legs, almost the same face. A dash more seriousness about the eyes, from hardship encountered and sadness endured. A jot more purposeful set to the chin, on account of having to save the whole future.

Otherwise the identical boy. Same and very different. Jack and not Jack at all.

Who am I now? I don't know. Does Dargon know more about me than I do myself? Seems likely. Are the pets he's threatening to introduce me to the same ones who chewed off the arm of the captain of the *Lizabetta*?

Three soft knocks on the door. *Bap, bap, bap.* Uh-oh. I remember this knock. As if I don't have enough trouble.

I open the door. Kylie stands there, dressed like a Victoria's Secret model in a mood to flaunt. "Can I come in and join the party?"

"There's no party, it's just me," I gulp as she steps in and shuts the door behind her. "What are you wearing, or maybe I should say not wearing?"

"I call it a thong sarong," she giggles, and flashes me a smile that could melt an igloo.

Flirting? Teasing? Thong sarong indeed!

"Why? Does my outfit make you uncomfortable?"

"It doesn't leave much to the imagination."

"Then you don't have a very good imagination," Kylie purrs. "I can think of a few things we haven't shown each other yet." Her eyes slide appraisingly up my body, as if she's trying to decide what weight class I belong in.

"Aren't you forgetting someone?" I ask.

"Who?"

"Dargon."

She shrugs. Steps closer. "Why bring him up now?"

"Seems relevant. How long have you been together?"

"Not very long. We met in Spain. At a nightclub." As she prattles on, I see Kylie's eyes flick quickly around the corners of the room. What's she looking for? Hidden cameras or microphones? If she's afraid we're under surveillance, why is she flirting with me? "He invited me back to his yacht. Hard invitation for a girl to refuse."

"And then, I suppose, he invited you back to his island. Another tough invitation to refuse?"

"Well, I was a little curious," Kylie admits with a chuckle. "Never met a guy who owns a whole island before."

"Now he owns you, too, right? So I'd better not trespass."

Kylie shakes her head and her blond hair dances. "Wrong, Jack. Nobody owns me. I'm a free spirit." She does some carefree dance steps to prove her point. Twirls and pirouettes closer. Sings as she dances: "I'm free! Free as the wind. Bright as the rainbow. Light as the air."

Now she's right in front of me. Stops dancing and breathlessly whispers her life story: "Raised in the beach towns of southern California, where blond chicks rule. I go where I want, hang with whoever I want, and party hearty. Nobody has ever owned me, and no one does now. You need proof?"

"I doubt that Dargon . . ." I start to object.

"I think you do need some convincing," Kylie coos. Stands on her tippy toes. Puts her arms around my neck. Grabs my hair with either hand, gently yet firmly, as if I'm a puppy dog that needs to be correctly trained.

Pulls me down. Kisses me on the lips.

Smooch must last a minute. I want to disengage but can't find the release lever.

She's got soft, pouty lips. Hot breath and tongue. Kissing her is like being sucked into a sexual vacuum cleaner. Never kissed anyone like this before.

Feel something wet. Tear sliding down her cheek.

Why is this blond beach goddess crying? Do I kiss so badly? "What's wrong?"

"I thought we'd have more time," she whispers.

"Time for what?"

"Be very careful, Jack. It will happen today."

"What will?"

Before I can try to find out, a voice from the doorway makes us break apart fast. Dargon stands there, not smiling. "I see you're making yourself right at home," he observes.

"Maybe you should learn to knock," I suggest.

"I make the rules in my own home. Shall we go now? Kylie, I'm going to have to ask that you don't accompany us. Under the circumstances, you'd be a distraction."

She's had a chance to recover. Gone are the tears and the heartbreak. She's a fun and flippant beach twit again. "Fine," she says. "I'm going to the pool. It's noon now, and you know what that means. Daiquiri time!"

She danced into my room and now she sashays out.

Stops in the doorway, right in front of Dargon.

They look at each other. Pissed off? Turned on? Both at once?

She gives him the same kind of long, hot kiss she just gave me.

No. Wrong. This one is longer. Hotter.

Breaks away, panting slightly. Looks up at him and says, "Jack's right. You should learn to knock." And then she's gone.

Dargon looks after her for a moment, and then turns back to me with a bemused smile. "It's amazing what you can pick up in a Barcelona nightclub."

"Especially when you have a yacht and an island."

"I think she may actually like me," he says. "Come. We have a busy day ahead of us, so we're going to travel fast. I hope you don't mind going off road."

✳

63

Racing down sandy track on monster of an all-terrain vehicle. Must weigh three thousand pounds. Brutish engine. Giant tires. Completely different animal from the antique motorcycle with the sidecar that Hayes's biker gang sold me.

This is a hyper-modern four-wheeled beast, with attitude, power, and kick. Doesn't need the smoothness of tarmac. Looks and feels like it will go over anything.

Dargon racing next to me. I'm wearing a helmet. Gloves. Leg pads. He's just in shorts and a shirt, his long brown hair flying in the wind. Fool. Show-off.

Wind whipping at us. Gravel pelting us. Sunlight reflecting off sand. Road winding around mountain.

Dargon takes his right hand off the handlebars. Signals to me. Gestures down steep rocky slope. Pointing a direction? Offering a challenge? Suggesting suicide?

He veers sharply off road. I take a breath and follow him down the rocky mountainside.

Bumpada-bumpada-bumpada. I nearly fly over the front of the ATV. Kick it into a lower gear. Lean backwards. Don't lock your arms, Jack, or you're a goner. No switchbacks possible. If I try to turn, this brute will roll.

Only one thing to do. Point the nose down and hang on.

ATV bounces off boulders and plows through deep sand. Nothing slows it. I speed across a rock face that suddenly disappears beneath me.

Rock cliff becomes ski-jump ramp, launching my three-thousand-pound ATV into the air. Uh-oh. Flying along on the back of a roaring metal stegosaurus.

I'm sure I'm going to die. Time stands still. I feel someone there with me. See ghostly hands holding the handlebars. Old but strong hands. Feel a presence on the bike with me. Guiding me. Warning me. My father's raspy voice. "Close, Jack. You're close."

"Close to what?" I try to ask. "Close to death? Help me out here!"

"Beware," he whispers, fading as quickly as he came. "Snarks. Find Snarks, but beware . . ."

He's gone. It must have happened in a fraction of a second.

I'm still flying through the air on my ATV. Haven't tumbled forward or lost control. Thanks, Dad.

Hidden bay reveals itself far beneath me. Trawlers tied up at a secluded marina. Must be more than a dozen of them, each the size of the *Lizabetta*. And a strange little domed building made all of tinted green glass.

Corporate retreat for dwarfs? Mini-laboratory or high-tech outhouse or Snark shelter? Definitely needs investigating . . .

If I make it. Can't stay airborne long with three thousand pounds of metal beneath me.

Land with a CRASH. Big, knobby tires skid and scrape, clawing for traction on gravelly slope. Engine roars and howls like Godzilla with strep.

I arm-wrestle handlebars. Nearly roll ATV. Somehow manage to regain control.

Dargon watching me. Looks surprised but pleased that I made it. And on we go, racing down the hill, side by side, neither turning or giving an inch.

Make it to the bottom, still neck and neck. Brake to a stop near glass dome. I take off my helmet. Sweaty. Scared. Thrilled. Pumped.

"You drive well," Dargon says. "Have you gone off road a lot?"

"First time," I tell him.

"You're kidding?"

"I only joke with friends."

"Then you should feel proud," he says. "Experienced drivers have died trying to do what you just did."

"I don't take pleasure in other people's deaths."

He climbs off his ATV and I dismount from my own beast. "Come," he says. "Try to lose that bad attitude for a few minutes. I want to show you my business secrets."

64

As we walk toward the gleaming little building, I feel a stronger pulse from Firestorm. It's much closer. Maybe inside these green-tinted glass walls.

Is Firestorm alive? A force? An intelligence? Does it know I'm coming? I feel some deep personal connection.

No doors visible. Dargon steps to a hidden camera. "Open," he says. Flash from camera. "Iris scan and computerized voice analysis," he tells me. "More personalized than any fingerprint."

"Since it's your island, I wouldn't think security would be a problem."

"Security is always a problem." The glass doors slide open. We walk in.

No security guard behind a desk to greet us. No Firestorm. Also no Snarks, whatever they are.

Strange. Where have I heard the word before?

Nothing inside glass dome. Just an empty room. "Stand here," Dargon says, walking to the center.

I join him.

"Down," he says.

We sink into floor. Elevator platform goes down shaft at an angle. Rock walls all around us. Light dwindling . . .

Platform slows and stops. We are in darkness.

"Lights," Dargon says.

They come on overhead.

We walk down long hallway. "Where are all the people?" I ask him.

"Rule one of protecting business secrets," he explains. "The more people who work for you, the more who can steal from you."

We reach big double doors. "Open," Dargon intones. His voice registers and I hear a series of bolts unlatch. The doors swing open. I catch my breath.

The scene reminds me of the war room in an old World War II movie, with generals clustered around a giant map of Europe as assistants move mock-ups of ships and troops.

But there are no generals or admirals here. Only a half-dozen young men and women, dressed informally. They could be nerdy grad students at Cal Tech or MIT, hanging out in a student lounge, brainstorming on a common problem.

They're not pushing models of tanks around Europe. They're using computers to plot the courses of simulated trawlers on enormous "maps" of all the world's oceans.

"Maps" is too simple a word. These are massive art projections, beautiful and functional. Contours of ocean basins and other topographical features like trenches and seamounts are "sketched in" with three-dimensional holographs.

I walk over to the Atlantic "map" and follow the Mid-Atlantic Ridge eastward with my eyes, toward Africa. Find the Azores island chain. North of that chain, off by itself, a tiny island blinks with a distinctive blue light.

I suspect that's where we are now—Dargon's island. Simulated trawlers are clustered there, no doubt the part of his fleet I saw right outside, moored to the long dock that juts out into the hidden bay.

Oscillating red lines surround the Azores. Similar red lines are visible in all the world's oceans, blinking like an endless chain of warning signals. Most are close to land, but the red lines also wink on and off in mid-ocean.

"Red for reefs?" I ask Dargon.

He nods, pleased. "You're looking at the most accurate model of ocean reefs extant in the entire world."

"Based on information you were able to bribe or steal from research organizations?"

A few of the young technicians glance at me. I guess no one questions Dargon in his inner sanctum.

He shrugs. "My information comes from many sources, Jack. You saw half of my fleet outside, being refitted with special new nets that are virtually unbreakable. I have forty trawlers, each of them equipped to fish the deepest coral reefs. That's more than a third of the global trawling fleet. And I'm steadily increasing my market share. Since the world's need for fish protein is skyrocketing, the next ten years look very profitable indeed."

"Till you wipe out your inventory," I say.

Again, several technicians look in my direction, and then quickly go back to work. Do they feel guilty about what they're doing? Is he paying them enough not to care?

Dargon doesn't even bother to lower his voice as he explains: "Once we fish out the deep-ocean reefs, there are thousands of shallow-water reefs with billions of dollars' worth of exotic fish. Enough to keep my fleet busy for another ten years at least."

"You're still just postponing the inevitable," I point out. "So you get another ten years. How does it make sense to destroy a resource that can never be replaced?"

I look around at the young scientists. "And how do the rest of you deal with it?" I ask them. "Doesn't it keep you up at night? And by the way, do any of you know what a Snark is?"

A gentle-looking young woman turns away from her computer for a moment and says, "Isn't that a made-up animal in *Alice in Wonderland*?"

"Thanks," I tell her. It comes back to me. Not *Alice in Wonderland*. "The Hunting of the Snark." By Lewis Carroll. A masterpiece of poetic nonsense. But not very helpful to Jack Danielson.

"You're not going to find anyone too sympathetic here," Dargon assures me, ushering me out of the vast chamber. The doors click locked behind us, and he leads me back to the elevator platform. "Your problem is actually a matter of vantage point," he says. "Up, please."

And up we go, through darkness to sunlight. The glass dome appears overhead. We step off the platform.

"If you kill all the fish, and there's nothing left to catch or eat, how can you possibly come out ahead?" I ask him.

He smiles. "You've been indoctrinated, Jack. Are you willing to open your mind?"

"To what?"

"A slightly more solipsistic approach."

"I don't know what that means."

"Then allow me to broaden your horizon." Dargon leads me out the sliding door.

The warmth and the sunlight hit us full on. He steps toward the long dock where the trawlers are moored. "You're a survivor," he says. "I like that about you, Jack. You make up your own mind."

I have a gut feeling that my survival skills are about to be tested in an extreme manner.

We walk down the dock, passing one enormous trawler after another. Half of Dargon's fleet. A significant part of the entire world's fleet. At the very end is a particularly odd-looking boat. It must be forty feet long but only eight feet wide. Small cockpit in the back. Enormous engines. Looks like a floating rocket.

Dargon heads right for it.

"Where are we going?" I ask him.

"Since you're so fond of sea life, I thought I'd show you mine," he says.

"Your what?"

"My reef. It's one of the finest in the world. It's where I keep my special pets."

✳

65

Strange-looking boat. Jack and Dargon standing in padded cockpit in bow. Looking up long and narrow hull. Nothing else in cockpit but tightly secured yellow barrel. Extra gasoline? Expandable safety raft for when we crash?

"Called a cigarette boat," Dargon informs me as he uses a small motor to guide us slowly away from the dock. "Ocean racer. They don't make many of them anymore."

"Why not?"

"People flipped them. Hulls shattered. Too dangerous. But it all depends on perspective. I have a less complicated perspective than you do, Jack."

He touches his hand to his forehead. Left eye pops out. Empty socket exposed.

I'm grossed out, but I'm also thinking: He shouldn't have shown me that. A weakness. If I ever fight this guy, that's the side to attack from.

"But I've seen your pupil move," I say.

Dargon shakes his head. "Don't be fooled. It's useless. And yet, in a way, perhaps it helps me to see more." He pops it back in. "Something I have in common with my role model. Hannibal lost an eye crossing the marshes on the back of an elephant. I lost mine on an even stranger journey."

"Across time?" I guess.

He doesn't deny it. Just speeds us out into the bay. Something about the way he looks as he steers the boat provokes me. The smugness with which he's dragging me along on this death-defying journey, from yacht to ATV to rocket boat. He knows where we're going and why. I don't have a clue.

"You're from the future, aren't you?" I demand. "Why did you come back a thousand years to start a fishing business? Who sent you? What the hell do you want from me?"

An amused shrug. The brown hair blows in the wind. "I didn't start this trawling company. I just took it over from the gentleman who did, when he met an untimely demise. I promise to answer your other questions very soon. But we were talking about Hannibal. Do you like mysteries, Jack?"

"I have enough of them."

"This is one of the great riddles in military history. Hannibal was raised from the cradle by his father, Hamilcar, with a single great mission in mind: to conquer Rome. In 221 B.C. he got his chance. Carthage declared war and Hannibal crossed the Alps into Italy. He destroyed one Roman army after another. But he never laid siege to Rome. He spent the next fifteen years marching around Italy with his army, never once defeated in battle, but he also never tried to knock down the walls of Rome and take the city he had come so far to destroy."

"Why not?" I ask.

"Military historians have had a field day with that," Dargon informs me. "Hundreds of theories. Carthaginians weren't good at siege warfare. Hannibal was waiting for his brothers. He was betrayed by the merchants of Carthage, who didn't want to spend money on the necessary reinforcements. None of the theories make sense. Why would the most brilliant and inventive general in history spend fifteen years marching in circles around the country-side? If he couldn't take Rome, for whatever reason, why didn't he simply go to some Plan B?"

"You know why?" I ask him.

"I have my own personal theory," Dargon admits, and switches on the power boat. The loudest roar in the history of overjuiced engines erupts from the outboard.

The ocean racer darts out into the bay.

"LIKE IT?" Dargon shouts.

"NO," I tell him honestly, holding on for dear life.

He laughs and starts up the second outboard. A much louder roar. Thunder in a tin can. The boat leaps forward.

I fall back against cockpit padding. Bump hard into yellow barrel. Spray splashes us. Wind howls around us.

"LIKE IT?" Dargon wants to know.

"YOU'RE GONNA KILL US."

"WE ALL HAVE TO DIE SOMETIME," he shouts back and switches on third outboard.

Forget thunder. Much too tame. This roar is beyond deafening. Outside earsplitting.

The boat leaves the water and takes off. Literally. The only parts that are still touching are the propellers. We are soaring between sea and sky with wind and spray whipping our faces and a rocket engine blasting at our backs. The hull is vibrating, crying out, shaking apart.

We're going to die. He's brought me here to kill me on this rocket boat. Don't know why, but it'll be over in seconds . . .

And then, quiet. Dargon shuts off the engines and the boat glides forward in silence. I let out my breath.

"Did you enjoy that?" he asks.

"I thought you were going to kill us."

"I was tempted to," he admits. "But I thought, why take the easy way out? Are you ready?"

"For what?"

"A swim," he says, and dives gracefully over the side. I instantly think of starting up the engines and driving the hell away. But whatever's down in his reef can't be as dangerous as this rocket boat.

At least I hope not. I dive in after him.

66

Two surprises.

First, Firestorm. It's very close. And it somehow knows that I'm in the neighborhood. Pulsing, tugging, drawing me in. At last. You've come. Finish. Find me.

Second surprise is how cool the water is. For some reason I thought it would be tropical. Wrong. The weather may be bright and sunny, but this is still the Atlantic.

Crystal-clear cold water. Less than forty feet from surface to bottom. I have a strong intuition we're about to go down.

I consider swallowing a red bead from Eko's necklace. But Dargon is watching me. I decide to try it without the bead. Can't show a guy like this weakness. If he can tolerate this, I can, too. It's mano a mano from now on.

We're treading water five feet apart. "Ready to swim with the sharks?" he asks.

I'm not crazy about the sound of that. "You're speaking metaphorically, right?"

"Come and see," he invites, and dives.

I suck in a deep breath and follow him down.

Not a reef so much as an underwater volcanic playground. There are lava caves, grottoes, and chimneys.

Sea life is everywhere.

We're not talking about small fish, either. Groupers that must weigh two hundred pounds chug along like tugboats. A dolphin and a tuna, sleek as race cars, flash by in a duel of speed demons.

Dargon swims well. He smiles at me and dives deeper.

I feel pressure in my ears, but no way I'm going to wimp out.

I couldn't dive to the wreck in the Outer Banks without help, and I needed one of Eko's oxygen beads to make it to the seamount, but here I can see the bottom. I summon my courage and follow him down.

A loggerhead turtle, big as a Ping-Pong table, paddles past. Dargon playfully hitches a ride on its back, just as Eko once did. It's so strange to watch him on the turtle's back—the despoiler of the ocean playing with the gentle old giant of the seas.

For a second I flash to the sea turtle I dragged across the deck of the *Lizabetta*, while its shell went *pap, pap, pap*. The look of pain in its eyes as I shoved it down the stern ramp. If only this one knew.

Suddenly a shadow seems to fall over the entire ocean floor. Bigger than the shadow of the cigarette boat. Longer. Wider.

I look up and see it.

My first cetacean! I'm no expert, but I'm pretty sure it's a sperm whale. Blunt head. Underslung jaw. Wrinkled, brownish body, with light streaks and scratches.

How can something so big swim so effortlessly?

I try to hail it on all frequencies. Hello, whale. Yo, Moby. Here I am swimming with the devil. Stick around and protect me. And, listen, where's Firestorm?

The big whale doesn't even give me a glance. Swims majestically away. Eko could have gotten through to it. Gisco, too. Too bad I don't have that phone line.

Running out of air. Maybe twenty seconds left. Should definitely head back to the surface.

But instead I follow Dargon a little farther down. My competitive side. Always gets me into trouble.

An enormous manta ray skims the bottom like a hovercraft. The biggest lobster I've ever seen in my life emerges from a dark grotto to shake its claw at me.

Firestorm calls out to me. So very close. Come, Jack. Find me. Finish. Feels like I could almost touch it with my hand.

Could it be in that lobster's grotto? Or in the mysterious lava cave leading away into darkness?

I'll find it on the next dive. My lungs are starting to burn. I made my point. Time to head up.

As if on cue, that's when I first sense it. Uh-oh. Something evil swimming nearby. I remember the electric current of pure evil I sensed from the bull shark that attacked Eko and me in the Outer Banks. This is far more powerful.

Whatever is directly above me is of another whole order of evil magnitude. But I'm running out of air, so I have no choice but to swim up toward it.

Dargon follows me. He knows what's up there, so he intentionally lags, letting me go first.

I can't hesitate or I'll open my mouth and swallow seawater. No time to fumble with Eko's necklace and try to unstring a red bead.

I head for the narrow shadow of the boat. The evil vibe amplifies. The whole ocean is buzzing with it.

Hidden in the shadow of the boat, another, darker shadow moves.

I know what it is before I see its rows of teeth. Before I see its massive jaws.

My father wasn't warning me about Snarks. It was sharks!

A great white!

67

Nearly twenty feet long. Two tons of predator. It sees me and turns in my direction.

Why do they call them great whites? It's pale gray. Narrow eye slits. Beady gray eyes.

Watching me swim toward it. Wondering how I'll taste. Which limb to chew off first.

Opens its mouth. Like the window display of a knife store. Row upon row of gleaming ivory razors.

I'm ten feet away. Can't stay down to avoid it. Can't go around it because it's right under the boat. Have to go past it, by it, through it.

No weapons except my bare hands. A blue flash! My father's watch!

I remember Eko taking on the bull shark in the Outer Banks. The jeweled pendant on her necklace flashed like a disco ball, blinding it for a second.

A second is all I need. Burn, baby, burn. Disco inferno time.

Nothing happens.

I'm so close to the great white that I can see which rows of triangular teeth will clamp down on me first, and which will grind me up later.

Those jaws open to an impossible circumference. I can almost feel the teeth. So here it all ends—

SSSSZZZIIIP! Disco ball supernova. Blinding flash from my watch shoots toward shark's eye slits. Great white looks dazed and confused. I swerve and put everything I have into one tremendous kick upward.

Enormous jaws close viciously, but miss me. They snap open and then whip closed again, inches from my right foot. Bad news. Shark vision improving. It sees me now.

Good news. My hands grasp side of boat. As shark swims in to finish me off, I pull myself up and over the side.

Great dorsal fin circles dejectedly and then the dental nightmare swims off in search of prey with less bling.

Hands grasp the other side of the boat. Dargon pulls himself into cockpit. Sucks air. "Well done, Jack. Bravo."

"How come he didn't go after you?" I gasp. "Let me guess. They're man-eaters and you're really a reptile?"

"They're actually more man-snackers," Dargon quips. He's no longer gasping. Barely breathing hard. Amazing recovery time. Must be in fabulous shape. "The captain of your former trawler is proof of that. He misbehaved, so I had to disarm him, so to speak. It's only when great whites smell blood that they become really nasty."

"Looked badass enough. Took two chomps at me."

"Playful nibbles," Dargon assures me. "We were swimming upward, and great whites almost exclusively strike at prey above them. But he thought about it. Did you see how he hid in the shadow of the boat? They're so cunning. If he'd been in the mood, he could have gotten both of us. I'm a man, not a reptile, and there's nothing wrong with the way I taste. Do you have any other questions?"

Dargon leans back in the padded cockpit, half closes his eyes, and waits. If he's really in a mood to answer my questions and tell the truth, that can only be very bad news for me. We must be at the end of our journey.

Still, I can't resist. "How do you breathe fire?"

"It's an old carnival stunt. The most dangerous of fire-breathing tricks. Called a blowout. You spit out a thin stream of fuel and ignite it. It makes a great impression on sailors, who tend to be a superstitious bunch. Come, what do you really want to know?"

"Why did you bring me here to swim with the sharks? You're not suicidal, so you must have had a reason."

"Well, I do enjoy taking occasional walks on the wild side," Dargon admits. "But I did have another reason. I wanted you to know how close we are to Firestorm." He pronounces the word with the same awe that Gisco used. "I wanted you to feel it."

"So you know what Firestorm is?"

"As much as anyone. Which is not much. I know you have a connection to it. I know what the prophecies say."

"Then you *are* from the future?"

"We're cousins, Jack. Distant, perhaps, but from the same era. We've been sent on long journeys, and they've converged at this moment in time. An island. A sunlit cove. Two strong men."

I hesitate. Decide to ask the million-dollar question. "I know why they sent me back a thousand years, but what's your mission?"

Dargon sits up. Sunbathing over. He's dead serious now. "The exact opposite of yours. To find Firestorm, and destroy it." He locks eyes with me and speaks softly, articulating each word: "And I was supposed to kill you at the first opportunity."

"You've had lots of chances to kill me," I point out with bravado. "On the boat, the yacht, the island. What are you waiting for?"

"I killed the man who ran the trawler business, and took it over more than two years ago," Dargon says. "Since then I've searched every inch of this damn island. I know Firestorm is here, somewhere. It has to be." His voice sinks to a frustrated whisper. "But I can't find it."

He looks across the water at the mountainous island that rises above the tranquil bay. I follow his gaze to the highest volcanic crags, and then I look back at him.

"That's why I didn't kill you, Jack," Dargon says. "I need you to find Firestorm for me. So I thought we might make a deal."

68

What could possibly be in a deal for me?" I ask. "If I find Firestorm, you'll just destroy it and then you'll kill me."

Dargon nods as if what I'm suggesting makes perfect sense. "That's what my mission would dictate. But it's not that simple."

"Why not?"

"I haven't told you my theory about Hannibal," he says, and he smiles cryptically. "Hannibal Barca. Son of Hamilcar. He was brought up in Spain. Do you know what his father's army was doing in Spain?"

"No."

"Pretty much anything they wanted," he says with a chuckle. "Conquering it village by village with a brutal mercenary army. That was Hannibal's grammar school. Raiding trips. Mercenary campfires. Then his moment came and he went over the Alps. He apparently decided he couldn't take Rome. So he spent fifteen years riding in circles around the countryside of Italy. What was he waiting for? What was his plan?"

"Why do you think he did it?" I ask, intrigued.

"Ever been to the countryside of Italy?" Dargon asks.

"No."

"Nice," he says. "Nice now, and nice then. Vineyards and villas. Great wine, tasty food, beautiful women. Military historians have endless fancy strategic theories about Hannibal's motives, but sometimes the simplest explanation is the best. He was a marauder, born and bred. Leading a ravenous mercenary army. Maybe they were just having too much fun to leave."

I try to take this in. Figure out what Dargon's really getting at.

"But wouldn't that mean he was betraying the people who sent him? Who were counting on him?"

"So what?" Anger rings in Dargon's voice. He's talking about Hannibal, but he's clearly thinking of his own life. "What did he owe those cowardly merchants in Carthage? What did he owe his monomaniacal father, who had ruined his childhood, beating him out like a piece of steel to prepare him for a deadly mission? He owed them *nothing*!"

BAM! Dargon slugs the boat hard enough to put a noticeable dent in the super-strong fiberglass hull.

He struck with his right. Remember that, Jack. And don't ever get on the wrong side of one of those punches, because he hits harder than anyone you've ever seen.

Dargon flexes his hand. Takes a second to regain control. Finishes in a voice charged with emotion. "Maybe Hannibal had the courage and vision to think for himself, Jack. To figure out what made him and his men happy and cut the false cords of loyalty and obedience to some faraway masters who didn't give a damn about him. To eat the fat of the land and drink the fruit of the grape and enjoy his hour in the sun. People say he failed. But maybe he succeeded, on his own terms."

He breaks off. Stands, as if embarrassed that he's showed me too much of himself. Walks to the yellow barrel. Leans against it for a second. I see his right hand move. He turns back to me. "Do you understand?"

"Completing your mission is no longer your priority?"

"Both of us, Jack. In the exact same bind. My father was horrible. Yours is no better. They're birds of a feather, locked together with centuries of hatred and venom. What right did they have to map out our lives? If I kill you and destroy Firestorm, and cross back to the future, it'll be to take up my father's war and finish off the People of Dann. And then what? Rule among the cinders? Scratch out a royal reign in a barren world of darkness? Doesn't sound like much fun."

"Not as much as you're having now?" I suggest quietly.

"You don't remember it," he tells me. "I've seen the future, Jack. A scorched wasteland, riven by fanatics who have hated each other for so long they'll each do anything to win. Do you really owe them your loyalty? They didn't treat you particularly well."

I think of my childhood—nothing but a lie and a masquerade. "No, they didn't," I agree.

"So cut them loose. Join me. Find Firestorm, and instead of destroying it, I'll use it. We'll use it, to enrich ourselves. It's a weapon, Jack, that no one can stand up against. With Firestorm we'll be unstoppable. I won't have to hide on this wretched island, cowering in international waters, extending my influence by baby steps. Find Firestorm for me and I will move mountains! We can be kings, Jack! The power of the pharaohs! That's what I'm offering you."

"What about the future? My father? Your father?"

"Let the future unravel as it will. Define the universe around yourself and your own happiness. That's solipsism. Be strong and embrace it! I have enough lobster tails and caviar on ice to last us the rest of our lives. After we're gone, who cares? When I die, the universe dies, or at least the only part of it I care about. Join me, Jack. Find Firestorm for me. We've reached the end of our journey. It's a yes or a no."

I stand and look back at him. What he said has struck a deep chord. We do have many things in common. We have both lived distorted lives. We've both been used, and possibly betrayed, by our fathers. But I'm not interested in the power of the pharaohs. And I know a bad dude when I see one. Also, I don't think he'd be such a great business partner. I recall that lovely reef on the seamount, and what he was going to do to it. Nope, not for me.

"No, cuz," I whisper. "That's my answer. No way. Not now. Not ever. Go ahead and kill me. You'll never find Firestorm. Maybe my father will send somebody else. I understand the Mysterious Kidah has gone missing. Maybe he can locate Firestorm and use it. You'll never be sure."

Dargon gazes beyond me, at the bay. Lost in thought for a second. No, wait, scratch that, he's not gazing out at the bay. He's looking at the water.

I smell something.

Then I see it for the first time. A vast red puddle, gushing out of the yellow barrel, forming a crimson slick over the surface of the rippling waves.

A nauseatingly thick, sweet smell.

Blood.

"Do you by any chance know what the ampullae of Lorenzini are?" Dargon asks.

69

Blood spreading over water.

Dargon standing with his feet spread to width of shoulders. Arms away from body. Ready to kick or punch.

Fight coming. No doubt about it. Dargon said I wouldn't last twenty seconds. Based on the dent he put in the fiberglass hull, I'm inclined to agree.

Gisco may be right, Dargon may well have enhanced genes. He may be a composite of all that's dangerous in the animal kingdom. How can I fight someone who has the eyes and reflexes of a raptor and the muscles of a bull, and strikes with the speed and fury of a lion?

I move into a fighting position of my own. Ready to shift in any direction at the slightest sign of trouble. "No," I tell him.

"I don't know what the ampules of ziti are. Sounds like a pasta."

"Ampullae of Lorenzini," he corrects me. "Two things you need to know about great white sharks, Jack. Some people think that when you're confronted by a great white, the best thing to do is to freeze. But they have unique jelly-filled canals in their heads called the ampullae of Lorenzini that allow them to sense the tiniest of electrical fields. If you so much as twitch—if one of your muscles undergoes the slightest involuntary contraction—a great white knows you're alive and just trying to play possum. Makes them even hungrier."

"Thanks," I tell Dargon. "And that's important because—"

"Of the second thing you need to know about great whites," he continues. "They have an absolutely remarkable ability to smell blood. They can sense a few drops of it at a great distance. I've just dumped twenty gallons of human blood into this bay. There are at least a dozen great whites nearby. Their top swimming speed is about twenty miles an hour. So you do the math."

"They're on their way," I mutter.

"Lunchtime." He nods. "Goodbye, Jack."

I know it's coming, and I'm still too slow. It's the same right hand that dented the hull. I raise my left to block it, but the punch pulls into the station way ahead of schedule.

Cranial cave-in! Feels like it crashes right through the side of my head.

I don't think it actually cracks my skull, but it does knock me across the cockpit so hard that I bounce off the padding. Reel back, dazed, right into Dargon's arms.

Next thing I know, I'm high off the ground. Lifted in a combination jujitsu hold and judo throw that wasn't covered in any of Eko's combat lessons. The jujitsu part immobilizes me while inflicting indescribable pain. I hear myself whimpering like a baby.

Twenty seconds must be up, because the judo throw part

commences. Dargon tosses me far out over the bloody bay. "Goodbye, cuz," he whispers as he releases. While I'm flying through the air, I hear the rocket boat's engines switch on.

Splash down into the bloody water. Cold revives me. Bay water no longer crystal clear. Visibility severely restricted by thick crimson fog.

I surface, and shake my head to clear it. See the rocket boat speeding away. Dargon waves once in farewell, and shouts something in Latin: *"Frater, Ave atque Vale."*

I recognize it, from Tennyson. It means "Brother, hail and farewell."

Goodbye, rocket boat. Hello, great white.

Two dorsal fins cutting through the water toward me. Several hundred yards away but closing fast.

Think, Jack. You have maybe a minute.

All I can think is that I'm about to be eaten.

Buzzing panic.

Paralyzing hysteria.

I fight it down. Fifty seconds. THINK!

Here's what won't work. Trying to swim out of danger. They're much faster and you're in the middle of a bay.

Also, playing possum's not a great idea. Because eventually you'll twitch and their ampullae of Lorenzini will chime like dinner bells.

What does that leave? Nada.

Great whites like to strike upward. So get down.

I fumble with Eko's necklace. No time to unstring beads. I gnaw two of them off. Swallow. Feel them breaking apart in my stomach. Dive straight down.

Two sharks speeding toward me like twin torpedoes through the red haze. If there's anything on this earth more frightening than a pair of great whites racing toward you through a fog of blood, I can't imagine what it is.

Fifteen seconds. I'm below them now, so they adjust their trajectories. Fish in the area start clearing out fast. Some sixth sense warning them. Feeding frenzy on the way. Alert! Alert! Leave the area!

Schools of mackerel dismissed. Eels evacuating. Grouper ungrouping.

I need help. No one left to help me. And even if there were, I've not been able to communicate with wild creatures.

Then again, help is my only chance.

There's a first time for everything.

I summon all my psychic energy. Everything Gisco and Eko ever taught me. If I'm really the beacon of hope I should be able to do this. Desperation helps. I feel a moment of pure primeval energy—as if I've returned to a wild state myself.

I suck it up. Roll with it. Spit it back out in a distress bulletin on every channel in the band. "HEEELLPP! SOS from the beacon of hope. Sharks coming! I'm your only chance! The ocean's only chance! I'm the guy who's supposed to save all of you, but you have to save me first! NOW! HEEEELLLPPPPP!"

Nothing. I might as well be praying to the Great Dog God.

Sharks now thirty feet away.

What would Gisco do in this situation? What escape would present itself to that great genius of cowardice?

Easy. He'd hide. Crawl in a hole.

But there are no holes. This is the ocean. Water above. Ocean floor beneath.

And in that ocean floor . . . lava caves!

Great whites less than twenty feet away. Jaws opening. Rows of teeth flashing.

I dive for bottom. There's a cave. No, not quite a cave, but a little grotto, protected by an overhang.

I reach it just before the killing machines reach me. Squirm my way in. Hope there are no eels around.

Great whites circle grotto. They can see me. Smell me. No doubt their ampullae of Lorenzini are picking up my fearful contractions. But they can't get at me.

One of them tries to poke its nose into grotto. Nope. Shark too big. Grotto too small.

The other one decides to gnaw off overhang. Uh-oh.

If they can remove my ceiling, they'll swim into this grotto and chew me up like a doggie biscuit.

I can hear their teeth grinding rocks and lava. The overhang is cracking and powdering. Another five seconds and they'll have ripped open my hole. Four, three, two, one . . .

BAM. Great white pushed sideways by sudden impact.

It's a beautiful sleek dolphin! Jaws looks at it, irritated.

BAM. BAM. Two more dolphins hit other great white.

Sharks momentarily distracted.

I stick my head out of grotto. See yawning entrance to deep lava cave twenty feet away. The sharks will get me if I try to cross that much empty ocean floor.

Great whites fight back. Lightning-fast strikes at dolphins. Bullies of the block. Reassert their authority.

Dolphins outmatched. In the wrong weight class. Great whites are too big, too tough, too mean.

Thanks, guys. You tried. Very brave of you. I'll try to do as well when they come for me . . .

Which they are doing . . . Gnawing off the final piece of the overhang . . . Looking down at me . . .

A SHADOW FALLS OVER THIS WHOLE SECTOR OF OCEAN FLOOR! Sperm whale! Diving out of nowhere, taking a chomp out of the side of one of the great whites!

Sharks don't flee. Don't even retreat. Go right after Moby. Battle royal in water. Sharks, whales, and dolphins. Teeth, fins, and flippers.

Monday Night Raw, forty feet down.

I make my move. Squirm out of grotto. Swim and run and wiggle at top speed over ocean floor, toward cave.

Twenty feet of ocean floor to cross. Fifteen.

A great white sees me. Wheels in my direction. It's a race. I'm horribly slow. He's gonna catch me.

Cave mouth yawning just ahead of me.

I make one final effort to throw myself in.

Not enough. Shark catches me. Bites my head off.

Injured. Dying. Dead. Yes, I'm dead. Death is inky black. The blackest black there is.

Cold, too. And excruciatingly painful.

No, wait. How can being dead be painful? The flashing, shattering agony I'm feeling is because I bashed my head on the lip of the cave as I threw myself inside.

Shark missed me! I made it! This isn't death. This cold blackness is the inside of an undersea lava cave!

70

Blackest black imaginable. Suffocatingly dark. Like being trapped inside a chunk of carbon.

Freezing. Feels like the refrigerator door just swung shut. Lights out. Cooling system on full. So silent.

Need light or I'll go crazy! My watch. Switch it on telepathically. Illuminates cave. Warms me.

Tunnel twists down toward the center of the earth. Looks like an indirect route to hell. I hesitate.

Caves have always scared me. This one looks particularly

creepy. What kind of cave starts under the ocean? Then again, what choice do I have?

Doesn't make much sense to go back the way I came in. Great whites lingering there.

So I swim forward, deeper into underwater cavern.

Steep downward slant. Swimming and crawling through tunnels that interconnect. Some I can barely squeeze through. Cold, lifeless volcanic rocks. Sharp edges.

Heading where? I don't know. Hopelessly lost. But Firestorm is very close. Calling me. Summoning me.

I use it as my compass. Every time I have a choice of direction, I head for the mysterious pulse beat that seems to rhythmically chant my name: "Come, Jack. Come, Jack."

Maybe I am fated to find it. But then what? Will I know how to use it? How can one man stop the destruction of the oceans?

If someone had found King Arthur's sword, could he have staved off the Dark Ages with it? Would finding the Holy Grail have ushered in an age of light? Or are quests really just wild-goose chases, embodying man's desperate hope that if he strives for something impossible with all his might, divine assistance will be forthcoming?

"Come, Jack. Come, Jack."

Exhausted. Numb. But I haven't come this far to lie down and give up in some lousy tunnel.

Suddenly the water's moving. Swirling. Whirlpool!

Trapped before I even know what it is. Scylla and Charybdis. I'm being flushed down a bottomless toilet. Slamming off walls. One crashing blow after another.

I use my arms and legs to push away from sharp rocks and try to protect my face as I swirl down and around, deeper and deeper.

Grab a ledge. Yank myself out of swirling current and plunge into a side channel. How deep am I now? Who knew the earth had this volcanic plumbing system?

71

Throne room. That's what I think of first. The ornate gallery in the palace where the King presides in all his royal glory.

Don't get me wrong, no King here. No sycophantic courtiers. No haughty Queen. No one at all, in fact. Just a bleeding, befuddled jester, Jack Danielson, limping in.

But it is gloriously ornate. A crystal coronation room. Folds of thin, translucent calcite billow like drapery from the walls in orange-brown beaded patterns. White gypsum snowdrifts layer the floor. Crystals of every color glitter from the walls in the pulsing, silvery light that emanates from . . . a throne!

I step farther into the room. No, not a throne. A shimmering platform. Some sort of glowing dais. Could it be one enormous diamond? No, that's impossible.

"Come, Jack. Come, Jack." It's reaching out to me. With each step I feel like I'm going to meet an old friend.

My body tingles. Every cell being zapped with a tiny electric charge. I'm terrified and at the same time exhilarated. I keep advancing. Moses tiptoeing near the burning bush. This is what my parents sent me back a thousand years for. This is what my whole childhood was about. This single moment in time.

I see it. Encased in the shimmering crystal dais but clearly visible. Heart-shaped. Silvery-white. With every pulse beat its form appears to shift slightly. Cardioid. Spherical. Crescentic. Conchate.

But that's not the strangest thing.

It seems to have a consciousness. I swear I can feel it. It's alive, albeit in a way I can't understand.

Powerful emotions bubble beneath its surface. It's angry. No, not angry. Wounded. It's been grievously hurt.

I'm standing right above Firestorm. Reach out one finger. Tremulously touch the hard rock of the dais.

As I reach down for Firestorm, I feel it reach up to me through the impenetrable, shimmering crystal that encases it. Suddenly I'm bathed from head to foot in silvery light. It cascades around me. Inside me. A bright memory . . .

A summer's day when P.J. and I went on a picnic. One of our first drive-away-from-home dates.

We drove along the bank of the Hudson and parked on a grassy knoll by the water's edge. Spread out a blanket, sat down side by side, and kissed passionately.

Touching Firestorm, I'm transported back there. My God, I am right there on the blanket!

The feel of P.J.'s lips. Honeyed sweetness of her breath. Wide river flowing by.

We ate lunch and kissed some more, and then P.J. fell asleep in my arms.

Half dozing myself. Lying with my head turned sideways. Watching her shut eyes. Each separate breath making her chest rise and fall. Hot summer sun baking bristling stubble tips of grass.

That's when it hit me, for the very first time. I realized that I loved P.J. But not just that. Love itself! It existed. Not just in poems and movies. It was a real thing, a powerful thing, and it was possible for me to feel it! The most spiritual moment of my life. Closest I've come to making sense of life or believing in God or accepting death. And also the least complicated moment of my life, a waking dream, wrapped up in the simple sunlit gauze of a July afternoon, the hungry chirping of the crickets, the musty smell of river clay, the tuneless fiddling of breeze-stirred reeds.

P.J. woke and saw tears on my cheeks. "What's wrong?"

"Nothing," I told her. But I couldn't stop the tears. "Must be allergies," I mumbled.

Somehow, she understood. Held me close. Tenderly. We watched the afternoon come on.

And that was it. An epiphany. A break point. I never saw the world quite the same way again. Can't explain it. But that was the day and the hour.

And there are tears streaming down my face as I stand in the crystal throne room touching the shimmering dais.

I still don't know what Firestorm is, but I now know what it's not. It doesn't come from outer space. Nor was it created by a wizard.

It's of us. Of the earth. It has the depth of life. The joy of our own love. The pain of our guilt. It has power. Fantastic power. Maybe even the power to save the seas and change the future. And it's been waiting for me.

But what do I do now? How do I use it? Or even get to it? If I had a diamond drill, it would probably take hours to dig it out.

I close my eyes. Empty my mind. Focus on my own breathing. Racing faster and faster.

No. Not breathing.

Footsteps!

I turn.

Dargon. In an elegant black robe. Parrot perched on shoulder. In his right hand is a very large and unusual gun.

72

Thank you for finding Firestorm for me," Dargon says.

He's bone-dry and his robe is neat and clean. He didn't swim through the tunnels or clamber up a steep shaft. "How could you possibly have followed me here?" I gasp.

His gray eyes seem to pulse with the silver light from Firestorm. "Questions, Jack, always so many questions from you. Why do you think I cut off your finger joint?"

"You were punishing me for damaging your boat."

"No. I was creating an opportunity. Femi bandaged you up and placed a little tracking bug in your plaster cast. I knew you were fated to find Firestorm, so I took you as close as I could to it in the boat and let you lead me the rest of the way. I followed your signal, down through the island's cave tunnels, which I have explored for two years. And here we are. You found it. It's time to complete my mission."

He aims the enormous gun and hits a switch. The weapon starts to power up. It reminds me of the gun my father fired when he made his valiant last stand. I'm pretty sure it doesn't fire bullets. Some kind of laser or beam of energy. But my father's gun was relatively small. This looks like the laser equivalent of a howitzer.

"Destroy it," the parrot trills. "Destroy Firestorm. Kill Jack. Shoot now. Blast away."

"Patience, Apollo. We've come a long way for this. A few more seconds to power up and we'll be ready."

I'm seized by an urge to protect Firestorm. I step between him and the dais. "Why are you going to destroy it?" I ask. "I thought you wanted to use it yourself. To be a modern-day Hannibal."

"You didn't buy that story before, so why would you buy it now?" Dargon asks. "No, my place is in the future, Jack. That's one difference between us. I know who I am."

Gun powered up. His finger tightens on trigger. The laser will slice right through me. I dive behind the dais.

There's a flash of tremendous light and heat. But the shimmering dais protects me. Maybe it is one enormous diamond after all! The hardest substance known. Whatever it is, it repels and reflects the beam from Dargon's super-gun.

He's momentarily blinded by the flash that bounces back at him. Rubs his eyes, furious at being thwarted. "Get it for me, Jack," he hisses. "You found it. Only you can free it. Get it and I'll spare your life. You have my word. Otherwise you'll die an agonizing death."

A figure materializes behind him. Stepping soundlessly in and out of shadows. A woman.

Dargon doesn't see her because he's circling the dais, blinking his eyes, trying to corner me.

But I see her. She holds her finger to her lips, signaling for me to be silent.

Her blond hair seems aflame in the silvery light.

She's wearing a thong sarong.

Kylie.

Dargon circles back unexpectedly and traps me. He smiles and takes careful aim. "This is your last chance . . ."

Kylie leaps. Sails through the air. Kicks the gun out of his hand. It clatters to the cave floor.

Parrot knocked off perch. Cursing and flapping wings.

Dargon doesn't even look to see who's behind him. He dives after gun. But she gets to it first and kicks it away.

Enormous laser gun spins and clatters across the bumpy cave floor and disappears down a deep crevice.

Only then does Dargon look to see who attacked him.

It registers that he's been ambushed by his own beach bimbo. I never saw Dargon surprised before, but for a second he's incredulous. Shocked. Aghast. Then furious. "What the hell are you doing here, you fool?" he demands.

"One of us is surely a fool," Kylie tells him in a surprisingly strong voice that sounds oddly familiar.

✳

73

Dargon steps toward Kylie. "You don't know what you've done, twit, but I'll tear your brainless head off your shoulders. And then I'll rip your new boyfriend apart with my bare hands." With his fighting skills, those aren't idle threats.

"Kill her," the parrot trills. "Break her bones."

But then Dargon stops walking. Parrot stops whistling.

Because she's changing.

Blond hair darkening. Features of face realigning. Eko! Holding a samurai sword. Its tip pointed threateningly at Dargon's throat. Her voice unmistakable. "Jack, this is your moment. You are our beacon of hope!"

Dargon apparently knows her. And he's not that thrilled at her little masquerade. "So you tricked me, High Whore of Dann!"

"Found you, tricked you, and now I'll kill you if you take another step."

"I think not," he says. "Apollo."

Treacherous bird has circled behind her and silently climbed cave wall. Does a little hop, skip, and comes down with a jump on her face, bright feathers flapping.

Dargon uses her momentary blindness to kick the sword away.

He bends to pick it up, and is knocked off his feet by a growling gray-brown blur.

Gisco! Powering forward like a canine locomotive.

For a minute the cave chamber echoes with blows and cries. Dog trying to devour parrot. Parrot pecking at canine eyes and snout. Eko spinning like a dervish, kicking at Dargon with either foot. Dargon punching back at her so hard his fist goes right through a stalactite.

And then they all stop. Everything stops. It must stop. Because there's a CLAP OF THUNDER.

Firestorm! It's had enough. I can feel it, reaching out to me through the dais. The clap of thunder echoes. Crystals peel off walls. Dust rises from the floor.

Firestorm is no longer a warm, silvery presence. Now the silver light is tinged with red. Angry. Vengeful. It wants to act. But it needs my help.

"Seize the moment, Jack," Eko urges. "This is what your father sent you back a thousand years for!"

"NO!" Dargon's voice is loud and desperate. "Don't do it. She's using you. Manipulating you for an evil end. The Dannites are a suicide cult, Jack. They don't want you to save the future. THEY WANT YOU TO WIPE IT OUT. They've lost, so they're willing to destroy everything!"

"Don't listen to his lies," Eko urges. "Every second is crucial. Do what you were born to do!"

But I am listening to Dargon. Can't help it. He's making sense. "You have lost in the future," I say to Eko. "Gisco told me that."

She doesn't look happy to hear this. Searches for the right words to argue.

Dargon beats her to it. "Yes, they've lost! So they sent you back in time on a suicide mission. If you use Firestorm to save the oceans, you'll drastically change the future. A thousand years from now, everything will be different. Not just coral reefs, but also the people. Your father and mother will never have been born. If you do what they want and change the present, your parents will cease to exist in the future. And then you, their son, must also cease to exist. A few minutes after you do it, everyone in this room will blink out. You will be committing suicide, killing both your parents and the whole world from which you come!"

He's lying! Gisco assures me. *Don't think! Just do it!*

You're the one who told me my fate would be worse than Oedipus's, I remind Gisco. So killing my parents sounds just about right. What he's saying makes a lot of sense. If I change something important now, I will be altering the whole future. How can I not be?

Because time doesn't work that way. It's not a river, where if you move a stone upstream, you change the entire flow downstream.

"That's true, Jack," Eko agrees. "This man is a clever and desperate liar. He's using a simplistic and outdated model of space-time to fool you. We can't explain it all to you now. Your father is wise and good, and he sent you here to save and preserve, not to destroy. Now you must rise to your moment and assume your destiny!"

I'm dizzy. Punch-drunk with their arguments. They play into my greatest fear and insecurity. I don't know who I am. Who sent me back. What their real motives were.

They continue to argue. Their words and thoughts swirl around me.

I search my soul. What is right? What is wrong? Eko and Gisco seem good. Dargon embodies evil. My father in visions seems wise. Dargon's father haunts my nightmares.

I remember the reef I dived down to. An undersea garden of

Eden. The oddly shaped sponges. The magnificent corals. The weird and wonderful creatures of the deep.

Dargon was ready to destroy it all.

Somehow I figure out what I have to do.

74

I step forward and in an instant clear my mind. The throbbing silvery light seems to pulse right through me. I reach down for it, as if reaching for a part of myself. This time my hand doesn't stop on the top of the dais. That incredibly hard surface that repelled Dargon's laser puts up as much resistance as a pool of water in a mountain spring. I reach into the pool. Touch the warmth that is Firestorm. My right palm just covers the glowing orb.

I withdraw my hand from the dais, and Firestorm comes out with it. It's free. I did it! Don't ask me how.

I hold Firestorm above my head.

Suddenly my hand is burning! I scream. YAAAAAAAA!

Try to hurl it away. No response. I'm paralyzed. It's not just my hand that's on fire. My arm, my shoulder, my whole body is suddenly searing, charring, roasting! Enveloped in orange-red flames.

Is Firestorm burning me, or am I somehow doing this?

Neither. It's a connection. A coming together. Something inside of me is unlocking it. I have some link with this primordial force, a spiritual connection far deeper than cells or even my DNA. This has nothing to do with science. It's magic, or beyond magic.

The moment I was born for! The Mysterious Kidah divined it,

my father learned of it and sacrificed my whole childhood to bring this about, the couple who pretended to be my parents spent years loving me and lying to me because of it, and now the fateful moment is here!

This pain has to be worse than being born, worse than dying. But those are the images I'm seeing. Birth and death. Creation and destruction. As if I'm inside Firestorm.

Lightning lashing lifeless molten seas. A one-celled animal dividing and feebly propelling itself. The first and smallest worm in the long history of worms uncurling. A tiny proto-fish emerging from an egg. A snake with winglike appendages rising above an ocean for a few seconds, as if no other creature has ever made it aloft before. A dinosaur chasing a squealing rodent-like mammal across a swamp, catching it, and devouring it. Neanderthals throwing spears at a great woolly mammoth. What looks much more recognizably like a man, grinding two rocks together, kindling a spark. Fire.

Yes, FIRE! Fields ablaze! Coal furnaces glowing! A mushroom cloud rising above the city-incinerating heat of an atomic bomb! Airborne gaseous chemical flames sweeping through a marsh, driving frightened wildlife before it. The eyes of the terrified creatures as they realize there will be no escape. Mothers herding their children desperately forward. Planes dropping napalm on virgin jungle. Oil geysering from a crack in the hull of a tanker, befouling a pristine sea, and then igniting, so that that water itself is on fire, and the birds and the fish flee before it like the terrified animals of the land.

Firestorm! The wound was undoubtedly inflicted by the hand of man. Firestorm! Is it the earth itself trying somehow to fight back? To reverse centuries of man's befoulment and abomination? Yes, that's it!

Worshipping the earth is mankind's oldest form of devotion. Earth gods pictured in cave paintings or on ancient rock carvings are always bestial and terrifying, the stuff of childhood nightmares.

Now those images sweep around me, and I hear frightening names, whispered from afar, "Gaea, Anath, Huemac, Aruru, Chantico." Horned gods, lion bodies with serpent heads, goat-faced deities with burning eyes, an Aztec god of earth and fire, with cactus spikes and a red serpent. "Dagda, Jord, Phan Ku, Geb." A green-skinned Egyptian god with an enormous upright phallus looks back at me and opens his mouth, spewing out a red vapor that makes the crystal throne room tremble. "Pele, Tekkeit-sertok, Kali." The dark Indian earth mother moves her four arms, and her necklace of skulls rattles.

Firestorm is fully alive now. Its spirit free. To create or to destroy. I feel its rage sink down, deep beneath this volcanic island, to the molten bedrock—

A galvanic sound rings out, ten times louder than the thunder-clap we heard earlier. Not a roar or a bang. More like a cosmic string that has been stretched tighter and tighter is suddenly snapping, and nothing will ever be quite the way it was again.

The cave rocks violently side to side. Boulders shift and rub and grate. I'm tossed away, head over heels, still holding on to Firestorm.

Flying through the air. Hurled sideways, high off the ground. I smash into something unyielding.

The walls are coming down around me. Dust. Rocks. The smell and heat of magma seeps up from gaping fissures.

"Come," a voice says. "Can you make it on your own?"

I look up. My vision clears. Eko.

"The whole island's going to blow apart. Can you walk? We've got to get out of here."

Based on what I know of vulcan speleology, she's absolutely right. This is going to make Krakatoa look like Jiffy Pop, old bean. Gisco stands next to her, bracing himself on his four sturdy legs as the cave shakes. *There's one other thing about the chimera of Greek legends worth mentioning—it was a portent of great natural disasters, particularly of the volcanic variety. We've only got a few minutes to get off this rock.*

I struggle to get to my feet. Gisco and Eko help me as best they can.

The ground is shaking so much that we have to lean on each other to walk.

They lead me away, out a side tunnel. I stop for a second. Half turn. Look back.

One last peek at Dargon, pinned to the cave floor by an enormous chunk of fallen stone. His parrot flits around him, trying to help but clearly useless and panicked.

Dargon's eyes meet mine. A burning stare of unmitigated hatred. If looks could kill, this one would finish me off.

But they can't kill. I'm heading out a side tunnel. And he's about to find out what it's like to be inside a lava cave when the molten magma comes bubbling back up.

I raise one arm. Mouth four Latin words back at him: *"Frater, Ave atque Vale."* Brother, hail and farewell.

And then I head up the tunnel and away, as fast as I can go.

75

Dargon's island doing the twist. Shaking, rattling, and especially rolling. Probably not fun if you're standing near his hilltop compound, or riding in a boat on the usually tranquil bay. But definitely a drag if you're in the upset stomach of this volcano when it's preparing to blow chow on the scale of Armageddon.

Best thing to do in such a situation? Flee!

We're running for our lives. Or, to be more accurate, climbing, sometimes on all fours. Don't ask me where we are, but I do know that we're heading almost straight up. Through steep, dark cave tunnels with treacherous footing.

Firestorm lights our way. It's barely flashing now, its energy released, its anger spent. I hold it tightly.

Eko is in the lead. I'm chugging along in second place. Gisco brings up the rear, huffing and puffing.

I don't mean to complain, but climbing steep caves is not what large dogs are best known for. Swimming, yes. Jumping, sure. Any of the field events, except pole vaulting, I might well medal in on a good day . . .

Less communication, more speed, High Dog of Dann, Eko admonishes him telepathically.

That's what I'm trying to tell you. Anatomically superior though the canine is in more ways than I can list right now, I'm incapable of climbing any faster. In fact, I need to slow down. I would suggest leaving me behind, but I know you'd never do that, so we might all pause for a brief subterranean siesta . . .

I know this four-legged fur pile well enough to suspect the prospect of being abandoned will make him run faster. Yes, he's right, we'll have to leave him behind, I suggest to Eko telepathically. There's no choice.

No choice at all, Eko agrees, instantly catching my telepathic drift. *He was a great dog once. You should have seen him in his glory. But he's too old now. Too slow. Poor fellow, it will be lonely lying here by his lonesome, waiting for the walls to cave in.*

You two are kidding, aren't you? You wouldn't abandon dear old Gisco? Trustworthy, gentle Gisco who knows more about how to find the exit from dark lava caves than a beacon of hope who's been chopped up and bloodied like a piece of hamburger, or a High Priestess of Dann who's been consorting with the enemy.

Consorting with the enemy? Eko sounds truly insulted. *How dare you, High Mutt! You know very well that was the only way I could position myself to assist Jack—*

Sensitive, aren't we? I'm sure you positioned yourself in some very interesting ways—

What the hell's that supposed to mean?

I try to mediate. Easy, you two. Gisco, if in fact you do have any idea how to get out of this cave, this would be a good time to—

The dark tunnel rumbles and shakes so violently we are all hurled to the ground. I cover my head with my arms as rocks rain down like hailstones. Somehow we survive. But that was close. We won't live through the next one.

Gisco appears unfazed. *You, who were about to abandon me, were saying?*

I respond quickly, brushing pebbles and grit out of my hair and eyes: That if you do know a way out of this lava cave, which I doubt but am willing to admit is possible, since cowardly dogs know more about hiding in holes than most higher animals, this would be a very good moment to let us in on the secret.

Gisco draws himself up in a huff. *Well. That's not really a very polite way of asking me to share centuries of secret canine lore. Is it now?*

More cave rumblings and tremors. We'll be entombed in a few seconds.

Please, High Dog of Dann, Eko pleads.

Oh, so it's High Dog now? What happened to High Mutt?

That was a term of endearment, she explains. And then adds a telepathic but heartfelt: *Please, Gisco.*

Yes, you sweet-faced bighearted pooch, I also beg. Save us if you can. We both love you.

Well, when you put it that way, I suppose I'll help out. Did you two happen to notice that the dust is moving?

Eko and I look at each other. The cave tunnel we're in is indeed suffused with rock dust from the recent near cave-in. The gritty miasma does seem to be moving slowly.

No. Not moving. Circulating.

No, not just circulating. Flowing.

Eko sees it, too. We look at each other, and then back to the dog. What does it mean, Gisco?

Caves breathe. He delivers this informational nugget as if he's imparting great wisdom.

We don't have much time, I remind him. Less mystery, more doggone clarity. Exactly why do caves breathe?

Changes in barometric pressure. But it's not a why so much as a where that you need to know about. The air flow accelerates near vents. So if the dust is moving this quickly, we must be near—

An exit! Eko finishes the thought.

But I'm way ahead of her, already following the flow of dust . . .

Through a winding corkscrew shaft that narrows and then veers around several tight corners. Suddenly there's light ahead, literally at the end of the tunnel, as it widens so that the three of us are running, sprinting side by side, and we pop out into . . .

Dazzling sunlight. We're on a cliff. Far below us on one side is the glittering blue Atlantic. On the other is the crater of the volcano. I look down into that pit and see, far below, molten red lava bubbling, foaming, and clearly getting ready to blow skyward.

Toward us.

"There's no escape," I say to Eko. "We'll never get off this island. It's a death trap, and all we've done by climbing up here is find three ringside seats. When the volcano erupts, it's going to fry us alive."

✳

76

Eko reaches inside a small pouch. Comes out with three shirts that look familiar.

No, not shirts. Thick, like life jackets. But form-fitted, like padded wet suits. They glow slightly, as if made from phosphorescent material. "Put these on," she says. "I assume I don't have to tell you to hurry."

The antigravity jackets we used to fly in the Outer Banks! I have mine on in a heartbeat.

I bend and help Gisco get his paws through his own jacket. As I straighten up, a voice from behind me calls, "All flights off this island have just been canceled."

Dargon. Less than ten feet away. Sweating. Drenched in his own blood. A deep gash down one side of his face. But standing strong and steady.

He's holding the large laser gun in his right hand. Aims it at me. "I should have killed you on the trawler, when I first had the chance. But I'll do it here and now."

I see it unfold in slow motion. Dargon's trigger finger moves. A deadly beam shoots out of the gun. There's no possible escape. It will vaporize me. No time to dodge. It's over.

Something dives in front of me. Takes my bullet, or my laser beam, or whatever. There's a scream.

Eko! She saved my life. But at what cost?

A throaty growl. Gisco sinks his teeth deep into Dargon's right wrist.

The gun falls away, over the edge of the embankment, into the crater of the volcano.

I kneel down next to Eko. She looks up at me. Winces, but manages a slight smile. Not in great shape. I'm pretty sure she's dying. "I think I would rather have been eaten by a bull shark," she gasps.

Dargon has pried Gisco off.

His parrot and Gisco begin fighting tooth and beak.

Dargon steps toward me. "I don't need a gun for the likes of you. I'd rather do this with my bare hands."

I stand up to face him. He's just mortally wounded the most

beautiful and interesting woman I ever met, who sacrificed herself for me. That's pretty strong motivation. For a minute I forget all about Dargon's mastery of the martial arts. All about the volcano that's about to erupt. I just want to put my fist through his face.

He beats me to it. Uncanny speed. One of his right-hand hay-makers. I get my left arm up to block it, but the force of the punch sends me spinning to the ground.

Stuns me. Rocks my world. Everything twirling.

No, it's not that my mind's spinning from his punch. The island's doing somersaults! Ground shaking. Lava exploding up from the crater. I get to my knees.

And here Dargon comes again. He jumps so well in a fight it seems as if he's flying. Reminds me of Eko in that barn, gliding down toward me in the ninja outfit.

Dargon lands on his right leg and uses his left foot to kick me in the chin. Faster, more precise kick than anything I've ever seen before. Knocks out a few of my teeth. I fly backward.

Grab a boulder at the edge of the crater. Look down into bubbling lava lake far below.

Here Dargon comes to finish me off. Leaping toward me, almost flying. His next blow will end this one-sided battle.

I've got to strike first. But he's too fast. Too skilled. Anticipates my every kick. Beats me to every punch.

I flash to Eko in the barn. The way I finally got the drop on her. When she was in the air, gliding down, I anticipated her landing.

Dargon's flying through the air now, heading for a rock outcropping near me. He'll land and instantly launch his final assault.

I ignore him. Roll over and do something very simple, yet at the same time unexpected. Kick away the rock outcropping.

He's still in the air, on his way down. Sees what I'm up to. Gives a guttural shout. Fear in his eyes . . .

His landing pad suddenly gone. He doesn't come down grace-fully, like a gazelle. He spins down like a helicopter on the side of a glacier. His legs splay at incredible angles, searching for pur-chase . . .

He slips and skitters along the lip of the gravelly precipice. Somehow manages to slow himself. His toes must be as strong and limber as fingers! They dig into the gravel. He stops himself, and starts to turn back . . .

I'm right there, waiting on his blind left side. He doesn't see me right away because of the glass eye, but he senses me and starts to raise his hand.

Too late. All it takes is a single light push, administered to the center of his chest with my right hand, holding Firestorm.

The orb flashes brightly as it touches Dargon's chest.

He looks back at me incredulously. Circles his arms. Slips over the edge.

Starts to fall. A cowardly death scream. WWWAAAAAAA!

I should check on Eko and Gisco, but instead I stand there and watch Dargon all the way down, till he disappears into the bubbling, molten lake.

Goodbye, cuz. You really had that coming to you.

Loud parrot shriek snaps me out of it. I pivot. Gisco has just bitten off Apollo's head. Headless parrot runs around in a circle and then stumbles off cliff and follows its master, flapping down into the molten abyss.

Gisco and I both run back to Eko.

77

Leave me," Eko whispers.

"No way," I tell her. "Come, let's fly off this rock together, before it vaporizes."

"I can't. Look. My jacket!"

I look. The beam from Dargon's laser gun sliced through her antigravity jacket. It's in tatters. Two humans. One dog. Only two functional flying jackets.

"Just go," she urges again. "Save yourselves."

I pick her up in my arms.

"No, Jack. I'm too heavy. You can't fly with the extra weight. Leave me."

"I'm the beacon of hope," I remind her, "and I have mental powers you never dreamed of. Now be quiet."

He's right. Be silent. Gisco seconds the motion.

"But we'll never get off the ground . . ." Eko objects.

"We are off the ground," I tell her.

And we are. Fifteen feet off the volcanic cliff, soaring up and out over the Atlantic.

Not a second too soon. A rumble wells up from deep in the bowels of the volcano below us. It builds and builds. Clouds of steam and gas flicker up over the lip of the crater in a red and orange fireworks display.

Fly faster, Gisco urges. *It's about to blow its cork.*

The rumbling gets louder, swelling and roaring, till it seems like the volcano will erupt at any second.

Everything that can get off the island is doing so in a hurry. Birds rise from the trees, circle and caw, and then speed off over the Atlantic. Bats fly out of caves. Dogs, goats, and even pigs wade into the ocean and swim straight out to sea, while rats throw themselves off rocky cliffs.

I see the trawler fleet trying to put to sea. But the big ships were being refitted and were moored to the dock. Men are desperately casting off and jumping aboard.

This is my top speed right now, I tell Gisco, as I clasp Eko tightly. You go on ahead. We'll catch up.

"You both need to go," Eko pleads. "Drop me in the ocean, Jack. I'm dying anyway." She struggles to get loose.

I hold her even tighter. "You're not going anywhere."

I'm staying with you two, Gisco announces. *We should have enough time to get away. Based on my unparalleled knowledge of vulcan speleology, this baby won't erupt for another half hour.*

Hardly are the words out of his telepathic mouth when the volcanic island rises to meet afternoon sun. Never saw anything like it. Hope I never do again. But it is glorious. Red fingers of molten rock claw up from the depths, reaching through white clouds as if to rip apart the curtain of blue sky.

I always thought an eruption was a quick, one-time event, like a bomb detonating. This powder keg keeps exploding and exploding.

The rock-splitting chain reaction of a mountain range ripping itself apart from inside.

The sibilant screech of rivers of molten lava searing red snake-like trails into the cold Atlantic.

The meteoric hiss as huge boulders take wing, spewed up from the crater, like a flock of newly hatched comets. Any one of them will kill us if it hits us, but our luck holds.

I see them raining down on the trawler fleet. One ship after another buckles and flips.

The green-domed entrance to Dargon's reef information center melts as a geyser of magma shoots up from the depths. Gone is the map room with all its stolen information about the location of the seamounts.

We're very high up now. Above the inky dust cloud that spreads out over what used to be Dargon's island. There's not much island left. Now it's just lava and water, and even that is soon hidden by volcanic soot.

But we're not down in that darkness. We're up in the clear heavens. It feels like a day trip to paradise. Warm sunlight. Endless layers of unsullied cloud.

I feel Firestorm changing. Look down at it in my hand. It's turned blue-green, the color of the ocean far below. It feels smooth and cool. I know what it wants.

I hold it for a second more and then let it drop. It falls like a turquoise teardrop. I think I see it land with a tiny splash. Whales and dolphins circle the spot.

"Strange," Eko whispers.

"What's that?" I ask her.

"That I'm dying."

"You're not. Cut it out."

"All the other prophecies were true," she gasps. "You did just what the Mysterious Kidah decreed. Strange that what he said about the two of us will never come to pass."

"What did he say?" I ask.

She looks up at me as we soar in and out of clouds. "Why did you think I was so hard on you in that barn?"

"You were teaching me how to defend myself. Time was short. You had to do what you did. I forgive you."

"I had another reason," Eko admits. "The Mysterious Kidah said that if you found Firestorm, we would one day be married. Have long lives together. Our descendants would be as numerous as the stars in the sky. So I was breaking in a future husband. But apparently even the Mysterious Kidah is wrong sometimes . . ."

"No, he wasn't wrong . . ."

Her body quivers. The lovely eyes half close. "Goodbye, Jack. I'm glad we had some time together."

"You can't die," I plead. "You're the only one who understands me. The key to my past. The key to my future."

Somehow she finds the strength to raise her head and plant a final soft kiss on my lips, and whisper, "Farewell."

"No," I say. "You can't die! *Fight it, Eko! Stay!*"

But I'm losing her. I can feel her slipping through my fingers. No, wait. She's not slipping away because she's dying. And I'm not dropping her, either.

She's blinking out!

Eko feels it, too. Holds me tighter. Whispers my name in a frightened voice. "Jack." The pressure of her fingers on my arms lightens, lingers on my skin, and then vanishes. She's gone. Like a beam of light. Poof.

Gisco!

I saw it.

Dargon was right! We're all going to blink out!

No. We would have gone together. We're staying, Jack. We're okay. She's the only one who's gone.

Where?

I don't know, old bean, the faithful flying hound admits, tears running down his snout. *But how I'll miss her! We crossed the centuries together. I'm so broken up over this, I actually feel like I'm breaking up.*

I look over. He is breaking up! Dissolving into air.

Don't go, Gisco! You're all I have left. I don't know where to go or what to do next! Stay! I beg you.

Don't worry, Jack. The one thing you can count on is that I'll never, ever leave you, the flying fleabag promises, and promptly flickers away into nothingness.

Gone. Both of them. Like candle flames.

Dargon's island is gone too, now, just a smudge of dust far below.

The sun shines above me, the clouds are cottony and cheerful. It could still be a day trip to paradise.

Not only that. I think I just saved the seas. Changed the future. Accomplished my father's grand design. The mission impossible he sent me on is over.

But I don't feel so good about it.

No, I don't feel good about anything. I feel empty. Drained. Terribly alone. Because I've lost my companions. The friends who could have helped me make sense out of it all. My sole remaining touchstones. The only way home.

Now the winds may blow me where they will. They sweep me eastward, toward Europe, and far below, the blue Atlantic churns endlessly.

ACKNOWLEDGMENTS

I could not have written this book without the scholarship and wise counsel of Dave Allison of Oceana, Dr. Elliott A. Norse of the Marine Conservation Biology Institute, Dr. Les Watling of the University of Maine, and Karen Sack and Sara Holden of Greenpeace International.

I am also greatly indebted to trusted family readers Orlando Klass and Sheila Solomon Klass; my intrepid researcher, Christine Bailey; my adviser on all variety of action scenes, Ed Nicholas; my wise agent, Aaron Priest; my indefatigable copy editor, Elaine Chubb; and my peerless editor, Frances Foster.

Special thanks to my supportive wife, Giselle Benatar, and my joyfully destructive kids, Gabriel and Madeleine.

Firestorm more insistent. Come, Jack. Hurry.

So I come. Swimming. But no longer sharply downward. The tunnel stops descending! Maybe I've reached the mezzanine of hell.

No life at all here. No crabs. No spiders. No cave-dwelling eyeless fish.

Tunnel starts to slant upward.

Water subsides. Hip-deep. Knee-deep.

Soon I'm crawling rather than swimming. Knees bloody. Exhausted. Legs cramping.

Minutes twisting into hours. Hours knotting into what feels like days. How far can this tunnel system possibly reach? Am I heading back toward Dargon's island, or out under the Atlantic?

Tunnel ends. Nowhere to go. That's it.

I look up. Vertical shaft gaping above me. No ropes or ladders to scale it with.

I brace my back against one wall. Hands and knees on other wall of shaft. Squirm and claw and snake my way up.

Don't look down, Jack. One slip and I'll plummet. Crack bones. Die slowly in dark chimney. No one to hear my cries.

Arms aching from the climb. Feels like crawling upward through my own coffin.

Am I already dead?

My thoughts bouncing off the stones. A white spot on the shaft's rocky wall. I fix on it.

It's growing, morphing . . .

The face of death that has haunted me throughout my journey, in visions and nightmares. An older version of Dargon. Looking back at me impassively.

No, it's the pained face of my imprisoned father, with his flowing white hair—a face that has reached out to me across the centuries, as he's tried to warn me.

Strange that I never noticed how close the two faces are. What did Dargon say? Two old foes, locked together.

I blink. It's a white speck on a dark rock wall again. That's all. I look up. See the lip of the shaft. Reach for it. Pull myself up and over and out of my own coffin. Lie there, gasping. Agony. Muscles cramping.

Somehow I get back to my feet.

Larger chamber. I can walk upright.

Drip, drip of water.

Things growing on the rocks. Plants? No, minerals.

Stalactites like daggers pointed down at me. Stalagmites like lost souls reaching out to me from the river Styx.

Firestorm pulsing: Come, Jack. Come, Jack. The walls of the cavern seem to shake with every throb.

My watch dimming. Wait! Don't go out yet!

A little light. Less. Complete and utter darkness.

No, not complete. Far in front of me I see a silvery radiance. Flickering. Twinkling. An underground star.

I head for it. Silver light grows stronger.

I know what it is. What it must be.

Firestorm!

Right here. So close it's now lighting my path.

I fumble along and reach the rock outcropping that separates the cave chamber I'm in from the next one. Like a dark doorway. Separating me from my fate.

I stand very still. Hesitate a long beat.

Take a deep breath.

And then I step inside.

✳